O'Cimarron!

O'Cimarron!

a novel

FELIX E. GOODSON

Red Hen Press Los Angeles 2001

O' Cimarron!
Copyright © 2001 by Felix E. Goodson

All Rights Reserved

Cover photograph courtesy of
George Morgan
Fort Collins, Colorado

Book and cover design by Mark E. Cull

ISBN 1-888996-31-5
Library of Congress Catalog Card Number 00-109462

First Edition

Red Hen Press
www.redhen.org

Acknowledgments

My greatest debt is to my enduring friend George Morgan who not only herded this book through to completion but drove me from Fort Collins, Colorado to the Cimarron Valley, in New Mexico in order to take pictures for the cover of this book and to allow me to become reacquainted with the people. I also want to thank my nephew Kelly Collins who served as our guide, Ina Kay Labrier and her family who showed us every hospitality. I am also grateful for the thoughtfulness and consideration of Kate Gale and Mark E. Cull, my editor and publisher who did the editing and organization of many parts of the book. And Maxine Davies, how grateful I am to you, for the typing, copying and letter writing. And I am perhaps most grateful to my friend Louis Smogor, who sent and received the endless number of e-mails necessary for the completion of this book.

Contents

Forward

This book is dedicated to the people of the Cimarron Valley, a valley which runs for eighty miles parallel to and just south of the Colorado border in northern New Mexico. This is a harsh, isolated and strikingly beautiful land and the people, both as I knew them as a child and as they live there now, are suitable reflections of this loneliness and austerity. I urge you to visit this valley. It is a land apart, even unreachable by cell phone as my companion, Gorge Morgan, discovered when we made a recent visit to take pictures for the cover of this book. Yes, the land is harsh, but it still retains its wild beauty in its many hued mesas, natural monuments, scrub oak, cactus, and wild flowers. And it still retains its rugged and resilient people: a few now grown old who were children when I lived there and knew them, a few descendants who went out of their way to be generous and helpful to George Morgan and myself when we visited, and a few newcomers, captured by the haunting beauty and loneliness of the place. They all shared and still share an admirable courage, tenacity and character, fitting attributes and reflections of the land.

As I look back, I salute these people, those from the past which this book is about and those who live their now. Though I left this valley early, something about its people, their ruggedness, their passion for living, their politeness and generosity have, I hope, become a part of me. Their mild manners belie a rugged individualism as will be encountered often in this book, a smoldering capacity for extravagant action and violence.

This book is about this land and these people, but it is a novel, not a memoir. The land is still much as I describe it, but features are sometimes displaced in their location. The characters of the book are all fictional, but they represent composites and reflections of people I knew then. Many of the events actually took place, but they are sometimes juxtaposed and occasionally altered in time and context.

There have been some questions by early readers and the publisher about the rawness of the language and the erotic starkness of some of the events. But the people talked and acted that way back then, as indeed, some of them still do. It would be unfair to the people of the valley, both past and present, to softpedal or censor or temporize or to make them less vivid and memorable in order to accommodate the sensitivities of the judgmental or squeamish. My effort has been to create a realistic portrait of this wild country and these vital and admirable people as they struggled and endured during those hard years of the 1930's. The people of that time who still live will understand. They were there.

O'Cimarron!

CHAPTER 1

Golden Bat

They climbed over a pile of rocks and there it was: a dark square hole made all the more black because of the bright sunlight on the white limestone.

Lonnie stood still, staring at the black hole. "I don't see why I have to go in there without a light to become a Golden Bat. Why won't you let me have a light?" His voice trembled a little.

"Well for Christ sake," Jimmy Joe Morgan was smirking down at him, "Do you think bats got lights when they go in there? Shit no! They ain't got no lights. They just go in there, that's what they do. And if you wanna be a Golden Bat, you don't get no light neither. But if you're too scared to go, you don't have to. Then we can call you the Golden Chicken." He let go his braying laugh.

Jimmy Joe was a broad shouldered skinny kid who went swaggering around bragging and showing off his hundred dollar kangaroo boots. He was big, fifteen years old, the oldest kid in the school except for Toad Thompson, who was feeble minded and kept taking the same stuff over and over. And he was good looking! Everybody was always saying how good looking Jimmy Joe was with his pale white skin, agate eyes, jutting jaw, and blond curls that covered his head and fell down on each side like he was sprouting horns. But Lonnie didn't think he was good looking. He hated his guts. The son-of-a-bitch, always going around hurting little kids by bending their arms back. Lonnie really hated him, standing there with that shitty smirk on his face, and he hated his brother Sam who was doing nothing except look uncomfortable.

"I think he's too chicken to go," Jimmy Joe said. "Let's quit fuckin' around here in the heat and go home." He let go his braying laugh again, then flapped his arms and crowed like a chicken.

"Fuck you," said Lonnie. He reached down and picked up a rock with sharp edges. "I'm going in there. And if that flashlight ain't there at the end of it, I'll kill you, I'll take a rock and kill you."

"Sure you will, you and how many other chickens? It'll be there; how else could we know you went to the end of it if you didn't bring it back?"

Lonnie glanced at Bobby Leo standing there with his black eyes peering into the darkness of the cave. How could anybody as shitty as Jimmy Joe have such a nice little brother? But he was nice and Lonnie's friend, even though he was only five years old and could barely climb on a horse.

"I'll go with him," Bobby Leo suddenly said. He walked over and stood beside Lonnie, but Jimmy Joe reached out and shoved him away.

"Shit no. To be a Golden Bat you gotta go in alone. Next year will be your time."

Nobody said anything for a long time, then Lonnie heard Sam's voice. "Shit, there ain't nuthin' in there but a lot of dark and a lot of bats. There ain't anything to worry about. When you run out of light, just follow the left wall." He pointed. "Not the right one, you might get lost in one of the side shafts."

There was silence again then Lonnie said, "Well, I'm goin'." He walked to the entrance, turned and waved, "So long, you assholes, everybody but you Bobby Leo."

As he walked along, he looked back occasionally at the square of light which was getting smaller and smaller. Ahead, nothing but darkness, and on each side everything was getting dark too, so that he could barely make out the walls. He moved to his left and began to feel along, his hand making raspy sounds on the rough surface. When he looked back, he could see only a faint glow. Then he heard the sound of the blow hole, panting and huffing like some kind of big animal breathing heavy. Another sound was mixed in with it, a high warbling, whining that undulated and shifted in pitch like a taut rubber band singing in the wind. It sounded like a ghost crying.

He heard his own voice, "Shit, there ain't no ghosts, and anyway, they don't cry. They just moan a lot and drag chains around. Shit there ain't no ghosts." As he moved closer, he could feel the warm breath of the blow hole pulsating around him and the eerie whining, wailing right above him.

"Nothing but a lot of hot air," he said aloud. "Just hot air, that's all."

2

And then he was past it, its panting and whining diminishing until it was a hushed wheezy whisper.

It kept getting colder and the wall kept getting wetter. Drops of moisture were coming from someplace, dropping on his face and hands. He stopped and listened. From above, there was a muted rustling mixed in with barely perceptible chirps and clicks. He stood there in the darkness thinking about the three matches he had in the band of his hat that they had missed when they searched him. Even more drops were falling now. "Bat piss!"

He started walking faster, his hand brushing along the damp wall until he was walking on a soft carpet which muffled the sound of his foot steps. "Bat shit!" A musty dank smell permeated the darkness. He could hear wings fluttering all around him and feel small puffs of wind as they came close to him.

He was thinking about why they never hit him when he heard a new sound. Something was moving ahead of him. Crunching, scraping. As he listened, the sound stopped and he couldn't hear anything but his heart hammering away in his chest. "Probably nothing." He kept moving, under another bunch of bats, the same piss drops and carpet of bat shit. Even above the sounds of his own movements he heard it again. No doubt about it now, directly ahead of him crunching, scraping sounds, getting louder and closer. "Maybe a rattlesnake!"

He stood stricken, hugging the wall, staring out into the dark. Shaky hands got a match out of his hat band and rubbed it on the stone wall. It sizzled, a momentary glow. He tried the next one on the seat of his pants, something he had practiced a lot after he had seen Old Man Dick light his pipe that way. It flared and made a pool of light. Hunched over, holding the match out, he stared toward the scraping sound to see a kite string on the floor of the cave, and for a brief moment before the match went out he saw the board, a two-by-four about a foot long dragging slowly as the string became taut.

There in the darkness, with the after-image of the match floating in his eyes and his burnt fingers stuck in his mouth, the fear gradually went away. He reached down, scrabbled around in the darkness until he found the string. He gave it a sharp pull, felt it grow taut, then limp, then screamed into the darkness. "Fuck you, you prick, and I hope I pulled your fingers off." He gave it another yank but there was no resistance. For just a second, he was almost sure of it, he heard laughter. "That Goddamn Jimmy Joe, that dirty prick."

He turned in the direction of the wall, inching along with his hand outstretched, but there was nothing but empty air. His panic increasing, he changed directions and suddenly, there it was solid and damp and comforting. Then he felt his panic rising again. Which wall was it? He stood there immobile, fearing to go forward, fearing he was following the wrong wall, that he might get lost in one of the side shafts.

No use waiting, he started moving again, feeling it get colder as he inched along, brushing his left hand along the wall. Then a knowledge came to him, canceling out the panic. If he was going wrong, it would be getting warmer rather than colder. He moved a little faster, and the minutes stretched out with nothing to fill them but the crunching of his footsteps and the sound of his own breathing.

Then everything changed. The floor of the cave began to slope up and to be filled with large rocks that he stumbled over. His right hand, which he had out in front of him, struck the end of something. He dropped down on his knees, his fingers running over the broken stones until in a wash of relief he touched the flashlight. But even as he touched it, he knew something was wrong; it was too light; it didn't have any batteries! He crouched there holding the empty flashlight, feeling something wet running down his cheeks dripping on his hands, then he heard his own voice strangled by sobbing. "Those pricks, those dirty pricks." He started feeling around, thinking maybe they had left the batteries. "Nothing but rocks and batshit."

The sobs gradually subsided, replaced by a curious calm, "By God, I done it, and I done it without any flashlight." He remembered what Fred Clafin had told him a long time ago when Fred had found him crying after Mama had whipped him for whirling a cat around by the tail and throwing it into a wall, "No use crying Lonnie. Sniveling don't help. Since crying won't make any difference, just as well be brave." He wiped his nose and eyes on his shirt sleeve, inched over to the wall and started moving, letting the empty flashlight scrape along the damp rock.

As he moved down the wall clicking the flashlight against the rough stone, he thought about the match in his hat band. He reached up and touched the oblong bulge it made, and felt better. He felt even better when far ahead in the darkness he heard the blow hole muttering and panting, making that scary whining sound. Then he was under it feeling the warm air pulsating around him.

"By God, I did it, back to the end of it and out again with no light, except for a match." He laughed a little, enjoying the sound of the flashlight clicking along the wall. At last, ahead of him, he saw a vague paleness, a square of dimness fixed there against a frame of total black. Faintly, he heard his brother Sam's voice strangely distorted by the echoes coming off the walls. "Hey Lonnie, you okay? You been in there a long time, you okay?"

He didn't answer but he reached down and dragged his hand through the sand and gravel and came up with the kite string. So that's why he didn't see it, they had buried it until it got dark. He sat down, grinning, holding the string in his hand, listening to them calling his name. They were all hollering now, even Jimmy Joe, sounding like he was scared as hell. Just when Lonnie figured they would start looking for him, he got up and ambled toward the mouth of the cave. He could see them walking around, peering into the darkness, hollering. He quickened his pace, shading his eyes from the brightness at the entrance and walked out.

"Shit, I'm okay, what you hollerin' like a bunch of scared old women for? Shit I'm okay, you think I'd be afraid of a little dark and a bunch of bats?" He paused looking at them, "Or a stinkin' piece of wood?"

He walked over to Jimmy Joe and handed him the flashlight. "I was gonna kill you for that board trick and for takin' out the batteries, but that board just made the trip more interesting, and hell, I didn't need no light. Hell, I've even got a match I could have used."

He took it from his hat band and struck it on the seat of his pants, and they all watched it flare briefly for a moment before it went out. "I didn't need it because I like the dark. I'm a bat now, a Golden Bat."

Bobby Leo was looking at him like he was the king of the world. "I wanna go in there," Bobby Leo proclaimed in a high piping voice. He started running into the cave shouting, "I wanna be a Golden Bat too."

Jimmy Joe caught him and whacked him a couple of times. "You little creep, you'll get your time. Now come on out before I beat the shit out of you. It's time we went home."

Bobby Leo and Jimmy Joe rode away from them across the alkali flats toward the Morgan ranch house which could be seen vaguely through the dust and haze of the afternoon. It was hotter than hell. Sam led the way on Old Dutch with Lonnie tagging along behind trying to keep Baldy from running away.

Running away whenever he was pointed home was just one of Baldy's bad habits. He had a bunch. He would puff his belly way up every time Lonnie tried to cinch the saddle tight, and then, when least expected, he would un-puff so the saddle would turn and dump Lonnie. He would run under branches or clothes lines or anything else that came handy, trying to scrape Lonnie off, which had happened twice. Two other times, when drinking water at the pond, Baldy had suddenly moved into deeper water and laid down, leaving Lonnie floundering around in the mud.

Baldy was always full of surprises. Right now he was trying to run away, but Lonnie had him under control. He had Baldy's head pulled way over to the side by wrapping one of the reins around the saddle horn and cinching it tight. Even with that, Baldy made little trotting shunts back and forth, catching up with Old Dutch for a moment before falling behind.

Lonnie was surprised to hear his brother's voice drifting back to him through the dust, which kept rising every time Old Dutch put his foot down. "You did pretty good at the cave Lonnie, nobody could have done it any better even though you're just eight years old. But be honest, you were scared to death weren't you? You were probably pissin' your pants the whole time."

"I didn't piss my pants." Lonnie let Baldy have a little slack and he lurched ahead until he was even with Old Dutch. "See look at my pants. They're as dry as a bone." He raised up in the saddle to let Sam have a look. "See, I didn't piss my pants, and I'm a Golden Bat now. Even if you and that prick Jimmy Joe tried to trick me."

They were crossing the Cimarron now, down the bank into the muddy bottom where just a trickle of water ran. Sometimes when it rained a lot somewhere up the valley, it could widen out to maybe a half mile of rolling dirty water. But now, with no rain for three months, it was just a trickle. They went up the far bank, then up a steep rise to a small circular pile of red boulders. From there Lonnie could see up the valley, maybe for thirty miles. To the north, Black Mesa stood out like a crooked black snake disappearing into the haze of the far distance. It was flat on the top, crowned by a black malpai bluff, the leftover of a lava flow that came down from volcanoes further west millions of years ago. The top of the black rim was a valley back then, filling up with lava which hardened to provide a rimrock which remained as the softer clay and sandstone to the south eroded to create the Cimarron Valley. Old Man Dick, who was an expert on things, practically everything, had told Lonnie all about it. How certain places like the Spire and Old Battleship and the Wedding Cake were once hard red rock which remained where they were as the softer stuff eroded around them.

As Lonnie looked up the valley, he could see the perfect concentric rings of the Wedding Cake, layer after layer of rock, some reddish pink, others blood red, others a mixture of blue and green with a white granite crown. It sure looked like a wedding cake!

To the northwest, right in the middle of the ranch, Old Battleship stood out, with its sharp prow cutting through the cactus, mesquite and dry grass on the valley floor. To the south there was a rugged arrangement of mesas, separated by lots of deep canyons and breaks which had been gouged out by millions of years of wind and water.

In between Black Mesa and the rugged mesas on the south was the Cimarron Valley, maybe ten miles wide in some places, but narrowing toward the west where the Cimarron river came down out of the highlands just east of Folsom. To the east, the valley simply disappeared just after Black Mesa, the highest point in Oklahoma, and melted into the flat lowlands of Kansas and the panhandles of Texas and Oklahoma.

CHAPTER 2

Jake

Lonnie looked back toward the cottonwoods which lined the bank
of the river. A rider was coming out of the trees headed toward
them. Lonnie couldn't make him out at first, too much dust haze,
but after a few minutes that crazy bastard Jake Veeder and his huge
horse, Macon, named after Macon, Georgia, where all the Veeders
had come from a few years before, became clear and kept getting
clearer and bigger the closer they got. Lonnie never knew what to
think about Jake Veeder. He was as big as a barn and as strong as a
bull.

Once, coming back from Clayton in their Model A Ford after a
rain, they had got stuck in a rut. Daddy kept rocking back and
forth with his wheels spinning, going nowhere, digging deeper
and deeper until the bottom of the car was hitting the top of the
road. They were stuck like that when Jake Veeder came along with
Macon making thudding clopping sounds in the wet grass by the
side of the road. Jake had pulled up, stared at the car for a while,
then got down from Macon, walked over, lifted the rear of the car
out of the rut and set it over. Then he went to the front of the car
and did the same thing. He stood there watching, with a crazy grin
on his face, as Daddy got the car going and drove away.

Another time Jake Veeder had rescued Lonnie from that prick
Jimmy Joe and Sam when they were threatening to beat the shit out
of him. They had been playing Wild West with their rubber guns,
all four of them, Jimmy Joe, Bobby Leo, Sam and Lonnie, when
Jimmy Joe called time out to take a piss. He had just shot Bobby
Leo in the eye with a thick rubber band which had been stretched
from the end of the barrel of his wooden pistol to a clothes-pin
attached to the butt of the gun. Bobby Leo's eye was red and his
nose was running as he kept trying to keep from crying.

Anyway, the truce was called, and Jimmy Joe took out his cock
and started making a fine stream up against a post next to the load-

8

ing chute. Lonnie couldn't resist it. He squeezed the butt of his pistol, the clothes-pin released the stretched rubber band, and it made a fine splatting sound as it hit Jimmy Joe square in the cock. Lonnie started running, hoping to get to Baldy before they caught him. But he wasn't fast enough, Sam caught him first, then Jimmy Joe grabbed him too, and they both started whacking him around.

Suddenly there was Jake Veeder on his horse Macon. He reached down, grabbed Lonnie by the belt, lifted him and put him behind him, with Lonnie feeling like he had just been saved from being killed. Then Jake looked down at Jimmy Joe, who was rubbing his crotch and Sam, who was looking astonished, and said in his little boy's voice, his face beaming with his crazy grin.

"Now you li'l' ol' boys doan wanna go roun' hurtin' li'l' bitty boys, now do you. Now I'm gonna put this little ol' dogey caf down, and if you all pick on him, at all, I'm gonna rope and hog-tie the both of you. Do you all hea' me?"

Finally Jimmy Joe muttered, "Well he shot me in the cock." He was sniffling a little. "And it hurts like hell, an' we had a truce, but he broke the truce and shot me. While I was takin' a piss."

Jake Veeder grinned even wider. "Well he musta been a good shot to hit a li'l' bitty thing like that. Yank 'er out and let's take a look, that is if you can find 'er. Shit it's probably crawled way back in there, lookin' for a safe place to hide."

Jimmy Joe muttered something and sidled away toward the door of the barn.

Jake put Lonnie on the ground, then while turning Macon, announced in his little boy voice. "Now I doan wanta hafta hog-tie you yearlins, so you better leave this little bitty dogey alone." Then he looked at Lonnie.

"Now when you get home I want you to tell that little ol' sweet sister of yourn, that I saved yor li'l' ol' shifless ass."

As he was talking, he started squirming around in his saddle making crazy motions like he always did when he was near Lucy Lemur. Lonnie appreciated being saved from what he considered would have been certain death, but watching Jake Veeder do his wiggling and rocking while he was talking about Lucy Lemur made him realize again that Jake Veeder was crazier than a bull-bat and that sometimes he could be real scary.

Jake Veeder had this thing for Lucy Lemur. When he was around her, he would do a kind of prancing shuffle and talk baby talk in his little boy voice. Lucy Lemur couldn't stand him. When he would do his act, she would look away as if he didn't exist, but Lonnie knew that she knew Jake Veeder was interested, because she would always stand a little straighter with her back arched so her tits, which had been getting a lot bigger recently, were clearly outlined under whatever she happened to be wearing.

Actually Jake Veeder was famous for a lot of reasons. Not only for lifting Daddy's car out of the rut but for being an expert roper and rope twirler. At the last rodeo over at the Behimer place, he had given a show which everybody agreed was the best rope twirling exhibition they had ever seen. First he had done a little dance while whirling two loops from two ropes, dancing in and out of the loops without missing a stroke. Then he had two loops going in opposite directions, one around his knees and the other around his shoulders. As a finale, he had mounted Macon and made a huge loop which went round and round, while Macon was turning in the opposite direction. He finished his show by riding up to the grandstand where Lucy Lemur was sitting, still whirling the rope, the loop getting smaller and smaller until it was just big enough to whirl around his own head. Then he threw the loop around Lucy Lemur, who was half way up the grandstand looking embarrassed with her eyes darting everywhere except at Jake Veeder. But there was loud applause and shouts for Jake Veeder, and Lonnie, who was sitting with Bobby Leo near the chute, could see that Lucy Lemur was secretly pleased. She even nodded to Jake Veeder as she took off the rope and threw it at him.

And he was also famous for having the biggest, toughest horse in the Cimarron Valley. Macon was as big as a work horse and built like one with a huge neck and shoulders and a long sleek body covered with hair that was almost gold. But he could be as dainty as any cutting horse, something he was really good at. All Jake had to do was let Macon know which cow he wanted cut out of the herd and Macon would do the rest, moving back and forth, speeding up and slowing down, always anticipating the moves of the cow until she finally gave up and let herself be cut out of the herd.

And Macon was famous for trotting the seventy miles from Texaline where a number of ranchers had driven their pooled herd to the shipping yard there. Jake had volunteered to try for a record and he made one with hours to spare. Macon had trotted for eight hours without stopping with Jake, as big as he was, moving in graceful unison with the swaying movements of the horse. A big crowd was waiting at the Veeder ranch when Jake and Macon, moving relentlessly through the rising dust, came into view. When Macon finally came to a halt in front of everybody, Jake doffed his black hat, now turned grey from the dust, waved it, and did a deep bow.

There was lots of applause for Jake and Macon that day, and Lucy Lemur who was watching with a funny little crooked smile on her face joining in. The other riders kept straggling in all the rest of the day, and some of them didn't get back until way after midnight. Nobody even came close to beating Jake Veeder's record, and everybody agreed that probably no one ever would.

Now, with Macon moving at a half trot, Jake Veeder came riding up to them. He stopped in front of Lonnie and Sam and gave them one of his crazy grins. "Well, if there ain't two of my favorite people in the whole world, the mean yearlin' bull and the li'l' shifless dogey caf. I bet you guys been doin' somethin' real interesting like settin' off firecrackers in big piles of fresh cowshit."

Lonnie's eyes bugged out in surprise. He wondered if Jake had heard about the time when him and Bobby Leo had done just that. Lonnie had pushed the firecracker, a two incher, deep into a pile of cowshit until nothing showed but the fuse. He lit the fuse and ran, but Bobby Leo just sat there staring in fascination. Suddenly there was a muffled "blam," and a wave of cowshit spread out in all directions, some of it turning Bobby Leo green. They had washed Bobby Leo and his clothes in the horse tank, and they thought nobody ever knew the difference. But Jake Veeder was grinning even wider now, looking down at Lonnie who was about five feet below him because he and Baldy were so little and Macon and Jake were so big.

Lonnie figured he had to say something, so he blurted out, "I wish I had a stick of dynamite so I could put it under your saddle and blow you clear out on top of Black Mesa."

Jake Veeder looked serious and began wiggling and swaying in his saddle. "Hey you little farts," his speech became baby talk and

11

took on a cooing lisping quality. "You tell that li'l' ol' sweet sister
of yourn, that I was askin' 'bout 'er an' that one of these days I'm
gonna rope and hog tie 'er and carry 'er away."

With that, he turned and headed toward the Veeder ranch, with
Macon raising a plume of dust every time his foot struck the dry
ground. Lonnie and Sam watched him go, with Lonnie thinking
that Jake was probably the craziest son-of-a-bitch in the whole
Cimarron valley. And sometimes he was downright scary.

Lonnie was turned round in his saddle looking up toward the
Spire when Baldy got his chance. With all this looking around and
talking to Jake, Lonnie had relaxed. Baldy gave a sharp jerk on the
reins; they pulled out of Lonnie's hand and un-looped from the
saddle horn. Off Baldy went in a trail of expanding dust toward
the ranch buildings, which showed through the haze in the distance: the milk-house with the water tank on its top, the windmill
spinning away and the barns, all looking small against the back-
drop of the near mesa.

There was no stopping Baldy once he got started. Lonnie hung
on, enjoying the wind whipping in his hair and the rapid drum-
ming of Baldy's hooves on the dry ground. Baldy went under the
clothes line but Lonnie was ready for him; he ducked low in the
saddle and missed the line by six inches. Baldy headed for the pond,
but Lonnie was ready for him again. Just before they got there, he
jumped off and let Baldy wade in by himself. Baldy kept going in
until the water reached his belly, then put his head down and started
sucking in water, gulp after gulp. Lonnie stood there holding the
reins, watching Baldy's throat move up and down, listening to him
catch his breath every now and then as he drank, his breath making little feathers in the water every time he breathed out.

Just as Baldy raised his head for a break in drinking, Sam came
in with Old Dutch at a slow walk. "That Baldy's still got your
number."

He was laughing and it pissed Lonnie off. "I can hold him when
I want to; I just wanted to get home fast. And I did while you were
out there messing around with that old bag of bones you ride."

"Sure you can hold him, just as long as he wants you to. When
you take his saddle off, be sure you rub him down. Remember
what Fred Clafin said about letting a horse drink too much when

he's hot from runnin'. You better pull him away." Lonnie pulled Baldy away and headed for the barn.

He had just finished rubbing Baldy down when he heard Mama calling "Orlando Ray, Orlando Ray." Jesus he wished she wouldn't call him that! He let Baldy loose in the corral and headed for the house. She was standing in the doorway, a short Irish lady with long brown hair streaked with grey, hanging down on each side of her face, and slightly bugged brown eyes, always slightly teary and a little vague, blinking too quickly.

"Can you get us a rabbit for supper, Lonnie? I tried to get a chicken but I couldn't catch one. Lucy finally caught one. A rabbit to go with it would help, if you think you can shoot one for supper." Her voice was hurried, a little breathless.

"You bet, Mama, you know I'm a Golden Bat now. I went clear to the back of Morgan's cave, in the dark, and I wasn't scared a bit, Mama."

"That's nice, Lonnie. Now go get your gun and get us a rabbit."

CHAPTER 3

Rabbits And Chickens

Lonnie walked through the kitchen where the cook stove was making popping and cracking sounds from the cedar Mama had just fed into it and down the hallway which separated the living room from the bedrooms to the gun cabinet. It was full of guns, maybe eight or ten from Daddy's 30-40 Craig to Sam's 30-30. There was Mama's 410 shotgun, Lucy Lemur's 30-30, and other rifles belonging to the hired men, Fred Clafin's 30-06, and one ancient one, made around 1880, a 38-55 Winchester belonging to Old Bartolo.

And there, half-hidden behind other rifles, was his single shot 22. He took it out carefully, stroking the octagonal barrel, the glossy dark wood of the stock which he kept rubbed down with linseed oil. He pulled the lever down and checked to be sure it was unloaded, like Fred Clafin had showed him. He leaned down and sniffed the faint odor of burnt powder mixed in with the smell of oil that remained from the last time he had cleaned it. It was his!

He had worked for it watering the hogs last winter when it was so cold he had to break the ice so he could keep filling the trough, bucket after bucket, with the hogs pushing and squealing and grunting around his legs, sometimes taking a little nip at his pants until he kicked them away. Fred Clafin had paid him five cents a day, and he kept carrying water for the hogs until he had earned five dollars, which was almost what his gun cost.

He had gone to Trinidad with Fred Clafin to get it and was horrified to hear that the price had gone up, that he was forty cents short. He had stacked his money on the counter in bunches of ten nickels each and was standing there helpless, staring at his little piles, thinking he wasn't going to get his gun after all when Fred Clafin reached in his pocket and pulled out the forty cents. He patted Lonnie on the shoulder as the clerk gathered up all his nickels. "This extra is what's called a bonus, Lonnie, for doing such a good job." Lonnie couldn't think of anything to say; he just held the gun in his hands looking at it. All the way home from Trinidad he had held his gun close, rubbing it and smelling it, even as he did now.

From the lower drawer of the gun cabinet he took a little box which had Super X written in red on the side, and removed five long-rifle shells, the kind that made a lot of noise and had a lot of killing power, according to Old Man Dick.

On his way, out Lucy Lemur came out of her bedroom into the hallway and grabbed him. She was looking down at him, big and mean and scary, her huge black eyes boring into him, her hair black and flaring out on every side. "You got my fingernail polish, you little creep. I know you got it." She grabbed his hand, "See there's some on your hand."

He snatched his hand away. "I ain't got your fingernail polish. What would I do with your fingernail polish? You must be crazy." He tried to pull away but she held on tight.

"You better let me go. Mama told me to get some rabbits for supper. And you're bothering me and it's getting late. You just better leave me alone, or I won't get no rabbits."

"You won't get any rabbits anyway," Lucy Lemur's voice quieted, she shook her head, and her huge eyes seemed to glow in the dim light of the hallway. She looked just like the lemur Lonnie had seen in the *National Geographic Magazine*. A lemur from some island off the coast of Africa that had huge eyes and a black crown of hair, and which looked so much like Lucy that thereafter he always thought of her as Lucy Lemur.

"I know you got my fingernail polish." She let him go and he dodged around her and headed for the front door, passing Mama who was standing next to the stove, with her head cocked to the side as if she had been listening.

Some of the hired hands were just coming in, watering their horses at the pond. Bartolo Viejo, who was getting old and looking rickety, was staring at him, stroking his long white mustache. "Hey, Lonnito, you do good huntin'. Okay some fat rabbits for supper, maybe you get a deer."

"Sure he'll get a deer," it was that runt Dogey Allen, that little shit with a crooked sneer on his face, as he looked at Lonnie, "Or maybe a mountain lion! Or maybe a grizzly bear!"

"Fuck you," said Lonnie as he broke down his rifle, put in a shell and clicked it closed, careful to pull the hammer back half way, on safety. He started walking toward the near mesa where the scrub oak and mesquite and cactus clumps made good hiding places for rabbits—and rattlesnakes!

At the top of the white limestone outcropping where they had quarried out the rock for the ranch house, he stopped and looked back. The sun was lower now, long shadows made dark square blotches on the east side of the buildings. The shadow of the wind-mill wheel was turning on the dried grass. To the north, the long dark smudge of Black Mesa meandered away to the west and the east to become lost in the haze, dust and heat waverings rising from the alkali flats. In the middle of the valley, the cottonwood trees skirting the Cimarron river made a green undulating ribbon, and to the south, the hodgepodge of mesas riven by canyons and arroyos, leading, if one went up far enough, to the line cabin on the topside where one could see the Rabbit Ears way over toward Clayton. To the northwest, the Wedding Cake, red and white lay-ers rising to a conical point, looking small and perfect from where he stood but actually three or four hundred feet high, covered with rough black and red boulders, scrub oak and lots of soap weeds and cactus.

Much nearer, only two or three miles away, on the far side of the middle pasture—Old Battleship, its dull red bluffs gleaming in the low sun, cruised along through the cactus, mesquite and brown grass. To the east, the red crags of the Spire were brighter than he had ever seen them.

He started walking again, crossing the ridge of white limestone where they had quarried out the rock, his head down, looking for arrowheads and rattlesnakes. Occasionally he would stop and glance around him thinking that maybe just over the next rise he would see a rabbit. He usually didn't get any rabbits during these hunts, but it was fun anyway stalking along with his gun ready. He thought he saw something move, over by a huge boulder at the bottom of the near mesa. He paused and sure enough a roadrun-ner made a dash toward a mesquite grove, running like crazy, thirty miles an hour, Old Man Dick said.

Even as he watched, a rabbit, a fat cottontail, jumped up and skittered way, visible for a blurry moment before it disappeared behind a cactus. He pulled the hammer back, let his finger rest gently on the trigger and eased up on the cactus until he could see around it, but there wasn't anything there. Then he saw the rabbit only about twenty feet away, bunched up into a furry ball, ears laid back against its head, nose trembling, eyes bright and beady, staring ahead.

He raised his gun and saw the grey blob wavering in his sights, gently squeezed the trigger, as Fred Clafin had taught him, heard the sharp "chuff" of the rifle. The rabbit leaped straight in the air then fell on its side, its legs kicking, blood spreading darkly in its fur. He stood for a long moment his heartbeat and breathing slowing. By God he had done it. Even Old Man Dick would have to admit it now, that he was some hunter. He had killed six rabbits since he got his gun and this one was probably the biggest and fattest one of all. He picked it up by its hind legs and started for the house, still looking out for rattlesnakes and arrowheads.

When he came to the quarry ridge he stopped and pulled out a square stone. There in a hole was his treasure, contained in a cigar box that Old Man Dick had given him. He opened it carefully, smelling the lingering odor of cigars mixed in with the almond odor of fingernail polish. There were a lot of important things in that box, his arrowheads, a spearhead as big as his hand, red and white flint with serrated edges, a silver dollar that Old Bartolo had given him for holding his arm out for twenty minutes, his Barlow knife, a soldier's medal from the big war and a piece of petrified wood.

He had used the fingernail polish to paint it and it made all its colors stand out beautiful, shades of red and brown and yellow, overlaid by the pink of the fingernail polish. He picked it up and ran his hand over its smooth surface, smelling the almond odor. Yes, it sure was beautiful. He placed everything back in the box and was about the close it when he saw the nearly empty bottle. He put it aside and returned the cigar box with its precious contents to the square hole. He covered it with the stone and stood for a moment marveling that nobody would know anything was there even if they looked right at it. Then he threw the bottle as far as he could, saw it flickering in the light of the setting sun before it disappeared in the dry grass.

Lonnie put his rabbit on the anvil by the tack-room, watching the cowboys coming in. Dogey Allen sure was a scrawny little runt, and mean, everybody said. He was skinny, bucktoothed, a yellow complexion with lots of pimples, shifty eyes which never looked right at you. He got his pimples from beating his meat, Old Walt insisted, even though Dogey was twenty-two, which was supposed to be too old for pimples. When people kidded him about it, he would laugh, showing his big brown teeth which he got from chewing tobacco all the time. Old Walt, in particular, kept kidding Dogey about his meat beating, and Dogey would respond. "The trouble with you Walt, is you're so old and blind you couldn't find your own prick, and if you did, you wouldn't be able to get anything out of it, except maybe some dust."

Old Walt was old, maybe forty-five, and he did have funny eyes. He couldn't close them. Two or three years before he had had a bunch of warts on his eyelids and had gone to a guy who was supposed to be good at wart treatment. The guy had put medicine on some balls of cotton and bandaged them in place on Old Walt's eyes for a couple of hours. When he took off the bandages, Old Walt's eyes swelled up so much he couldn't see a thing. Then little by little he got so he could see again but his eyelids came off. He went around now just staring, not being able to blink, day and night.

Lonnie couldn't help being curious about Old Walt's eyes and once had asked him if he ever went to sleep. "Sure I go to sleep, people can sleep with their eyes open." He looked at Lonnie for a moment and his eyes seemed to twinkle, or maybe they were just shining from the drops he put in them. "I can sleep just like anybody else but sometimes its hard to get to sleep 'cause so much is happenin'. The trouble is they dry out a lot when I'm asleep so I have to put in some of these drops, when I wake up."

Old Walt had had a lot of jobs before Daddy hired him. People would hire him and then he would get fired. He always worked hard but people just couldn't stand having him around with him always staring like that. Lonnie's uncle Doc Wilson, the county sheriff, had hired him once, just before Daddy hired him. The sheriff thought Old Walt would be a natural as jail guard. He figured nobody would try to pull anything with Old Walt out there staring all the time, even when he was asleep. They had fixed up a comfortable chair in front of the door where Old Walt could see all the cells, and he was given responsibility for the night shift.

But one of the inmates, a regular visitor to the jail because of his screaming drunks, noticed a certain vagueness in Old Walt's eyes when he was sitting there staring. One night when the door to his cell had been accidentally left unlocked, this guy made a bunch of funny motions with his hands and put some wild expressions on his face, but Old Walt didn't make a move. Then the guy just walked out, right past Old Walt who was staring at him as he left.

Everybody thought it was funnier than hell except the Sheriff who was up for reelection. He hated to do it but he fired Old Walt after making sure Daddy would hire him.

Old Walt came out of the bunkhouse and watched Bartolo finish skinning and gutting the rabbit. Lonnie was watching too, thinking that maybe he was going to be sick. It wasn't the sight of the guts that got him but the hot sweet smell that came from the rabbit's naked body after its skin had been pulled off. He backed off a little and glanced at Old Walt. Not only did he have weird looking eyes, he didn't have any teeth, not a one, and he had a long nose which seemed to touch his chin every time his face collapsed while eating or chewing tobacco.

Old Walt examined the rabbit, all naked except for its feet which made it look like it had boots on. Old Walt took out his pocket knife. "There's lots of luck going to waste if we don't get them feet! I'm goin' to cut 'em off and we'll all have some good luck."

Lonnie was looking at the naked rabbit with its fur boots. "You mean them feet really bring good luck?"

"Sure they do, I had one in my pocket when I got rid of my warts," Walt made guttural cackling sounds, deep in his throat. Lonnie guessed he was laughing but couldn't figure out what was so funny.

"Now you guys hold him while I cut 'em off! One for me, it always pays to get a new one every now and then. If you don't, the luck wears out. One for you, Lonnie, one for Bartolo, and one for Lucy."

Lonnie helped Bartolo hold the rabbit, listening in fascination as the knife grated through the bone. He looked at his rabbit foot thinking maybe it was all a bunch of crap.

"Now you keep that foot on you all the time, both of you, and you won't have no warts."

Bartolo was grinning, his face all crinkled up, "Muchas gracias, amigo Walt, I keep, sure don't want no warts."

Lonnie shrugged his shoulders and put his rabbit foot in his shirt pocket. He took the rabbit from Bartolo and presented it to his mother who looked pleased. "That's fine, Lonnie, a nice rabbit. I'll cut it up so we can have it for supper." She paused for a moment smiling at him, then suddenly looked pained as she glanced at the chicken which was sizzling in the frying pan.

Lonnie didn't like to see her looking like that, like something was bothering her. "Go get washed up Lonnie, but bring in some wood first."

Lonnie listened, he could hear somebody chopping wood, probably Sam. He went out the front door, past the windmill to the woodpile next to the bunkhouse, where Sam was splitting pieces of cedar which had been cut into stove length pieces by the buzz saw. Lonnie loved the buzz saw, the high screeching sounds and cedar smells and sometimes smoke which puffed out when it ran into a knot. Old Walt was the expert with the buzz saw, placing the wood on the rack just right and pushing the rack in easy as the wood met the whirling teeth. He didn't seem to mind the sawdust even though it got in his eyes a lot and he had to keep cleaning them with a squirt bottle he kept in his pocket, dabbing them with a white rag.

Lonnie watched Sam splitting wood, balancing each piece on its end before whacking it right down the middle. He was really good at it. He stopped for a moment, looking at Lonnie, holding the two bladed axe out in front of him.

"Hey, Golden Bat, wanna try this? It ain't hard."

Lonnie backed away, "No thanks, that's okay, you go ahead. I'd probably cut my leg off."

Lonnie was enjoying the pungent odor of fresh cut cedar as he carried in the wood, when he saw a car coming in on their road from Highway 64, raising a billowing plume of dust.

"Daddy's comin', Mama," he said as he put the wood in the wood-box. They both listened as a car came to a stop, the car door slammed and massive steps came up the walk to the front door. It opened and there he was, a huge man, filling the doorway, coal black hair with streaks of white falling down covering his ears. Heavy features, made larger by the small glasses he was always peering through without seeming to see anything. Broad shoulders, a big gut that fell down over his belt, and a stern expression that made everybody uneasy, even Lucy Lemur, who once said that when Daddy looked someplace it had dark shadows in it.

Lonnie could never figure out what Daddy was thinking. He was always sitting in his chair staring out the picture window toward Black Mesa, with his lips moving. Lonnie knew he must be thinking deep thoughts because his thinking was almost like talking, coming down to his lips as it did. But he seldom said anything out loud except when he made an announcement or gave directions to Fred Clafin. Lonnie had heard him make a speech once when he was running for county commissioner, and was amazed that Daddy could say so much about buildings and roads and bridges. He could barely read and could only sign his name. He was always saying, "Blanche, you got the education, read this to me," or sometimes, "Get a piece of paper, Blanche, we're gonna write a letter." And Mama always went running with that hopeful expression on her face, glad to be of use.

Lonnie loved Daddy more than anybody but he was afraid of him, the way he looked when his lips were moving or the way he sounded when he came home drunk, cussing and shouting.

But he could be kind and gentle too. One day a long time ago when Lonnie was just a little kid, Daddy had found him out behind the barn trying to take a crap and getting nothing done. He had picked Lonnie up and carried him to the house, rumbling with concern. "Blanche, this kid's constipated, get him some draught to loosen him up." Lonnie hated it but he had to take it, a big spoon full of green powder that tasted like ground up hay. It was so dry and hard to swallow that he sneezed and produced a green haze in front of him, causing Mama to sneeze and Daddy to laugh, which he seldom did.

Another time when they were going to have company, everybody was trying to catch some chickens to fry, that is everybody but Lonnie, who didn't feel like running just then. Daddy kept calling him to come out and run down a chicken. Lonnie was fast and could turn corners faster than anybody, even faster than some chickens. But that day he just ambled around thinking how silly they all looked running around like crazy with the chickens squawking and flapping their wings. Daddy finally got fed up, he

21

grabbed Lonnie and gave him a smack on the rear and told him to start running chickens.

Lonnie was offended and shocked. Daddy had never hit him before, except for that one really bad time which he didn't like to think about. Mama was the one who whacked him when he did something bad like the time he tied a string around Mike Collin's prick and his own so they could walk around feeling like real friends with a common bond.

How was Lonnie to know that Mike would suddenly start to run without any warning whatever? All Lonnie could do was grab the string just as Mike hit the end of it. They had a tough time getting the string off because Mike's prick swelled up and turned blue. Lonnie got a beating from Mama for that one, even though it wasn't his fault. But he had become famous. Years later when he came home from the army, people would sidle up to him with a funny look on their faces that Lonnie had come to recognize so that he always knew what was coming, "Did you really tie a string around Mike Collin's prick, and tell him to run?" Lonnie would always say something noncommittal. He didn't like to think about it particularly after the beating he got from Mama.

But Daddy had never hit him before, except for that really bad time. And just for not running down a chicken! For some reason that he couldn't figure out later, Lonnie reached down and picked up a large stick and turned on Daddy making motions like he was ready to hit him. Daddy just stood there with a hurt look on his face not saying a thing. Not doing a thing! Lonnie threw the stick down and started running chickens, looking back every now and then to see Daddy watching him.

But that was a long time ago. This night they were having chicken again, and Lonnie's rabbit. They were all around the table, Fred Clafin, Bartolo, Dogey Allen, Old Walt and Horse Womack on one side with Sam, Lucy Lemur and Lonnie on the other. Daddy was at the head of the table and Mama was at the foot, jumping up every now and then to refill a bowl or a platter. They had just started eating when something funny happened. Mama was talking about the chicken just as Lonnie was about to bite into a wing. Mama was looking at the chicken platter.

"I don't know what happened to one of these chickens," she said in her soft, always hurried voice, "Bartolo brought it in all torn up and bleeding, it was out behind the barn just lying there bleeding."

Lonnie suddenly couldn't eat his wing, he was looking at Sam who was giving him that shitty look he sometimes wore when he knew something about you. Sam glanced at Mama. "That sometimes happens, Mama," he looked at Lonnie again with that shitty smirk on his face. "Maybe Lonnie knows what happened."

Lonnie had stopped eating, everybody was looking at him, even Daddy. "I don't know anything about any chicken, why would I know anything about an ol' chicken." His voice sounded screechy in his own ears. He looked down at his plate and took a big mouthful of pinto beans.

They all started eating again, but Lonnie kept thinking about the chicken. Bobby Leo had been over the day before and had brought a bunch of firecrackers, big long ones, two inchers. They had been dropping them into one of the pipes which worked as a handle for a post hole digger. Lonnie would drop in a lighted firecracker and Bobby Leo would drop in a marble. They would both aim it and could hit damn near anything, the fan of the windmill, a cow out in the pasture.

Then Lonnie thought about the chicken. He had run it down inside the big barn where nobody could see what he was doing. And he had performed the operation, putting the firecracker up its ass. Bobby Leo lit the fuse and he let the chicken go.

Sitting there munching his beans he had a vision of the frenzied flight, the flapping wings and heard again the soft "blam."

Lonnie knew that Sam was still watching him, could feel his eyes. Jesus Christ! "Maybe you better eat some of that rabbit you killed Lonnie, I think you might like it better than the chicken."

"Yea, pass the rabbit," said Lonnie. "Boy you should have seen this guy jump when I shot him, straight up in the air." He hoped his voice sounded okay He looked around but nobody was looking at him, they were staring at Old Walt whose eyes were watering so much that tears were running down his cheeks and dripping onto his plate. Lucy Lemur was making small disgusted sounds deep in her throat, but Lonnie could see that she was concerned. What in the hell was wrong with Old Walt? Lonnie figured he had maybe thought about something sad or maybe he had taken a bite of real hot chili.

"My goodness Walt," Mama said, "I hope you're not crying because my corn bread is so bad." Mama laughed a little, in self depreciation. She got up and found a white cloth for Walt, "Here's something for your eyes."

Old Walt took it and wiped his cheeks and dabbed at his eyes. Lucy Lemur made more disgusted sounds. Everybody else at the table kept looking down at their plates except for Horse Wommack, who was staring at Lucy Lemur. He was always staring at her when he thought nobody would notice, and his eyes looked funny when he stared, kinda like Old Growler's eyes when he was watching every move you made when you ate something.

Horse was well named. He looked like a horse with his long thin face, bent nose and buck teeth. And he sounded like one when he laughed, a kind of high pitched whinny. He hardly ever said anything except in the evenings when all the cowboys sat around exchanging bullshit stories. Then he would tell a bunch of big lies or dirty stories which he would always spoil with his whinny before he got to the end of them.

CHAPTER 4

Evening

Daddy got up and left the table, he always left the table first which was a signal that the rest of them could leave if they wanted to. Lonnie jumped up and headed for the door. He was afraid somebody might say something else about that chicken. He started up the slope towards his treasure box on the quarry ridge, looking out for arrowheads and rattlesnakes. The sun had gone down but there was a bright glow from some patchy clouds. To the west, the mesas and canyons were black with shadows, but to the east they were suffused with a soft light that brought out the hues of the rimrocks.

The many rings of the Wedding Cake were fired by the fading light, but toward the southwest in the far pasture, Old Battleship plowed along in the semi-darkness of its own shadow. As he stood there on the ridge looking about him, Lonnie was struck with the strange place he lived in, way down in a valley separated from the rest of the world by mesas to the north and the south. It was a lonely place he knew with just a few people scattered miles and miles apart, all doing pretty much the same thing—raising cattle, riding horses and looking at mesas.

A full moon was showing above the Spire that jutted up out of the plain in the distance, just sitting there like it had been put there with a big hand. Even as he looked at the moon, the air was full of bull-bats climbing and swooping making "eoos," "eoos," as their wings slanted into the evening air at maybe two hundred miles an hour, or so Old Man Dick maintained, as they reached the bottom of a dive before they went shooting up again, beating for enough altitude to make another dive.

Down below, the lights of the house were just coming on, Mama going from room to room lighting the oil lamps and the big Aladdin lamp that used a gossamer filament and had to be pumped up all the time.

The darkness of the evening was gradually offset by the rising moon which created a soft sheen on everything; the dry grass, the white rocks, the ranch buildings. Down below, a dog was barking and way out in the pasture a calf was bawling, once every minute or two.

After a while, the glow in the west was gone but the valley lightened up as the moon rose creating black shadows on the west side of everything. It made the tops of everything shine, sharp contrasts of dark and bright with no color anywhere. The wind was rising now, coming in from the north causing the cactus to rustle and the scrub oak to sway. Winter was coming! Lonnie shivered a little as he thought about it, wind whipping snow into high drifts and ice on the pond and on the Cimarron. He didn't like winter, particularly when he had to ride out with the cattle. The coldest place in the world, on top of a horse in the winter.

Then, from below, he heard his mother calling, "Orlando Ray, Orlando Ray." God he hated that name, the way the other kids were always mocking his mother calling him "Orlando Ray," at the top of their voices, just to piss him off.

"Okay, Mama, okay, Mama, I'm coming," he screamed as loud as he could just to stop her calling. As he made his way toward the house, the light from the moon tinted everything with a glaze of silver; the house, the milk-house, the barns, the windmill, the bunkhouse, even Horse and Dogey who were walking from the tack room to the bunkhouse, and Lucy Lemur who was coming up the incline toward him. He stopped, waiting for her to start screaming at him but tonight she was strangely different. Her large black eyes seemed luminescent beneath the helmet of her black hair. She looked more like a lemur than ever as he edged away, ready to run in case she tried to grab him.

"I know you got my fingernail polish, you little creep. What I can't understand is why you would want it. Why would you want it enough to steal it? If you'll tell me I won't hit you. I promise I won't hit you."

Lonnie couldn't think of anything to say for a minute. Then he blurted out. "Well why do you want to put fingernail polish on your fingers?" he hesitated, "And lipstick on your lips? I know you been using some of Mama's lipstick, when you think she won't notice." He suddenly shouted, "I know! I know! You want the men to notice you."

He had seen how Dogey and Horse and even Old Walt kept throwing hidden glances her way when they were working around the barn or in the tack room. Had seen how she knew she was being watched and moved loose legged with her back arched, stopping every now and then to glance around her, at the mesas and across the pastures, how she would turn and walk away from them swaying a lot to emphasize her hips which were getting broader and her breasts which were getting bigger.

"You little creep, I'm gonna tell Mama what you said. You little creep. You know I don't do that. You think I'd like to have that runt Dogey, or that silly Horse, or that watery eyed Old Walt, looking at me?" She made a grab for him but he was too fast, he ducked away and started running back toward the quarry ridge. He stopped and looked back, she was walking rapidly toward the house her hips moving in easy rhythm, her black hair swinging above the whiteness of her blouse and the whiteness of her arms.

She glanced back at him over her left shoulder, "You can have the fingernail polish, it was just cheap stuff anyway." With that she disappeared into the shadow of the house and then was briefly outlined in a momentary flare of light from the open door.

When he went into the house, Mama was getting out what he hated most in the whole world, a bottle of cod liver oil. He was the only one who had to take it because he had rickets as a little kid, whatever that was. It must have been something terrible because she made him take three tablespoons of the stuff every day. Jesus Christ! She always had a determined look on her face when she came toward him with the bottle.

"Now don't argue about it, just take it."

"I don't see why I have to take that stuff Mama, you don't make Lucy and Sam take it. Why do I have to take it?"

"Because you had rickets, when you were little," Mama repeated again for the hundredth time. "Get up here and take it."

"I just can't do it three times. Maybe just one time. Put it all in a cup and I'll take it down in one big gulp."

She hesitated, then went to the cabinet and got a cup. The thick yellow green liquid made soft "blub, blub"s as she measured out three tablespoons and put them in the cup. She handed him the cup and stared at him expectantly. He looked down into the cup. Jesus Christ! It smelled terrible, like rotten fish. His brother Sam came in just then, sized up the situation and came over to Lonnie looking smug and superior. He and Mama were both waiting so he turned up the cup and filled his mouth. And it just stayed there. It wouldn't go down! He tried to swallow again and again but nothing happened except his throat moved up and down and his eyes bulged spasmodically.

Sam kept shouting "Swaller it, swaller it" and Mama looked worried. Finally Sam hit him on the back three or four times and he swallowed convulsively in synchrony with the blows.

He stood there for a while on the edge of puking, gasping for air, looking at them through tear filled eyes. Little by little he got things under control. He shrugged his shoulders and licked his lips. It didn't taste so bad now.

"Can I sleep in the bunkhouse tonight Mama, there's lots of room? I can sleep in Old Man Dick's bed. I like sleeping in the bunkhouse with all the other cowboys!"

"Yes you can, yes you can." Mama's voice was hurried as usual, "But go ask Daddy. Just to be sure."

Lonnie went to the living room where Daddy was sitting in his big chair looking out through the picture window toward Black Mesa which appeared as a long dark smudge above the moonlit plain. The white light from the Aladdin lamp on the big dining table struck his forehead but his eyes were lost in shadows. He was rocking back and forth a little, thinking, Lonnie knew, because his lips were moving.

He was probably thinking about money, about how he could pay the bills and the cowboys and for the mortgage, whatever that was. A few nights before when it was really late, Lonnie had gotten up to take a piss and heard Mama and Daddy talking about it. Lonnie had peeked through a crack in the hallway door and had seen them sitting at Daddy's big desk. Mama's back was to him but Daddy was facing her and Lonnie could see him clearly. He looked really worried and suddenly Lonnie felt a clutch of fear in his chest. He had never seen Daddy look that way, like he was afraid.

Daddy's voice was low. "Are we gonna make it?"

Mama was staring at some papers. "We can make it for maybe

three months if nothing really bad happens. Maybe until we sell the cattle."

Daddy's voice was grim. "There ain't no market for cattle. Nobody's got any money, and the bank won't lend any more. The Raton bank has already gone broke and the Clayton bank is close to it. Hell, we can't even begin to get through the winter. There ain't no grass, the cattle are starvin' and we ain't got the money to buy cake or hay. Hell, we ain't even got enough money to buy salt. In two or three months I'll have to let the hands go."

There had been a long silence. Then Mama said, "I've asked Mr. Rutledge to put my name before the school board. Maybe I can teach school this year."

Another long silence with Lonnie standing there looking through the crack. He was trembling, thinking things must be pretty bad or Mama and Daddy wouldn't be talking that way and looking so worried.

After awhile Daddy's voice came through again. He sounded a lot better, almost cheerful. "Well that would help a lot. And maybe the government will buy cattle. Roosevelt said so the other day, I heard that in Clayton yesterday. And maybe he's gonna save the banks. Maybe it'll happen. Or maybe the oil men will come, and lease our land."

There had been another long silence. Then Daddy said, "One thing for sure, we ain't gonna give up."

Lonnie guessed he must have made a sound because Daddy suddenly looked straight at the door. He got up and started walking toward Lonnie who tip-toed back into the bedroom and crawled in next to Sam. He couldn't go to sleep for a long time, thinking maybe they were all going to wind up in the poor house, as Granny Martin was always saying when she was real old and feeble, just before she died.

Now Lonnie approached Daddy and touched his hand which lay on the arm of the chair, occasionally twitching in unison with his moving lips. Daddy turned his head and looked at Lonnie, his dark eyes, bigger than Lucy Lemur's behind his small glasses, were wide with surprise and irritation.

Lonnie hurriedly broke out, "Can I sleep in the bunkhouse tonight, Mama said it would be okay"

The irritation in the huge eyes died and left them suffused with amusement, and something else, perhaps pride. "Sure you can, but don't pay any attention to those stories they tell. They're just bullshit, all of them. You remember that. Just bullshit."

"I'll remember, Daddy." Lonnie turned and scurried toward the hallway fearing Daddy might change his mind. He stopped suddenly when he heard Daddy's voice. He turned and looked at him thinking the worst but Daddy was smiling.

"Oh, you can sleep with the bullshitters tonight, Lonnie. That's okay. I just wanted to thank you for that rabbit we had for supper. That was a fine rabbit."

Lonnie stood there blinking back tears. He smiled back. "Thanks Daddy." He ran back and touched Daddy's hand then headed for the hallway. As he ran out of the house he knew he would never love anybody as much as he loved Daddy.

CHAPTER 5

Bunkhouse

The door of the bunkhouse was slightly ajar showing a vertical slit of dim yellow light. The rumble of voices came to Lonnie as he walked along enjoying the way the moon cast bright light on everything. As he got near the door he could make out the voices, somebody was telling a bullshit story, Dogey Allen. He was always telling stories about fucking women, with lots of dirty words.

"Well look who's here," it was Old Walt looking up from his cards. They all sat around a small table directly under an oil lantern; Dogey Allen, Old Walt, Fred Clafin and Horse Wommack, playing pitch. Near them, where the light was best, Bartolo was mending harness, making holes with a leather punch and spreading rivets with a ballpeen hammer on a small anvil.

Lonnie pulled up a chair next to Bartolo. "How'd you learn to do that?"

Bartolo put two pieces of leather together, fitted the leather punch in place and squeezed. The punch made a quick crunchy sound as it bit into the leather. "Ah Lonnito, *muchos años*, many years ago my daddy he taught me. When I was little chiquito, like you." He leaned over and gave Lonnie a poke with the ballpeen hammer.

Dogey Allen looked up from the circle of card players, he was grinning. "That must have been about a hundred years ago, you're such an old fart."

Bartolo was grinning too. "*Sí, señor Dogey, muchos años.* Here, Lonnito, you brad down a rivet." Bartolo shoved a rivet through the hole he had just made, put a little washer on it and handed Lonnie the ballpeen hammer. Lonnie placed the leather on the anvil and began to whack away at the rivet, watching it spread a little each time he hit it. Soon it was spread way out and the two pieces of leather were fixed together.

He looked up to see Fred Clafin watching him. "That was a good job Lonnie. You're good at hunting rabbits and you're good at fixing a harness."

Lonnie felt great. They were all looking at him now. He held up the harness and saw the light gleam on the brass rivet. He handed it back to Bartolo and then sat back watching the card game. Horse had just finished playing a card and was looking back at his hand. Old Walt was studying his. At least Lonnie thought he was, but how could you tell, his eyes were so bleary it was hard to know what he was looking at.

"I'll bet you been to a lot of places, a lot of far off places," Lonnie said to Bartolo who was punching more holes in pieces of harness. "Where have you gone to?"

Horse whinnied. "Yes, he's been everywhere. Probably to Clayton a couple of times."

"He's been a lot farther than that," Fred Clafin said quietly as he picked up a trick. He's been clear across the ocean, clear over to France, he got wounded twice in the war."

Everybody stopped playing for a minute, staring at Bartolo who was smiling a little as he beat on a rivet.

Lonnie liked watching the card games. They were playing pitch, something they played most every night except right after payday when they played poker. Lonnie enjoyed poker most, watching them bet and lose and win until somebody, usually Fred Clafin, had all the money. They would borrow some of it back with Fred keeping a record in a small book he carried around. He charged five percent a month, which came to a lot of money Lonnie knew, even though he couldn't figure it out.

"Did you ever do any traveling except going to war," Lonnie asked Bartolo who had stopped working and was looking out the small window into the darkness as if he was seeing something out there. His eyes became intense as he turned his head to look at Lonnie.

"The world is big, *muy grande.*" He made a circling motion with his hand. "I see the world. I go *vamos* on a boat, I work on a boat, *mucho trabajo*, we go round the whole world."

"I knew a woman once who showed me about goin' around the world," Dogey Allen said, looking up from his cards. "Boy, it was some trip."

"I'll bet it was," Fred Clafin fanned his cards out.

"Well it sure was, a whore in Trinidad, she showed me the whole thing, the whole world."

"That's a bunch of bullshit," Lonnie was looking bug-eyed. "How could she do that?"

Dogey had everybody's attention. "Well there I was in this whore house, in Trinidad. I was as naked as a jay bird, then this gal, a real good lookin' gal, she didn't have any clothes on either. Well anyway she dripped black strap molasses on my back right down my spine, around the crack of my ass, and all over my prick. And then she started going round the world licking the molasses off."

There was complete silence in the room, the card game stopped and even Old Bartolo quit fixing harness.

Dogey readjusted himself in his chair and continued. "When she got done on one side of the world she turned me over and started on the other side, her tongue traveling along licking up the molasses. Well she licked off the molasses, off my prick and balls, then she started sucking my prick while her hands were pumping my balls. Well I bet you can figure out what happened." Dogey stopped here, took out a sack of tobacco, and made a big operation out of rolling a Bull Durham cigarette.

"You fainted," Horse whinnied and exposed his yellow buck teeth.

"Hell no, I didn't faint. Do you think I'd faint and miss everything? Hell no, she kept sucking and pumping until I was about ready to explode. Then she gives one big suck and one big pump, and I came, and came, and came. That's what happened!"

There was a long silence, then Lonnie finally said, "You know what I think, I think that's just a bunch of bullshit."

"Shit yes," said Old Walt, "the only thing Dogey's been around is a big pile of shit, bullshit, cowshit, you name it. He's probably never had a piece of ass in his life."

"Oh yes he has," Horse was whinnying and simpering. "I saw him getting some up at the high corral. He had a heifer in there snubbed down in the chute when I rode up. He was spread out with his boots stuck in the sideboards of the chute, pumping away. I can still see his white ass bobbing back and forth."

"You know what he did when I caught him at it? He grabs up his pants and starts looking in that heifer's ears, first one and then

33

the other. Said he was trying to get rid of ticks." Horse let go his whinny laugh. "You know what I told him? I told him that was a hell of a way to get rid of ticks, to punch them out like that."

Horse whinnied again but nobody else was laughing, they were all looking at Dogey Allen. He was setting forward in his chair with a stricken look on his face which, even as they watched, contorted into seething rage. "You son-of-a-bitch, that's a goddamn lie." He jumped up from his chair and lunged at Horse who sidestepped and moved back against one of the bunks. His face was contorted too, with fear.

Dogey got to him and grabbed him by his shirt front, screaming "You goddamn liar, you better take that back, or I'll kill you, you son-of-a-bitch."

They stood there swaying back and forth with Dogey looking up into Horse's face and Horse not looking at anything. His eyes were strangely slitted, his face drawn until his teeth were bared. Then Dogey started pulling buttons off his shirt. He would pull off a button, show it to Horse who wouldn't look at it, then flick it across the room. Button after button. All the time screaming at Horse that he better take it all back. Horse just stood there, not daring to move, looking like a stray dog Old Growler, Old Man Dick's dog, had grabbed by the throat, trembling, not daring to move, laying on its back with its face so tight it was pulled back into a hideous grin with its teeth showing.

"When I finish pulling off these buttons you better tell everybody you was lyin', or I'll kill you, you son-of-a-bitch," and Dogey looked like he would and Horse looked like he believed him.

The last button went sailing across the room and Horse began to talk. "Jesus Christ, Dogey, you know I was just kiddin', I was just kiddin'. I was just makin' up a story."

He looked around at the others and Dogey loosened his grip. "Shit Dogey, everybody knows you don't go around fucking cows." Dogey let him go and the mood relaxed.

Fred Clafin, who had a hint of a smile on his face, observed, "Sure that's right, everybody knows that cowboys don't fuck cows. Now everybody calm down and I'll tell a story." Dogey sat back down in his chair and Horse started looking for his buttons.

Fred Clafin assumed a strategic position under the lantern. "Well all this reminds me of a story. It seems that there were these two old ranchers, two old cowboys, who had been friends for many years. They were taking a walk down toward the creek when they came to a large maple tree standing alone in the pasture. The first old cowboy stopped, looked fondly at the tree and said, 'You know, this tree brings back fond memories.' 'How's that?' asked the other old cowboy. 'Well, as a matter of fact I got my first piece of ass under this tree.' 'Yeah, I know,' said the other cowboy, 'I saw you.' The first old cowboy looked shocked and said, 'You're kiddin', you really saw me.' 'Sure did, and not only that, her mother saw you too.' The first old cowboy was truly astonished and said, 'For Christ sake, what did she say?'

'She said "Moo",' said the second old cowboy."

There was a moment of silence and then a burst of laughter, with Horse laughing loudest of them all. But Dogey Allen wasn't laughing. He was sitting hunched over with his lips set in a thin line, glaring at Fred Clafin, and then at Horse who suddenly shut up as Dogey's glance took him in.

Then they all looked at Lonnie who was having a fit of giggling and snickering, tears running down his cheeks. "She said Moo, she said Moo," he gasped. "Boy that was some Mama and some heifer, probably real good lookin'." He broke into another spasm of laughter. Dogey Allen began to grin a little and Horse started to relax. There was a moment of silence, then Horse observed, "I'll bet Dogey's was better lookin'."

It was like an explosion, like one of Lonnie's two inchers going off. Dogey jumped clear across the table and hit Horse so hard that his chair fell over backwards with Dogey on top of him. Dogey was screaming like a crazy man, his fists moving so fast they were a blur. Fred Clafin jumped up and started pulling Dogey who was holding on to Horse so tight they both came sliding along the floor. Fred kept shouting, "Cut it out. Now! Now! Now! Or I'll beat the shit out of both of you."

Old Walt jumped in and started helping Fred and together they finally got them apart, with Dogey making snarly animal sounds, and Horse making whimpering noises, his face red as a beet and his nose bleeding.

"Now both of you sit down at that table and if either one of you starts anything, I'll fire you." Fred Clafin looked like he meant it. They glanced at him once or twice then sat back down at the table, breathing hard, not looking at each other. Dogey gritting his teeth and Horse dabbing at his nose.

The door opened suddenly and Sam, carrying a lantern, eased up the step and looked in. "Daddy wants to see you, Fred."

Fred got to his feet. "Does he want to see me now?"

"Yes, he does." Sam looked full of important news but he wasn't telling. "He said as soon as it's handy for you."

Fred took the lantern from Sam and turned to the others. "Maybe it's happening, I better go right now." He and Sam walked toward the house, the lantern swinging.

There was complete silence in the room. Bartolo crossed himself, Old Walt mumbled something that sounded like he was mad at somebody, and both Dogey and Horse whispered "Jesus Christ," almost in unison.

The silence stretched out until Lonnie said, "Can I tell a story? I've got a real dirty story, about molasses. Like Dogey's."

The apprehension diminished and they all looked at Lonnie who was standing next to one of the bunks looking eager, occasionally giggling a little in anticipation.

"*Sí, Lonnito*, you tell good story." Bartolo was back riveting harness, and the others were back playing pitch, but they were all looking at Lonnie. Lonnie, sure of his audience, his freckled cheeks glowing in the lantern light, his brown eyes shifting from face to face, said in a shrill emphatic voice.

"Well this is a story about moles, you know the little rats which can't see, which are blind and have big front feet with claws for diggin' dirt, and live in long tunnels they dig with their claws. Anyway, this mole family, daddy mole, mama mole and baby mole were going to grandma mole's house for breakfast. Daddy mole was in front with mama mole in the middle and baby mole was last. When they were way down the tunnel getting close to grandma mole's house daddy mole stopped and sniffed." Lonnie started giggling and sniffing with his face pinched up, looking like a mole.

The others laughed a little and Dogey Allen observed, "Jesus Christ, he looks like a mole."

"Yea," agreed Horse, "look at his hands, they're turning into claws."

"Well anyway," Lonnie continued. "We're getting close, said Daddy mole, I can smell pancakes."

"Yes, we are," said mama mole, she was sniffin'. Here Lonnie screwed his face up again and started sniffing, with the others chuckling in appreciation. "Yes, we're gettin' close," mama mole said, "I can smell bacon fryin'." Then baby mole who was just behind daddy mole and mama mole said in his little voice as he was sniffin', "Yes we're getting close, I can smell mole asses."

Lonnie went into a spasm of snickering and giggling, "Mole asses," he repeated, and they all laughed with him. Old Walt said it was the best story he had ever heard, about moles, and they all laughed again.

They heard the door of the house closing and the heavy crunch of Fred Clafin walking toward them. Then he was there in the doorway, bright in the light from the lantern, framed by the darkness of the open door. There was complete silence, every eye on him. In a strangely subdued voice he said, "It's tomorrow," he paused looking at each of them. "It's finally come, our time."

There was another long silence, with everyone looking at him, and then at each other. Bartolo crossed himself again, and the others looked bewildered and frightened. "*Madre de Dios, mañana,*" Bartolo's voice was almost a whisper.

Old Walt was having another spell of watery eyes, he was staring out the window into the darkness with tears running down his face. "It just ain't fair, it just ain't fair. It's like doing away with our reason for livin'."

"Well it's gonna happen, and there's nothing we can do about it, there's nothing anybody can do about it." Fred Clafin's voice was harsh, almost angry. "Now get to sleep all of you, its gonna be a long day tomorrow."

Lonnie lay there in the darkness smelling Old Man Dick's bed, Old Man Dick's pipe, musty wool from an old army blanket, Old Man Dick's dog Growler who was always on the bed when nobody was looking. He listened to the heavy breathing of the cowboys and the snoring; one snore ran the entire scale from high whine to low shuffs. Probably Old Walt laying there asleep with his eyes open staring out into the darkness, seeing nothing. In the distance he heard an owl hooting and way out just on the edge of sound, coyotes yelping. Then he thought about tomorrow, hoping they would let him shoot.

CHAPTER 6

Beans

Like no time had passed, the barrel lid that served as a gong was sounding and Lonnie knew it was morning. The cowboys were crawling out of bed, putting on their shirts and levis and pulling on their boots, wheezing and coughing.

"Hey look whose still layin' in bed, probably playin' with his pecker, the mole asses kid. Get out of there you little bastard, you gotta do a lot of shootin' today, and today you gonna git somethin' bigger'n a rabbit." Dogey Allen was standing over him, poking him with a boot and grinning.

Lonnie pushed the boot away. "I'll get up if you'll get out of my way, you shithead." He crawled out from under the blankets, feeling the cold draft coming in from the open door, seeing that it was still dark out.

He put on his clothes, his checkered flannel shirt and his worn levis, pulled on his boots, the new ones Daddy had brought home, just like the cowboys all wore with three rows of stitches, made by Tony Spenelli. Finally his old hat, it looked pretty funny and was too big now that he and Bobby Leo had blasted it high in the air with a two-incher.

The cowboys were going out the door into the darkness of the early morning. Fred Clafin was last, he was checking his rifle, a Savage 30-06, that he had taken from a set of pegs over his bunk. Lonnie beat him out the door and headed for the stock tank where everybody was washing up, scrubbing down with Lava soap and drying off with towels Mama put out every week or two. Lonnie waited his turn, the Lava soap felt like a piece of sandstone and smelled like creosote. He got some in his eyes and it burned like hell before he got it washed out, splashing icy water in his face until the stinging went away.

A little bit of orange glow was showing above the mesas to the east when they all went into the kitchen and took their places around the big table. Daddy was already there eating his ham and bacon and three eggs, fried so hard the yolks wouldn't run. He was always poking at his eggs and if a little yellow ran out he would make Mama fry them some more. He was poking at them now, squeezing down on each of them and sure enough a little bit of yellow came oozing out of one of them.

He looked up at Mama, "Hey, Blanche, these here eggs are still a little bit bleedy, you better cook 'em some more."

Mama jumped up and put his eggs back in the skillet. Then she filled all the platters and set them on the table. They were having fried eggs and bacon and sausage, with large biscuits along with fresh butter and molasses.

Lonnie couldn't help giggling as he poured some of the syrup on his biscuit. "Mole asses," he said under his breath. Some of them heard him, a wave of snickering went around the table.

"What are you people laughing at?" Lucy Lemur wanted to know. She had stopped eating and was staring at Lonnie.

Nobody said anything, they just kept eating with Dogey and Horse sneaking occasional glances at Lucy Lemur who had on a bright white blouse which accentuated her breasts and made her black eyes look bigger and her black hair look blacker. She had a bright red ribbon in her hair which pulled it up so the soft whiteness of her throat showed. Lonnie thought she had never looked so pretty with her red ribbon and bright shining eyes.

Daddy got up and left the room. He always left the table first, and he always gave signals that he was about to leave; crossing his knife and fork on his plate, putting his spoon in his cup, making two or three bobbing movements before he finally pushed his chair back and got up. Lonnie knew he would go sit in his big chair and stare out the picture window toward Black Mesa, with his lips moving.

Fred Clafin was next. He pushed his chair back and then just stood there looking around the table. "All right, its time. We better go now. Get your guns and put them in your saddle scabbards then meet me in front of the bunkhouse, with your horses ready. You too Lucy, we'll need you too, and Sam and Lonnie, out in front of the bunkhouse in twenty minutes."

Lucy Lemur flushed, her cheeks seemed to glow. "You mean I can ride, and do some shooting? Mama, did you hear that, Fred needs me to ride today." She jumped up from the table and started for the living room, looking back over her shoulder. "I'll get my 30-30 and be right out, I'll be saddled and ready in ten minutes."

Mama looked at Fred Clafin, she seemed worried about something, then she glanced at Dogey and at Horse. "You let her ride with you Fred, I don't want her out of your sight." Mama's voice could be firm sometimes.

Fred Clafin nodded, "Yes ma'am, she will ride with me and so will Lonnie."

Lucy Lemur came back into the room carrying her 30-30 Winchester. She was looking sullen. "Oh, Mama, you always treat me like I'm just a little girl, I know how to take care of myself." Standing there with her Winchester and her flashing black eyes, she did look like she could take care of herself. Her face softened as she looked at Mama. "Don't you worry, Mama, I'll be okay, Fred needs me and I'll do a good job." She turned her glance full on Fred who was standing there looking embarrassed. "Thank you for letting me go Fred, I'll do a good job."

Lonnie headed for the gun cabinet for his twenty-two. He took a whole box of Super X long-rifle shells, figuring they would do a better job than just longs. Within ten minutes he had Baldy saddled and ready to go, his twenty-two in his saddle scabbard. He moved in among the cowboys who were standing around holding their horses by their reins scuffing at the dry ground with their boots.

Lucy Lemur had changed clothes. She wore a tight blue blouse made of some kind of velvet material, her new alligator boots, an old pair of levis with holes in both knees and a tear running up her right leg which let her thigh show as she walked, and a beat-up old canvas hat pulled down around her ears. Lonnie was amazed that anybody dressed that crummy could look so beautiful. When she saw the cowboys, Dogey, Horse, and even Old Walt, watching she got a funny expression on her face and started gazing at the mesas.

Fred Clafin was looking across the valley. "They're comin'." From the east a group of horsemen was just appearing over the rise next to the Spire and from the northwest another group was raising dust as it came toward them at a slow trot.

Soon the yard was filled with horsemen; the Beheimers, the Morgans, the Wagoners, the Wiggens from up the valley and the Sumpters came in, all with their hired hands. They watered their horses at the pond then gathered around Fred Clafin, who waited alone on his buckskin in the center of the yard. He raised his hand and everybody quieted down.

The sun peered above the eastern mesa and set his red hair and beard ablaze with copper light. He spoke in a low voice but everybody could hear him. "Thanks for coming, all of you. We got a big job. It's a sad job, but don't think about it that way." He paused, there was a murmur from the horsemen. "Let's just think of it as something we have to do." He paused as the horsemen crowded in a little closer. "You Beheimers and Wagoners take the canyons and uplands to the south. Drive them to the high corral. Cut out the strongest cows and bulls and the fall weaners, leave the rest in the corral until two o'clock then drive them into Black Smith Canyon. The Wiggens and the Sumpters, you guys do the Carizosa and the western canyons and the western mesas, drive them back here and cut them out the way I just said. My men and the Morgans will do the Kierkendahl and all the lower pastures. Lucy will ride with me. We'll be checking back and forth. They should all be in Blacksmith Canyon by three o'clock, and it should be all over by four. Are there any questions?"

"What about me?" Lonnie was right next to Bobby Leo, who was riding his big bay.

"And me," said Bobby Leo. "What about me?" There was a chuckle from the horsemen as Fred Clafin looked at them. "Lonnie and Bobby Leo will stay here and help Bartolo. I know you all brought your lunch, but Bartolo here will fix supper for everybody. Lonnie and Bobby Leo will carry wood and do what he tells them to do."

"That's a lousy deal," screamed Lonnie, "You said I could ride, and now you're making me and Bobby Leo into just wood carriers. I'm a rider and a shooter not a wood carrier."

"Yeah, what a lousy deal," echoed Bobby Leo. "We want to ride, not be a wood carrier; I'm not going to carry any fuckin' wood."

There was more laughter, Fred Clafin looked stern, but there was a smile just at the edge. "Hey you guys, Bartolo will need your help. You help him good until 2:00 o'clock, and I'll let you ride up for the shootin'."

"It's still a lousy deal," sniffed Lonnie, but he couldn't see any way out of it. He and Bobby Leo rode to the barn and unsaddled their horses.

And that was it. Men rode off in all directions, starting at the outer borders of their areas and herding them in; two thousand cattle, half in the high country on the plains toward the Rabbit Ears and half in the lower canyons and in the valley.

The sun came up fast making it hot by mid-morning. There was no wind, the dust from the cattle moved along with them, hanging in yellow clouds. Small spurts of dust rose where the feet of the horses and cattle struck the baked ground. There was hardly any grass anywhere, just occasional skimpy patches hiding under cactus or soap-weed. It hadn't rained for three months.

The cattle were skinny, even the bulls and the young yearlings. And some of the older cows staggered as they walked, weaving from side to side, staring through the dust, their eyes sunk deep in their heads. Toward noon, Lonnie could see them straggling in from every direction, moving slow, the riders weaving back and forth, vague images in the dust.

Jesus Christ, it was lousy work, carrying that goddamn wood, and hotter than hell, with the sun beating down and no wind. Every now and then, Lonnie and Bobby Leo would quit working to get a drink of water or to take a piss or to stare into the fire Old Bartolo had built, listening to the popping of the cedar, watching the smoke rise, looking into the bean pot where the water was just beginning to boil.

About noon Daddy came out of the house, stood for awhile watching the cattle as they spiraled in, then came over and looked into the bean pot. Lonnie and Bobby Leo began moving faster, carrying more wood, not screwing around. Daddy watched them for awhile, then turned to Bartolo. "There'll be lots of 'em Bartolo, the women and kids will be comin' too, so make a lot. You got everything you need?"

"Sí Señor, maybe some more potatoes."

"I bought a sack yesterday, plenty if you need 'em."

Daddy picked up a ladle and stirred. "Maybe some more side meat in here, Bartolo, beans need lots of side meat, and maybe some more peppers. You think you got enough beans in there?"

"*Sí, Señor, muchos frijoles.*" Bartolo cackled, "*Muchos frijoles* and *muchos petos.*"

He cut off another slice of salt bacon, plopped it in the pot, and put in two big handfuls of dried red peppers. Then he brought out another giant pot, one that Lonnie loved because Daddy used it for rendering hunks of hog belly, which started out as large chunks of white fat and wound up as gallons of bubbling clear lard with tasty crunchy cracklings floating in it. Bartolo hung it on a hook next to the bean pot and, as Lonnie watched him, his mouth started watering and he could almost taste the cracklings.

Bartolo looked at Lonnie and Bobby Leo. "Hey *muchachos*, bring water, *agua, mucho agua.*"

Lonnie and Bobby Leo started moving back and forth from the spout on the windmill. Carrying gallon buckets of water, which put up puffs of steam and started boiling almost as soon as they poured it in the pot.

"Jesus Christ, this is worse than carryin' wood!" Lonnie was panting as they carried bucket after bucket. "Everybody else is out there havin' fun and here we are carryin' water."

"Yea," whispered Bobby Leo as he glanced at Daddy, "we're really doin' good. Wood carriers and water carriers."

"Yea, it's a lousy fuckin' deal." Lonnie was watching his bucket fill in spurts as the sucker-rod brought up the water. "We should be out there ridin'."

"Hey *muchachos*, keep it comin', *de prisa, de prisa.*" That goddamn Bartolo was a slave driver, a goddamn slave driver. Lonnie and Bobby Leo speeded up a little, bucket after bucket, until the pot was half full.

Bartolo went to the house and brought out a big crock of peeled potatoes, then another crock filled with inch square chunks of beef. They went into the pot along with lots of onions and peeled green chili peppers and a handful of salt. And something else, five or six glugs from a large green bottle. Lonnie thought it was vinegar, but it could have been cow piss, which Bartolo maintained was his secret ingredient that gave his stew a distinctive taste. And it did taste distinctive, and good. Everybody agreed that Bartolo made better stew than anybody in the entire length of the Cimarron Valley.

"Hey *muchachos*, go get the boards, we gonna make a big table."

"Jesus Christ, Bartolo, you treat us like a bunch of slaves." Lonnie was thinking about just quitting, when Daddy looked at him. He and Bobby Leo went behind the bunkhouse and started bringing out the boards, long two-by-twelves that were so heavy they could barely lift them, and sawhorses which were not so heavy but awkward as hell to carry. Bartolo put the sawhorses in place and lined up the two-by-twelves side by side and end to end until he had a table about four feet wide and twenty feet long.

When it was finished he put a lot of stuff on it, including a funny looking brown bottle, which Lonnie could see was about half full. Bartolo went to one of the pots and started stirring and Lonnie saw his chance. He eased over to the table and grabbed the bottle thinking maybe he would take a sniff. But he didn't even get the cork out before Bartolo started hollering at him.

"Hey, *muchacho*, you leave alone, you put that down. Why you want to find out secret, old Bartolo's secret?"

"Well for Christ sake, Bartolo." He put the bottle down. "What's the big secret, what the hell is that stuff? Why do you put it in the beans?"

Bartolo took the cork out of the bottle and poured four or five glugs in the beans. "This make beans with no farts, eat lots of beans and no farts."

"Well, that don't make no sense. What's wrong with farts anyway?"

"Ladies no like farts, farts okay for men, ladies no like *los petos*, in *frijole* beans, *muchos petos*."

"That sounds like a lot of bullshit to me."

"Or bull farts," offered Bobby Leo, who was standing there listening with his eyes wide. "How come there are so many farts in beans anyway, where do all the farts come from?"

Bartolo seemed perplexed. "Farts in beans. *Muchos petos* in beans."

Lonnie was intrigued. "In every bean?"

"*Sí*, every bean."

"Well I got a question," Bobby Leo's voice was shrill with excitement. "How many farts are there in one bean?"

"*Madre de Dios*," Bartolo looked stunned and turned back to his pots.

Felix E. Goodson

Daddy stood there looking at Bobby Leo, then walked toward the house, his shoulders shaking.

There was a slight breeze now which made the heat more bearable but caused a lot of dust to start blowing toward them from the cattle which were being driven into the corral.

"Hey Bartolo, we better do something or we'll get dirt in the cookin'." Lonnie was trying to look into the bean pot, but the dust and smoke blinded him. "We better do somethin' or we're gonna have muddy beans."

"*Sí, sí*, okay, okay, dirt in beans okay. A little dirt in beans tastes good, make good beans, *comida buena*."

Lonnie tried to look into the pot again to see if the beans were getting muddy but he couldn't see anything but steam and dust. He was unconvinced. "I don't think Mama would like muddy beans, Bartolo. Maybe Daddy would like them but I doubt it."

Bartolo changed his mind. "Okay, okay, maybe you right, *muchachos* get screens from behind bunkhouse, bring screens, maybe keep out the big pieces."

Even more dust started blowing in from the corral where the men were wheeling and shouting, the cutting horses culling out the strong ones and the weaners. In an hour it was all done, a big bunch of cows tramped around in the corral, about three hundred looking like skeletons, their ribs and hip bones showing, sticking up sharp under the hide. Little skinny calves separated from their mothers in the turmoil bawled continuously, appearing and disappearing in the swirling dust. The keepers were kicked out of the corral in ones or twos or little bunches and moved away, some crowding around the pond drinking water, others straggling toward the windmill in the lower pasture.

Finally the men started coming out of the barn and down from the hitching rail where they had tied their horses. Bandanas were tied around their faces, their hats and clothes were white with dust. They all headed for the stock tank where they waited their turn to wash up, then stood in line holding tin cups under the stream which sprang out at each lift of the sucker-rod, drinking cup after cup.

Most of the dust had lifted when Lonnie looked up to see Fred Clafin with Lucy Lemur at his side riding down the slight incline which sloped from the quarry ridge where his treasure box was

45

hidden. After watering their horses, they came to the fire and looked into the cooking pots. Lucy Lemur had a sneaky look on her face as she turned to Lonnie and gave him a dig in the ribs.

"Hey Lonnie, I've got a present for you."

Jesus Christ! He knew what was coming. And sure enough there she was holding the fingernail polish bottle out toward him.

"You little liar, I knew you took my fingernail polish." She stuck the bottle in his hand but he dropped it like it was hot.

"Why you handin' that to me? I didn't take your fingernail polish, why would I take your ol' fingernail polish?" His voice sounded shaky to his own ears. Then he brightened a little. "I know what happened, I'll bet some animal took it, probably a skunk. Hell, everybody knows they like things that smell bad. I'll bet a skunk took it."

"Sure you little creep, I'm sure a skunk took it. A little one named Lonnie Wilson." With that she turned and walked toward the house, her head back, her hips swinging.

Jesus Christ! Just his luck. He should have buried it or left it in his treasure box. He felt guilty now that she knew about it. Like he really was a skunk.

Bobby Leo sidled up to Fred Clafin who was stirring the beans with a big ladle. "Lonnie and me been carryin' wood all morning, and we brought the boards for the table, and we hauled water."

"Yeah," Lonnie joined in, happy to get fingernail polish off his mind. "We did everything Old Bartolo told us. We worked hard."

Fred Clafin was tasting the beans, blowing and then slurping, smacking his lips after each "slurp." "Hey Bartolo, you better put some more seasoning in here, three or four more slices of sideback, and maybe a little more pepper."

"*Sí*, señor, okay" Bartolo was grinning, showing three teeth, about all he had, from under his handlebar mustache.

"Yep," Fred Clafin continued, looking down at Lonnie and Bobby Leo who were both looking up at him, eyes wide, filled with hope. "You guys go in and get some lunch and then get ready. We'll move the cattle out in about thirty minutes."

Lonnie threw down the wood he was carrying, and he and Bobby Leo ran toward the house. Mama gave them fried potatoes, beans and cornbread and a piece of ham. They sat at the table munching and talking. "It's about time," Lonnie observed. "We always get shit on."

Bobby Leo mumbled through a large mouthful of beans, "We always get shit on, just because we're little and they're big."

They finished lunch, ran out to the horse corral and were saddled up ready to go when Fred Clafin came out, without Lucy Lemur who was staying to help Mama get the dinner ready.

Dogey and Horse, both looking peculiar, rode over from where they had just got the cattle moving out of the corral toward the south mesas. They were acting like they had something to say but didn't know how to go about saying it. Horse started to speak, then whinnied nervously. Fred Clafin was looking from one to the other, like he was waiting for something. Dogey, his face red and his voice raspy, finally blurted out. "We want to know why you always ride with Lucy, you never let us ride with her," he stopped, even redder in the face.

"Yeah," Horse finally controlled his whinny, "like you are trying to protect her from us."

Fred Clafin kept looking at them, smiling a little. "Shit fire, you poor defenseless assholes, I'm not trying to protect her from you." His smile widened and his copper flecked brown eyes sparkled. Lonnie thought he was really handsome for an old man, almost forty, with his huge head covered with deep red curly hair, and his short red curly beard gleaming bright in the noon sun.

"Shit I'm not trying to protect her from you. You got it all wrong. I'm trying to protect you poor dumb bastards from her." His deep laugh rang out. "Now let's get off this shit and get these cattle movin'. Do you have the extra shells, like I told you?" They both nodded, looking dumb and helpless. "Well come on goddamn it, we got a job of work to do."

CHAPTER 7

The Big Shoot

Old Walt already had them headed out, moving at a slow pace through the rising dust toward the south mesas, toward Black Smith Canyon. After awhile the herd stretched out with the stronger ones leading the way, the weaker ones wavering from side to side, just barely moving along. Lonnie and Bobby Leo were bringing up the rear with Walt on one side, Horse and Dogey on the other, and Fred Clafin leading the way.

They hadn't gone far when Dogey left the herd and trotted his horse back to the corral. There were four heavy reports and Dogey trotted back to the herd.

"Did you shoot 'em?" Lonnie asked as Dogey passed him on his way back to join Horse.

"Right between the eyes," Dogey was grinning. "Shit it wasn't much, they were just layin' there, damn near already dead."

Lonnie and Bobby Leo kept pushing the stragglers, going out occasionally to get ones that broke away from the herd. It must have been three o'clock, getting hotter than hell, when the lead cattle, following Fred Clafin, turned the point and entered the mouth of Black Smith Canyon. In the distance, going up the Zig Zag, Lonnie could see riders moving up the trail from the valley floor to the top of the mesa. A cloud of dust appeared from their right, cattle from the high corral moving in at an angle, maybe three hundred, with the calves and the weak ones trailing.

Lonnie took a swig of water from his canteen and wiped the dust from his eyes. Bobby Leo was just a dusty shadow over to his left. "Now this is livin'," he murmured. "How you doin', Bobby Leo?"

"I'm doin' great," Bobby Leo's voice came out of the vagueness. "Man this is sure better than carryin' wood. You think they're gonna let us shoot?"

"Sure as shittin' they're gonna let us shoot," Lonnie felt great.

"Shit, that's what we're here for, for ridin' and shootin'."

They came to a rise where the wind coming down the canyon struck them from the side and cleared the dust away. Lonnie could see the mouth of the canyon in the distance and to his right the long string of cattle from the high corral angling in, joining the cattle they were driving. Riders were whooping and shouting, slapping their chaps with their lariats, and the cattle seemed to be moving faster. Jimmy Joe and Sam were riding back and forth screaming and waving their hats, having a good old time.

Gradually the herd disappeared into the canyon and the riders began coming out, riding along easy, taking sips of water from their canteens, talking and laughing a lot. Lonnie and Bobby Leo kept bringing up the rear, keeping the stragglers, mostly little calves, coming along with the herd.

Up above on the rim rock on both sides of the canyon men were sitting around on rocks or in their saddles or gathered together in small bunches looking down. Lonnie could see Fred Clafin up there on the left rimrock riding along, stopping every now and then to talk to somebody.

Lonnie and Bobby Leo drove the tail end of the herd into the canyon where Old Walt was standing guard to keep any from coming out. His eyes were watering bad from the dust and he kept dabbing at them with a dirty rag. He grinned at Lonnie and Bobby Leo. "Hey you guys are pretty good cowboys, you did a good job. I got 'em now, you go on up the Zig Zag."

They left the mouth of the canyon and headed for the point where the Zig Zag started. Jesus Christ it was great going up, first to the left then to the right, the horses straining, leaning way forward, their heads held high, their legs pumping. The higher they got the more everything down below looked little, Old Walt at the mouth of the canyon, the cows and the calves wandering around in the dust. Lonnie looked back and could see other horses straining up the Zig Zag, their riders lolling back in the saddles with the reins loose, just taking it easy.

And then it happened, that goddamned Baldy wouldn't move. He had stopped right in the middle of the trail between a zig and a zag and just stood there with his head down, heaving and panting. Lonnie tried kicking him, then he tried whacking him with the ends of his reins but he wouldn't budge. To make matters worse

Sam and that son-of-a-bitch Jimmy Joe came up from below and saw him sitting there beating the shit out of Baldy, going nowhere. They paused for a moment, looking at him with shitty looks on their faces.

Jimmy Joe let go that bray of his, "Well if it ain't the Golden Bat and his horse. Some horse! A little runt of a piece of shit. What the fuck you doin' just sittin' there on that little runt?"

"I'm sittin' here enjoyin' the scenery, you cunt-head. Now leave me alone or I'll hit you with a rock, a big sharp one that will knock your brains out if you have any."

"Why you little son-of-a-bitch, if you weren't so little, I'd drag you off that little piece of shit you call a horse and beat the shit out of you."

Sam was moving on up the trail, looking back, worried. Jimmy Joe turned his horse and started up the trail, giving Baldy a whack with a quirt as he passed. Baldy didn't even twitch, he just kept standing there like he was resting, taking deep breaths. Then he started going up too, not slow and easy but pumping hard with his head way down almost touching the ground.

Just before they reached the top Baldy with Lonnie hanging on to the saddle horn passed Sam and Jimmy Joe whose horses were gasping and foaming. Lonnie didn't even look back, it felt real good to pass those assholes.

Ahead, when he got on top, he could see Bobby Leo waiting over by the cap rock. He had tied his big bay to a tree and was standing there in the shade of a scrub oak, occasionally looking down.

When Lonnie got off Baldy Fred Clafin came riding up. "You can shoot, Lonnie, but only at the calves, try to hit them right between the eyes. Remember what I told you, aim low when you're shootin' down hill. It won't be easy, so aim the best you can. It's at least 300 feet down there to the canyon floor. And don't start shooting until you see me give the signal!"

He paused looking at Bobby Leo, "You stay behind him while he's shooting." With that he rode on down the line, stopping every now and then to give instructions or to answer questions.

Bobby Leo was making little snorting sounds. "Does he think I don't have enough brains to stand behind somebody whose shootin', and how could I stand in front, Jesus Christ there's nuthin' out there but 300 feet of nuthin'."

"Your right," Lonnie was laughing. "You'd look real funny standin' out there on thin air."

Bobby Leo didn't say anything. He was looking at Lonnie's twenty-two which was leaning up against a rock. "Let me shoot first," Bobby Leo's voice was shaking, "I've never had a chance to kill nuthin'. You get it all ready and let me shoot first."

Lonnie looked at him and then down at the cattle which were milling around raising more dust. He picked up his twenty-two, opened the breach and put in a long-rifle shell. "Okay, but wait 'til Fred gives the signal." He cocked back the hammer and handed Bobby Leo the rifle. "See that little one down there, bawling and running around in circles. You try to hit him right between the eyes."

Bobby Leo began making practice aims. He kept squinting down the barrel but his hands were shaking so much Lonnie was sure he couldn't hit anything. Lonnie kept his eyes on Fred Clafin who had ridden up on a high point where everybody could see him. He had his pistol out and was looking back and forth at the men on the bluffs. There was a moment of waiting then his pistol shot rang out and echoed off the canyon walls.

Bobby Leo pulled the trigger, there was a sharp snap and the calf jumped but didn't fall down.

"Okay, let me shoot now, you hit him okay, that was a good shot but let me shoot now." Lonnie's voice was shaking too but he could barely hear it, how could you hear much with the roar of the rifles all along the rimrock on both sides of the canyon.

Down below cattle were falling and running back and forth, bellowing and raising so much dust it was hard to see them. Lonnie loaded his twenty-two again and tried to locate the little calf but it had disappeared in the swirling dust. He tried to find another calf but just as he made one out it dropped to the ground before he could pull the trigger.

This happened three times. When he was about ready to pull the trigger on a decent target somebody else would beat him to it. Finally a cow ran to the side of the canyon and stood still for a moment. He fired and saw her shudder and drop.

"Jesus Christ, I got one, I got one, a big one."

"Yeah, I saw, I saw you, I saw you kill it. Let me have another shot. Give me a chance." Bobby Leo was grabbing at the gun, screaming at the top of his voice.

"Okay, okay, for Christ sake, let me load it," Lonnie screamed back.

The firing along the caprocks had become intermittent, heavy bursts and then sporadic shots, occasional intervals of silence. The bawling of the cattle diminished. Lonnie looked down, nothing much was moving, the dust was drifting away, leaving the floor of the canyon visible. Hundreds of cattle lay dead or dying. When one moved a little there would be a sudden burst of gunfire, the bullets raising spurts of dust around it.

Lonnie felt good, he had got one. He could hardly wait to tell Daddy about it, and Fred Clafin. He reloaded the rifle, pulled back the hammer and handed it to Bobby Leo. "Maybe you can get a shot, if you see one move, take a shot."

Bobby Leo took the gun and peered down. "Shit there ain't nuthin' to shoot at, there ain't a one movin', they're all dead."

"Well go ahead and take a shot anyway, maybe one ain't quite dead."

Bobby Leo sighted for a long time, then pulled the trigger. There was another sharp snap. He handed the rifle back to Lonnie. "Shit, it ain't no fun killing a dead cow."

Lonnie loaded it and gave it back to him. "Hey, a few are still wigglin', and look there's one over there trying to get up, see right over there."

Bobby Leo aimed the rifle and fired. Immediately the cow fell over on its side. "You got 'em, you got 'em." But Lonnie figured somebody else did it, or probably a bunch of guys, there had been a lot of firing and dust rose around the cow.

Lonnie looked down the caprock and saw Daddy standing there alone, looking down. To Lonnie's astonishment, tears were running down his face. He just stood there, not moving, not wiping the tears away. Jesus Christ! Lonnie couldn't believe it, Daddy was crying like some little sniveling kid.

Lonnie sure hoped Bobby Leo wouldn't see him crying like that but when Bobby Leo handed him back his gun he looked over and his eyes got round. "Hey, your Daddy's crying, your Daddy is over there crying."

Lonnie didn't look up, he was examining his gun. "He's probably drunk. Jesus Christ, this sure is a good gun, ain't it?"

He couldn't help looking again and Daddy was still there, looking down, crying. And to make matters worse, Fred Clafin rode
up and stopped about twenty feet behind Daddy, and damned if he
wasn't crying too. Lonnie couldn't stand it. He turned away, tears
streaming down his face. What the fuck were they crying for, it
was a good shoot, and he had killed one himself.

Some of the other men came along. A few of them started to
approach Daddy but turned quietly away and rode over to the Zig
Zag.

George Morgan, Bobby Leo's daddy, came up to Daddy and
handed him a bottle. He took a swig or two then passed it back to
George who took a swig or two. They stood there passing the bottle
back and forth and pretty soon they were talking loud and laughing.

George Morgan was a real good looking guy, looked just like
his kid that Goddamn Jimmy Joe, and everybody agreed that he
was the best cocksman in the Cimarron valley. "Old George is
hornier than a horned toad," Dogey Allen had once observed. And
Lonnie thought he probably was. Once when Lonnie and Bobby
Leo were hunting arrowheads on the hill behind the schoolhouse
they crossed Highway 64 where it ran through Emory gap and
caught George fucking the Indian Princess, and that was when she
was only fifteen years old. Not that he was robbing the cradle, far
from it. The Indian Princess, her name was actually Alma Ruth
Veeder, was so well known for being easy that some people who
wanted to be nasty about it called her Pokehauntus while others
being more polite called her the Indian Princess. Anyway her being screwed by George added very little to her reputation for being an easy poke and even less to his reputation for being a
cocksman. When Lonnie and Bobby Leo came around the tree
George had the Indian Princess spread out on the hood of his new
Model B Ford and was so hard at it that he didn't even notice
Lonnie and Bobby Leo who stared for a moment before they took
off for the school house, moving fast.

Once, George had grabbed Lucy Lemur when she wasn't looking and had squeezed her tit, and that was back when she didn't
have much, just little nubbins. She had turned on him suddenly,

her big eyes, or so it seemed to Lonnie, shooting sparks of fire and her face contorted in disgust. "If you try that again I'll tell Fred Clafin and he'll beat the shit out of you. And remember this, if I wanted anything to do with a man it sure wouldn't be an old man like you." Old George seemed to shrivel and get smaller. He backed away and Lonnie never saw him try anything with Lucy Lemur again. He didn't even get close to her.

George and Daddy apparently emptied the bottle. George threw it off the bluff and it went spinning down, glinting in the afternoon sun before it disappeared into the shadow of the west wall of the canyon.

He said something to Daddy then walked over to where Lonnie and Bobby Leo were just getting on their horses. His face was red and he seemed in a good mood. "Well, here are two of my favorite cowboys." He cleared his throat, he was always clearing his throat, little self-satisfied raspy sounds. "What're you guys doin'?"

Bobby Leo pointed down into the canyon where four pickups had driven among the dead cattle and a guy carrying a black book was walking around counting and making notes.

"We're goin' down and see what those guys are doin'." As they looked down three or four men carrying knives and chains got out of each pickup and started skinning cattle.

George was swaying a little. "They're gonna get all those hides and sell them, fifty cents a hide." He glanced at Lonnie, "But your daddy gets ten cents of that. And the government gives him twelve dollars for each cow we shot and four dollars for each calf."

Lonnie was stunned. "Jesus Christ, that's a lot of money. Daddy will be rich." Lonnie was thinking that now they wouldn't have to go to the poorhouse.

George cleared his throat again, rocking back and forth on the heels of his hundred dollar boots. "Yeah, he'll be rich alright." He turned to Bobby Leo. "Don't get in the way of those men down there." Then he walked over and joined Daddy. They talked for awhile then went over to where their cars were parked.

Bobby Leo didn't say anything for awhile but as he and Lonnie started down the Zig Zag he began making his little snuffing angry sounds. "All those son-of-bitches, even my daddy, thinks we don't have any brains at all. That we're just little kids."

"Yeah, well fuck them." Lonnie got Baldy moving down the

Zig Zag, which was easy because they were going in the direction of home.

When they reached the bottom, they rode into Black Smith Canyon over to where the men were skinning cattle, doing it fast. They would skin down the head, then the two front legs, then make a slit down the belly. When the skin was about half way off one guy would tie a chain that was attached to a pickup truck around the loose hide and it would peel off real easy, just like taking off a glove. There were five teams of three men each and they really moved fast, about five minutes per hide. Pretty soon there were lots of naked cows laying around already beginning to bloat in the afternoon sun. They didn't skin the calves, they lay among the naked cows some still bleeding from gunshot wounds.

The guy with the black book came down from the far end of the canyon, a skinny guy, with a long hooked nose and a sad look on his face. He stopped and peered at the boys from under his beat-up Stetson.

"How many out there?" Lonnie was thinking of the money Daddy would get.

The guy looked into his black book. "Six hundred and forty two cows and bulls, and three hundred and twenty-seven calves." He looked even sadder as he turned away and went to his car.

"Jesus Christ! Did you hear that, man that's a lot of money." Lonnie was thinking of how rich Daddy was, and wondered why he had been crying. Maybe he was so happy making all that money, he couldn't keep from crying!

They turned their horses and headed for the ranch-house, with Baldy pulling at his bit, trying to get some slack. Lonnie did the one rein cinch job around the saddle horn again which made Baldy trot sideways but it kept him from running. As they rode out of the mouth of Black Smith canyon Lonnie looked back. Some of the naked cows had two legs sticking out at a crazy angle, their white bellies bloated in the sun.

Other riders were coming down the Zig Zag moving out into the flat of the valley. It was getting cooler, the sun was way down, maybe only three or four inches above the far mesa. They rode into a long dark area, the shadow from Old Battleship and it got even colder. Lonnie shivered a little, thinking maybe next time out he better wear a coat.

CHAPTER 8

Party

Down below, there was a lot of dust boiling along their road, coming in from Highway 64, the women and children driving in for the big party. By the time Bobby Leo and Lonnie got to the pond to water their horses, a whole bunch of women and kids were gathered around the big table, laying out stuff, laughing and talking.

Then all eyes were on Lonnie. In his excitement he had forgotten about Baldy's bad habit and before he could do a thing about it Baldy waded out into the pond and laid down. Lonnie barely had time to get his leg out of the way and to grab his twenty-two out of the saddle scabbard. There he was waist deep in water, holding his gun in the air with everybody laughing. He couldn't stand it, that son-of-a-bitch Baldy was rolling around like a hog, having a good old time. And he kept it up until he was good and ready. Finally, he gave a snort, stood up and let Lonnie lead him off to the corral.

Fred Clafin had finished rubbing down his horse and was coming out the gate. He stopped short when he saw Lonnie but he didn't laugh. "Well I'll be damn, he did it to you again. That's some crazy horse, he did it to you again."

Lonnie felt like crying but he laughed, "Naw, I made him do it, he was so dirty he needed a bath."

"Sure," said Fred Clafin, not even smiling, "I know that."

Lonnie took off the saddle and rubbed Baldy down thinking maybe he would shoot the son-of-a-bitch, right between the eyes like he had shot that cow.

"Some day I'm gonna shoot this son-of-a-bitch," he said to Bobby Leo, who had tied his big bay to the hitching rail. Lonnie sat down on a feed bucket, took off his boots and poured the water out.

Bobby Leo didn't say anything.

More and more riders were coming in, watering their horses at the pond and tying them to the hitching rail. There was lots of joking about the "Big Shoot," and lots of bullshit claims of how many each of them had killed. Jake Veeder had been grazed by a ricochet and was proudly displaying the red mark on the side of his head. Somebody observed that someone on the opposite cap rock was trying to kill him but was a bad shot. Somebody else observed that he was probably a good shot but that Old Jake's head was so hard that no bullet could even make a dent.

When the gong sounded, everyone picked up tin plates and tin cups which Bartolo had stacked on the table and started lining up. It was some dinner. All the women had brought something: home made bread, five or six different kinds of salad, different kinds of vegetables, pies and cakes. Bartolo was ladling out his stew and Lucy Lemur was ladling out the beans. Lonnie, who was in the middle of the line, saw how the cowboys looked at her as they pushed their tin plates toward her. She acted like she didn't notice but Lonnie knew she did. She was wearing her ragged jeans, which showed part of her leg, a red blouse which matched the red ribbon in her hair. When Dogey and Horse came by, they both kept staring at her like a pair of hungry dogs hoping for a handout. She gave each of them a full ladle of beans without even glancing at them, a superior little smile on her face. And she didn't glance at Jake Veeder, who did a little prancing shuffle as he held out his plate toward her. After she had given him a ladle of beans, he said in his baby talk voice, "*Muchas gracias* fo' them beans, from the sweetest hand in this here whole valley."

"You're holding up the line," she said, still not looking at him.

That night the men drank a lot of booze. In the light of a bright moon, Lonnie saw them drift out of the house toward the pickups and saddle bags, and saw them drift back in, their faces a little redder, their voices a little louder. And everybody danced a lot. They would put a record on the old Victrola, wind her up, and let her go. They did the polka, the versuviana, and a lot of square dancing. Part of the time Lonnie had to play the piano. He was good at "Red Sails in the Sunset," and "There's an Old Spinning Wheel in the Parlor."

It was good to see Daddy having a good time, and Mama was dancing too, her face flushed and her eyes sparkling. Lucy Lemur danced with practically everybody, except George Morgan and Dogey and Horse. George kept away from her and Dogey and Horse skulked around looking silly, peering into the center of activity like two coyotes on the edge of a campfire. But Jake Veeder couldn't keep away from her. While Lucy Lemur was dancing with Old Man Beheimer he came prancing out, moving his arms around real crazy while doing a buck and weave and tried to cut in. But Lucy Lemur just kept hanging on to Old Man Beheimer while Jake followed them around making an ass of himself. Finally Daddy went over to him and told him to get out and stay out. Old Jake was half glassy eyed from booze and started arguing but when Fred Clafin showed up behind Daddy, Jake started saying all kinds of dirty words and went out the door.

Lucy Lemur was wearing a long white dress, made of some lacy stuff which billowed out as she moved, her hair was pulled back and tied with a red ribbon, and she had a blue Hollyhock just over her right ear. She was so beautiful and graceful everyone kept looking at her.

She did a great waltz, the "Blue Danube" played on the Victrola, with Fred Clafin who looked young and handsome wearing his new boots, new levis, and a new red and blue checkered shirt. He moved easy like he always did in the saddle even when his horse was trotting, not letting any light show, automatically adjusting to the rhythm of the horse. And there wasn't any light showing between him and Lucy Lemur who was moving easy too, right with him like they were just one person, making all the turns and whirls and dips just right.

When the dance was over everybody applauded. Fred Clafin bowed to Lucy Lemur who gave him one of her brightest smiles. Lonnie caught a glimpse of Dogey and Horse, looking like they had just received a big helping from a plate full of turds.

Nobody went home until it was late, at least ten o'clock, then the cars started leaving, following the track of their headlights through the plumes of dust raised by the cars in front of them until all were lost in the smokey billows which puffed over the road.

The riders were starting to leave when it happened. Jake Veeder was in one of his mean drunks. He was walking around the bunkhouse, screaming insults at everybody, particularly Daddy. He stopped by the windmill and took a piss and started screaming. "Hey Emmett, you big fat overgrown hawg, come out here and get this, you big slunchgut. And if you doan I'm gonna beat you 'til you'll be real happy to give me a suck job."

Daddy went out the front door and down the steps toward Jake who had finished pissing and was standing there, his head hunched down, wagging his pecker back and forth. A lot of people had crowded around taking in the show which was clearly visible in the bright moonlight.

Old Jake Veeder was something else. Everybody was afraid of him. He had bitten the ear off of one of the Eddleman brothers, and then had whipped all three of them when they came out to the Veeder ranch to settle up scores.

But Daddy didn't seem scared. He had almost reached the spot where Jake was holding forth with his cock hanging out when something happened so fast it was almost a blur. Dogey Allen came in from behind Daddy and hit Jake Veeder so hard in the crotch that his cock, as Old Walt who was close enough to get a birds eye view later maintained, shriveled up and withdrew like a worm trying to suck back into a worm hole.

Then they were on the ground, turning and twisting, fists pumping, snarling like two dogs in a dogfight. The snarling and fist pumping and dust raising went on for a few minutes then Fred Clafin and Daddy, working in unison, reached down and lifted them high over their heads and threw them into the pond.

There was a lot of laughter as they came up, spitting dirty water and slushing toward different banks of the pond. Jake Veeder didn't say a word. He went to the hitching rail, got on Macon and rode toward the near mesa. Dogey didn't say anything either. He just stood there on the edge of the pond looking wet and wilted. But of all things Lucy Lemur came out with a towel, went up to Dogey and dried off his face. He waited there in the moonlight, one eye already swelled shut, the other gleaming strangely as she handed him the towel and went back into the house.

The party was the talk of the valley, particularly the fight. And Dogey, even though he was a little runt, seemed to walk taller. And people regarded him with a little more respect, which wasn't much.

CHAPTER 9

The Spire

A week after the big party, Lonnie was carrying in wood for the cook stove when he saw two riders coming up the road that angled in toward the house from Highway 64. It wasn't long until they were close enough to recognize, Bobby Leo riding his big bay with the white splotch in its face and Jimmy Joe, the prick, riding his Palomino which always strutted along like it was doing something important rather than carrying the mean bastard. Lonnie shouted for Sam and they both waited by the windmill as the two of them rode up and got off their horses.

Bobby Leo was looking real eager. "See my new boots? I got new boots and a new red bandanna."

And the little bastard did look pretty spiffy with his bandanna and his new shiny boots which had four rows of stitching, which immediately made Lonnie jealous because his only had three rows of stitching. Jimmy Joe always looked real spiffy to other people, but never to Lonnie who hated his guts so much.

Jimmy Joe was drinking from the water can, surveying everybody with his agate eyes, his hair sticking out on each side like he was a short-horned bull wearing a black hat. He cleared his throat just like his daddy. "You know I been wantin' to take a look at that pile of rock sticking up over there." He was pointing at the Spire. "Shit, that thing must be two or three hundred feet high, just stickin' up by itself, out there in the pasture all by itself."

"Me too," chimed Bobby Leo. "Let's go over there an' take a look. Maybe I'll climb it. Shit, I wouldn't be afraid to climb it."

"You little prick, you can't hardly climb on that big dumb horse of yours, let alone climb something like that. Nobody can climb that thing, it doesn't slope at all, it's just sticking straight up, with no place to grab hold of, or no place to put your feet."

"I can climb it," Lonnie heard his own voice saying. "I can climb it. Shit, it would be easy. I've been over there and its got a crack running from the bottom clear to the top. All you'd have to do is just keep goin' up that crack 'til you got to the top. I can climb it."

Sam was looking at him. "Are you crazy, you'd fall and break your dumb neck. Anyway I don't think you got the guts to even start climbin' it."

"Well shit, let's go take a look at it. An' if that little piece of shit wants to break his fuckin' neck, well let him. But shit, he's too chicken to try." Jimmy Joe flapped his arms and crowed like a chicken. "And just to show my heart's in the right place I'll give the little bastard five dollars if he can climb it."

"Wait a minute." Lonnie ran in the house and put on his tennis shoes.

Then they all got on their horses, with Lonnie and Bobby Leo dropping behind, mainly because Baldy was going through his usual slow poke routine.

"You're really gonna climb that thing?" Bobby Leo's voice was quiet, almost a whisper.

"You damn right I'm gonna climb it, I ain't no chicken, and five dollars is a lot of money."

The closer they got to the Spire the taller it got until finally they were there at its base, looking up.

Sam look relieved. "Jesus, it's high, but there ain't no crack."

"The crack's on the other side." Lonnie was looking eager. "Let's go around, you'll see there's a crack that runs clear to the top."

As they rode around, they moved into an oblong swath of shade and it seemed cooler. The Spire was about a hundred feet square at the bottom and maybe fifty feet square at the top because it did slope a little. And sure enough there was a crack, one about an inch wide that ran all the way up.

Lonnie got off Baldy, ran over and started climbing. Shit it was easy. By turning his feet just right he could fit the toes of his tennis shoes sideways into the crack. His fingers, also turned sideways, fitted into the crack giving him a good hand hold.

He was about thirty feet up when he stopped and looked down. Sam was down there, screaming at him, waving his arms around. Bobby Leo and Jimmy Joe were looking up with their mouths open. Lonnie took three or four deep breaths and started climbing again. When he finally stopped and looked down everything looked crazy. Sam was still down there screaming at him and so were Jimmy Joe and Bobby Leo. All of them running around waving their arms, looking like assholes, little bitty assholes because from where he was, maybe half way to the top they looked small and ridiculous. Even the horses looked small. Lonnie was having fun, making assholes out of all of them, particularly Jimmy Joe, the prick, who would owe him five dollars.

When he got close to the top the face of the Spire sloped out a little but he kept moving up, both feet wedged, one on top of the other, up a hand and then the other hand, up a foot then the other foot. And suddenly he was there, removing one hand and then the other from the crack to grasp the sharp edges of the top. He pulled himself up and over and lay on the red flat surface breathing hard.

After a few minutes he crawled away from the edge, stood up and looked around. A number of red round boulders, some big and some small, were scattered here and there.

Jesus, he felt good. He sure wasn't no chicken. He had climbed it and that fuckin' Jimmy Joe owed him five dollars. He looked out across the valley and could see everything. Old Battleship was gleaming in the midmorning sun and the Wedding Cake looked a lot closer than it actually was. Hell, he could see clear over to the Morgan ranch-house. He walked around looking at the boulders. He had thought the top would be as flat as a pancake but it had all those boulders on it. He would have to ask Old Man Dick how they got up there.

Those assholes down below were still screaming at him, their voices small and far away, like mice squeaking. He crawled to the edge and looked down. Yep, there they were moving around like little dots, their voices small and insignificant. Then he looked down the entire stretch of the wall and he looked again, particularly at that part which sloped out. And suddenly he felt dizzy and something funny was happening to his stomach, like a big worm had gotten in there and was crawling around.

He crawled quickly away from the edge and lay flat on his stomach gasping for air. Jesus Christ, he had never felt this way before. And the horrible thought struck him that pretty soon he would have to crawl over that edge, get his feet wedged just right in the crack and let himself down. The more he thought about it the funnier his stomach felt, and the more he knew he couldn't do it. After thinking about it for a few minutes, in spite of the fact that he knew they would all call him chicken, particularly that fuckin' Jimmy Joe, he crawled to the edge and started screaming for help.

They must have heard him because in nothing flat all three of them were headed for the ranch-house at a dead run, their horses creating little plumes of dust which drifted away in the wind. Lonnie moved back from the edge. Jesus Christ, this was the worst fix he had ever been in. He figured Daddy would beat the shit out of him for this one. That is, if he ever got down!

Even though there was a good breeze it was getting hot and he was thirsty. He got up and walked over to a big red boulder and lay down in its shade. Jesus Christ, how in the hell was he going to get down. He racked his brain but couldn't figure any possible way. Then he began to cry, thinking it wouldn't be long until he starved to death. How could they get water to him? Maybe an airplane could drop some, and maybe something to eat. He cheered up a little and stopped sniffling. Then he thought that there was no way an airplane could hit a small target like the top of the Spire, and started sniffling again. Then he figured he was going to need all the water he had in him and stopped sniffling again.

Actually it wasn't so bad lying down in the shade of that boulder with the breeze wafting around him. And anyway he figured somebody, probably Fred Clafin, would know what to do. He dozed off for awhile then woke up with a start. A lot of noise was coming from down below. He crawled to the edge and couldn't believe it, a bunch of cars and trucks were parked down there and other cars and lots of horsemen were spiraling in from every direction. Jesus Christ, what a fucking mess. Everybody in Union County was coming, just to embarrass him. Then he thought that maybe it would be better to die and leave his bones on top of the Spire than face all those crazy people: people that apparently didn't have much to do or were really bored or they wouldn't be coming in droves like that just to see a little chicken kid kick the bucket on top of a tall rock.

After about an hour there were hundreds of people below, walking around chatting, looking up. Some of them had brought baskets of food, which the women were laying out on blankets and makeshift tables. The men were drifting out to their cars and pickups for a quick shot of booze. The kids were running around playing games. Jesus Christ, it was just one big celebration and he was the center of it all. Suddenly he didn't feel so bad. If he really had to die it was probably better to do it before an audience.

It was then that he heard the voice. He didn't recognize it at first but then realized it was Jake Veeder; Jake Veeder who could scream louder than a panther and always won the hog calling contest at the rodeo every Fourth of July.

"Can you hear me? Can you hear me? Come to the edge where I can see you. Hey little bitty Dogey, can you hear me?"

Lonnie crawled to the edge and sure enough it was Jake Veeder looking bigger than anybody else even though small at that distance.

"Yea, I hear you. Yea, I hear you." Lonnie figured everybody could hear him, even those clear over at Clayton if all of them weren't already down below there, having a grand time.

Jake was shouting again, and it came through loud and clear.

"I'm goin' to shoot up a line. Git yor ass behind a rock so you won't get hit. Git behind a rock so you won't get hit."

"I hear you," screamed Lonnie.

He crawled away from the edge, walked over to the big boulder and lay down behind it in the shade. Three or four times he heard something rattle on the side of the wall and then something with a string attached went arcing over his head and fell down the other side. Suddenly he had the string in his hand and understood what it was all about. He took out his Barlow, cut the string and tied it firmly around the big boulder. Then he crawled to the edge and looked down. Jake Veeder was shouting again.

"Now pull up the clothes-line. Can you hear me? Pull up the clothes-line."

"I hear you." Lonnie moved away from the edge, sat down and began pulling the string, winding it around and around his foot. After about ten minutes of pulling and winding, a clothes-line attached to the end of the string came over the edge toward him. He kept pulling until he had enough clothes-line to tie around the big boulder, using a double no slip knot Old Man Dick had taught him to tie. Then he crawled to the edge and looked down. Jesus Christ, there were hundreds of people down there now and more were on the way, plumes of dust were rising on their road from Highway 64 and others were rising from the roads across the flats from the Beheimer place. Jake Veeder was shouting again.

64

"Now pull up the rope. Pull up the rope. It's gonna be heavy but you got to do it. Can you do it?"

"Yea, I can do it."

Lonnie crawled away from the edge and started pulling the clothes-line, wrapping it around his foot. Then he thought about it and moved behind a middle sized boulder that he could brace his feet against. There was another boulder handy, a smaller one, that he wrapped the clothes-line around as he pulled. At first the pulling was easy but the longer he pulled the harder it got.

"Jesus Christ," he gasped, "that damn rope must weigh a ton." His arms and hands were getting tired so he took another loop around the rock and rested for awhile. Then he crawled to the edge and looked over.

A zillion people were looking up with their mouths open, shading their eyes.

Jake Veeder was shouting again. "What's the matter, why ain't you pullin'?"

"I'm restin', I'm restin'."

He looked down the wall and could see the end of the clothes-line with the rope attached to it only thirty or forty feet below. He crawled back, braced himself and started pulling again, winding the clothes-line around the boulder. At last the end of the clothes-line with the rope attached came over the edge and started moving toward him. He rested again, gasping and sweating in the hot sun. Finally with a few more heaves he had enough rope to tie around the big boulder and secure it with his double no-slip knot.

He was drenched with sweat. The breeze, which seemed stronger now, cooled him off as he rested in the shade of the boulder, getting ready. He had to do it! But shit he could do it. He had climbed down ropes lots of times, from the upper window of the barn and three or four times from the catwalk of the windmill. Finally there was no waiting, he went to the edge, closed his eyes, lowered his feet over, wrapped his legs around the rope, and began to slide slowly down. There was only one really bad time, when he had to let go with one hand so he could grab the rope below the edge. He let go with his right hand, and grabbed the rope. Then his left hand came over and grabbed the rope and he was moving down, hanging in the air because of the outward slant of the wall. Below him there was very little sound except a low murmuring and heavy breathing that reminded him of the blow-hole.

Down and down he went, hand under hand, legs wrapped around the rope. After awhile he started rubbing along the wall and felt a lot better. By God he was doin' it. And that asshole Jimmy Joe owed him five dollars. He even had the courage to open his eyes for a moment and then wished he hadn't. The ground was still way below. He closed his eyes but had noticed while they were open that everyone had moved away from beneath him, as if they expected him to fall, the sons-a-bitches.

Time after time, as he moved down, he came to a knot where ropes had been tied together. After awhile he stopped to rest as he came to each knot. Jesus Christ, his arms and his hands were tired and his hands were probably bleeding. He could feel them slipping more on the rope. But he kept moving down. And just when he felt he couldn't hold on any longer a bunch of hands reached up and pulled him away from the rope.

It was then that all hell broke loose. Everybody was screaming and clapping as Jake Veeder put him on his shoulders and started prancing around showing off, the big bastard. Mama and Lucy Lemur were over by one of the cars, both were crying and Mama was as pale as a sheet. Jake Veeder pranced over to them and deposited Lonnie on the ground where he staggered around until Mama grabbed him and started hugging him. Jake Veeder made a little speech.

"Well ladies here is yor little bitty dogie caf. He shore is sum climber, he's probably the best climber in the whole Cimarron valley, bar none."

Mama murmured, "Thank you Jake," and even Lucy Lemur smiled at him, also saying "Thank you," and then adding as her face contorted into a little superior grin, "He sure is some climber but you must be the best shot with a nigger shooter in the whole state of New Mexico."

Jake Veeder suddenly looked like a great happy puppy, but the longer he stood there the more he pranced and the redder he got.

"I need a drink of water," croaked Lonnie. He was watching some of the men as they tried out the nigger shooter. It was some nigger shooter, whittled from a crotch of wood taken from the big maple which grew by the cesspool. The handle and the branches were a foot long, the rubber bands three feet long and an inch wide, tied into slits cut in the large raw-hide pocket that held what was being shot. The men were having a tough time stretching the rubber bands. One after another tried and could only get the bands pulled back half way. Finally Fred Clafin tried and was able to sail a large iron nut like the one Jake Veeder had used to shoot up the line clear over the top of the Spire. But it was quite a strain, the muscles in his arms and shoulders bunched and writhed, but for Jake Veeder who went over to give them a demonstration it was as easy as pie. He stretched the rubber bands until they looked like they were going to pop and sent one of the nuts high over the Spire as everybody applauded.

Lonnie became almost as famous for climbing the Spire as he had for tying the string about Mike Collin's prick. A reporter from the *Clayton News* came out and took his picture and a picture of the Spire. Maybe the best part of it all was that Daddy didn't even get mad at him. When he got home from Clayton the day that it happened, he had stared at Lonnie for a long moment, then smiled a little and turned back to the coffee he was drinking. And when that week's paper came out there he was, freckled face and all, staring at him as he looked at it.

The bad part of it was that prick Jimmy Joe wouldn't pay him the five dollars. About a week after it all happened Bobby Leo and Jimmy Joe visited again. After some initial palavering, Lonnie broached the subject.

"You owe me five dollars."

Jimmy Joe cleared his throat, shook his hair horns. "I don't owe you no five dollars. Shit, you got scared and couldn't get down without a rope."

Lonnie felt like crying. "You shit, you do too owe me. I climbed it like I said I would."

Bobby Leo looked at his brother. "You do too owe him five dollars."

"In a pig's ass," said Jimmy Joe. "But here's two dollars, since I can't stand a snivelin' piece of shit." He took two silver dollars out of his pocket and poked them at Lonnie. Lonnie hesitated. Jimmy Joe clicked the dollars together, they gleamed in the morning sunlight, brand new, beautiful. Finally Lonnie took the two dollars, but he sure hated that Goddamn Jimmy Joe, the dirty prick!

Chapter 10

Gold Finder

Lonnie was letting surges from the windmill fill the tin cup so he could have a drink of good, cold water when Jake Veeder rode up. He let Macon drink from the pond, then came over and stared at Lonnie as he took one gulp after another.

"How 'bout fillin' 'er up for me an' then go tell your lil' ol' sweet sister that I've come a cortin'? I think she kinda likes Old Jake since I got yor lil' ol' ass down from that rock."

Lonnie stepped back a little and looked up at Jake Veeder. "I'll get you a drink of water but I ain't gonna tell Lucy nothin'. An' if I did, you know what she'd say. She'd say you're the last person on earth she'd like to drop dead with."

Lonnie filled the cup and handed it up to Jake who started drinking and looking toward the door of the house. He was grinning his silly grin.

"Well you tell 'er that one of these days, one of these ol' days, I'm gonna rope that lil' filly an' do some tamin'. She'll tame down real good, 'cus ol' Jake knows how to gentle down them wild ones."

Jake finished drinking and handed the cup back to Lonnie who hung it on the hook next to the sucker-rod. There was a hot wind, maybe ten or fifteen miles an hour coming out of the south, keeping the windmill churning along; the sucker-rod going up and down bringing up gush after gush of water which flowed into the stock tank and from there out into the pond which, in spite of the heat, was nearly full.

Jake had turned Macon and seemed ready to leave when he looked across the valley toward the Cimarron river. He shaded his eyes.

"Well I'll be damn, if it ain't the old fart comin', him an' his mangy, worthless dog."

Lonnie stared across the valley beyond the alkali flats and sure enough, angling in from where Highway 64 skirted the Cimarron river he could see the wavering image of somebody coming. Out in front, Lonnie could barely make out a moving speck. Old Man Dick never followed roads, he just cut across to wherever he was going.

Just then Lucy Lemur came out the door. She was wearing the superior smirk she always wore when confronted with Jake Veeder who started wiggling and swaying in his saddle as soon as he saw her. Lonnie noticed that Lucy Lemur had on one of her prettiest dresses, and that she stood slightly sideways with her back arched so that her hips and breasts showed good. Jake Veeder took one look at her out of the corner of his eyes and began shifting and wiggling even more. He didn't look directly at her, he never did unless he was drunk and then he stared at her like he was hypnotized. The same way he had looked when he was hypnotized at the school house in Kenton, when the magician gave a show and had everybody barking like dogs and generally making asses of themselves.

But he could talk and he did, his voice lispy and cooey, baby talk. "Well if it ain't Miss lil' ol' Lucy. Lookin' as sweet an pretty as I ever seen 'er. If you get any sweeter you gonna turn into a piece of candy or maybe jus' pure honey."

Lucy Lemur glared up at him. "Why don't you get lost you poor ignoramus. Why are you always coming around bothering people, particularly me?"

Jake seemed upset. "Well maybe I ain't so smart. But I can do some things. I can do lots of things like bulldog cows and bulls an' cut out cattle. An' you seen me with a rope. I'm real good with a rope."

"Big deal," sniffed Lucy Lemur and went back into the house.

Jake Veeder sat there on Macon looking like a hurt little boy. Then he muttered "I jus' doan savvy why she doan like me."

"Well, you're sure good with a rope," offered Lonnie.

"Yeah, big deal." With that Jake sniffed three or four times and rode off toward the Veeder ranch.

Lonnie could see Old Man Dick pretty good now and could make out Old Growler even though they both faded in and out in the heat warps rising from the alkali flats. Mama came out the door of the house and stared toward the oncoming figures. Then she shouted, "Bartolo, get hot water ready." It was amazing how loud she could be when she wanted somebody to do something.

Bartolo came out of the bunkhouse and started building a fire under the big pot which Daddy sometimes used to scald hogs when he butchered. "Hey Lonnito you bring water. *Mucho agua. Pronto Pronto.*"

Jesus Christ, he was always getting the shitty jobs to do. Just because Mama couldn't stand the way Old Man Dick smelled when he came in from one of his long trips. But there was no way out of it. Mama was looking at him with that expectant "do it now" look on her face, so he got the bucket and started making trips back and forth between the windmill and the big pot. Bartolo had the fire going, the cedar was popping and throwing off sparks. Flames reached up and covered the bottom of the pot.

Lonnie could see Old Man Dick and Growler clearly now, coming past the windmill in the lower pasture and finally up the long slope toward the house. Growler was leading the way as he always did, with the bent figure of Old Man Dick trudging behind. The distance between them never varied. It seemed like they were tied together with Growler pulling and Old Man Dick taking each forward step as if he would fall on his face if he didn't move. He had a long stick in his right hand which he moved in unison with each step, rowing himself along through the dry grass on the slope. A tableau of moving figures, connected by an invisible bond, coming around the edge of the pond toward the windmill. Lonnie had the drinking cup filled and handed it to Old Man Dick who gulped the water down, much of it draining from the corners of his mouth. Growler waded out into the pond and started lapping up water.

Old Man Dick was as skinny as a snake, with a bald head and a long crooked nose and little red bleary eyes. He never wore a hat and his naked head had little brown crusts all over it. He looked like an ancient bald eagle or maybe the California Condor Lonnie had seen once in National Geographic magazine, the same one that had the picture of the lemur that looked just like Lucy Lemur.

Old Man Dick had two or three more cups of water then handed the cup back to Lonnie, who rinsed it out carefully before he took a drink himself.

It was true that Old Man Dick smelled bad; a combination of stale sweat, urine, tobacco, dog, and something dead. He always slept with Growler on his trips, under the little tarpaulin he carried on his back with all the other stuff he needed, a skillet, lard, salt and pepper, a single shot 22 rifle, just like Lonnie's, and a forty-five revolver that had a brown wooden handle.

"Hello Miz Wilson," he said to Mama who was watching him from the door of the house. "How you been Miz Wilson?"

"I'm fine Mr. Dick," she answered in her hurried voice. "Did you have a good trip? It's nice to see you. Now you go and take your bath and I'll have something to eat for you when you're ready."

Old Man Dick looked and smelled like he really needed a bath. His face and clothes were caked with dust. Little rivulets of sweat made meandering grooves down his face following the course of his wrinkles. Lonnie followed him out behind the bunkhouse carrying the clothes Mama had just given him. They were clean and freshly ironed, an extra set she always had ready whenever he happened to come visiting for awhile.

Bartolo was waiting. He had a bucket with a wooden handle attached filled with water that he had taken from the big pot. When Old Man Dick took off his clothes Lonnie couldn't believe it, he was so bent and skinny his skin folded in a number of places, and he didn't have any ass at all, just loose skin covering knobby bones. His legs looked like poles with almost no thighs or calves. Jesus, he had legs like a chicken! And he looked just like a chicken standing there rubbing himself down with the soap after he was wet with the water Bartolo kept pouring over him. Just like a chicken, with chicken legs. A skinny chicken that had been fresh plucked, naked without feathers except for the long white eyebrows which were wilted down by the water.

He dried off with the towel Bartolo handed him and put on the fresh clothes and damned if he didn't look almost handsome. He seemed to be feeling good and kept grinning a lot at Lonnie and Bartolo as he rubbed the top of his head with his hand; something he did every few minutes, as regular as clock work. He put on a fresh pair of socks and some shoes that Daddy had given him and was ready to eat. And man could he eat. Mama filled his plate three times, pinto beans, fried potatoes, slabs of venison from a deer Fred Clafin had shot. Lonnie had never seen anybody eat as much or as fast.

"Boy you sure do eat good," Lonnie observed.

Old Man Dick peered at him from under his long eyebrows, then put down his fork and rubbed the top of his head. He glanced at Mama who was putting wood in the cook stove.

"I sure do thank you Miz Wilson, that was really good."

His voice sounded clear and strong, not the voice of an old man somewhere in his nineties. Actually nobody knew how old Old Man Dick was. He never mentioned it and no one wanted to come right out and ask him. But Lonnie knew he was old, really old and that he had been lots of places. Daddy had once said that Old Man Dick had a high education and that for a long time he had taught school at a place called Princeton, way back in the east. But that somewhere along the line he got tired of the rat race and started walking. And that was a long time ago. He had been walking up and down the Cimarron as long as anybody could remember. And he was always welcome any place he decided to visit.

"And here's something for Growler. Lonnie you go take this to Growler." She handed him a big platter filled with leftovers.

Old Growler ate even faster than Old Man Dick, making little growly sounds as he gulped everything and then looked up at Lonnie, hoping for more. Old Growler was old too, an ugly brown dog with a huge chest and bent front legs. Old Man Dick had said that Old Growler was part Bulldog and maybe some German Shepherd. He was a big dog with scars all over his face from all the fights he'd been in and from a badger he once tried to pull out of a hole. He had won all the fights except the one with the badger. Old Man Dick had observed that nobody could pull a badger out of a hole and Lonnie believed him.

A car drove up. Daddy and Sam and Lucy Lemur had gone to Clayton to pick up some groceries. They spotted Old Growler who was still looking hopefully up at Lonnie with his sad soulful eyes. Old Man Dick came out the door and Sam and Lucy Lemur ran up to him making a lot of noise, telling him how great he looked. Old Man Dick just stood there rubbing his head and then went over and shook hands with Daddy. Everybody liked Old Man Dick, even though it was generally agreed that he was a little bit crazy.

Like the crazy notion he had about cats. He had told Lonnie all about them last year when they were sitting on the bench in front of the bunkhouse. He had looked sideways at Lonnie and said,

"Now see there, there's one and he's watching us, trying to figure out where I put my gold finder."

Lonnie was astonished. "You mean that cat, that cat that's just sittin' there minding his own business. Why that cat don't care about nothin' except washing his face."

Old Man Dick put on his wise owl look, peering sideways at Lonnie, his eyes partly hidden by his long white eyebrows.

"That ain't no cat. That's a spy. All cats are spies. Don't they go around watching with their big slit eyes? Didn't you ever see one sneaking around watching you from around corners and watching you in the dark? They're spies all right."

Lonnie didn't believe it at first, then the more he watched cats the more he thought it might be possible. After awhile he started feeling real uneasy about cats, the way they looked at him, particularly when it was getting dark or the way their eyes glowed in the moonlight. And pretty soon he was not only afraid of cats, he hated cats, and that was what caused him to whirl one of them around and around by the tail and throw it against the bunkhouse wall. Mama had whipped him good for that one. He began to wonder about Mama, about why she would come to the defense of a bunch of spies.

Another time, also last year, they were sitting on the same bench when Old Man Dick surprised him by asking a funny question. He was looking sideways through his eyebrows with that know it all look on his face.

"You been getting sleepy lately?"

Lonnie was surprised. "Whataya mean, have I been gettin' sleepy? No I ain't been gettin' sleepy."

Then he thought about it awhile and said, "Well I do get sleepy some, just before I go to bed at night. An' then I'm sleepy for awhile after I get up in the mornin'."

Old Man Dick's "know it all" look got bigger. He was grinning a little, rubbing the top of his head.

"You know why you been getting sleepy lately?"

"Cause I'm tired, for Christ sake, why else should I get sleepy?"

"Well there's a damn good reason." Old Man Dick was looking serious.

"What reason?"

"You know them space ships in the funny papers that Buck Rogers flies around? And those space ships that evil emperor Ming flies around?"

"Sure I know about them space ships." Buck Rogers was Lonnie's favorite in all the funny papers. "But what's that got to do with gettin' sleepy?"

Old Man Dick nudged him. "Can't you see it, can't you figure it out?"

"You mean them space ships are doin' it?"

"Yep, that's exactly what I mean. One of them space ships or one just like one of them space ships is circling us right now, around and round this world, and its releasing sleeping gas. An' when we all get so tired and sleepy we can't do anything, funny looking creatures from another world, way out there, are gonna swoop down and land and take over. That's what's gonna happen!"

Lonnie was doubtful about it, but he had been getting sleepy and the more he thought about it the sleepier he got and the more he thought it might be true. Finally, a few days later, he asked Fred Clafin about it, and also about the cats being spies. Fred had looked at him for a moment, made little strangling noises with his shoulders shaking and observed, "Old Man Dick told you this stuff didn't he?"

"Yes he did, but what's that got to do with it?"

"Well Old Man Dick is sure a smart old guy, but he's got some strange ideas. I don't want you to go around believing in sleeper spaceships and spying cats." Fred Clafin looked serious for a moment, then said, "You don't tell him I said so but all that is just a lot of bullshit, and I better not catch you believing it."

Lonnie was relieved. He figured Old Man Dick was just having fun, spinning a lot of big whoppers. So he stopped believing in spying cats and sleeping gas but he still thought Old Man Dick could find gold with his gold finder.

After breakfast the morning after Old Man Dick came, he turned to Lonnie who was sitting by the kitchen cupboard watching them all work.

"Hey Lonnie," he was hanging up the dishtowel he had been using for drying, "let's you an' me go do some prospecting and some arrow head hunting."

So they started out, up the incline, across the quarry ridge with

Old Growler leading the way. Lonnie had his 22 rifle along, just in case. Old Man Dick had his six shooter with the brown wooden handle, sticking out of a holster he had strapped to a belt, hanging low, ready, also just in case. They were both looking for arrow-heads and it wasn't long until Old Man Dick spied one, half-buried beside a clump of dried grass. It was a beauty: perfect, with reddish brown and white stripes and slightly serrated edges.

It was generally agreed that not only was Old Man Dick one of the world's best walkers, he was also one of the world's best arrowhead hunters. As a matter of fact that was the way he made his living, selling arrowheads to the occasional tourist who, for reasons nobody could understand, sometimes came up the valley.

When they came to a large swell in the pasture, a dome from which they could see clearly in all directions, Old Man Dick took off his backpack and sat down on a rock that he had used before on prospecting trips. He reached in his backpack and took out a Prince Albert smoking tobacco can, opened it carefully, and took out his gold finder. Actually it wasn't just a gold finder, it could find the location of practically any metal, gold, copper, silver, or platinum.

"First we're gonna look for copper."

He took a penny from his pocket and held it to the end of the silk string of the gold finder which was dangling a few inches above the ground. At first it was steady then much to Lonnie's amazement, at least he looked like he was amazed, it began to swing back and forth, in cadence with little grunts of satisfaction uttered by Old Man Dick.

"Now you see that? There's copper over that way."

"How do you know it's not the other way since it's swinging that way too?"

"Cause the beam is one directional, that's why. There's copper over that way."

Lonnie knew there was. Everybody knew it. There had been a copper mine in the middle of the pasture which still had a lot of rusty machinery laying around and a big pile of copper ore that was waiting to be processed when the copper mine company went broke. Every time they had gone prospecting, Old Man Dick always checked out the gold finder, which was just a little bottle filled with some funny looking brown dust, hanging on the swinging string. And always the gold finder homed in on the old pile of copper ore.

"Let me try it." Lonnie was looking eager, holding out his hand.

"Okay, but you got to hold her steady." Old Man Dick got up. "You sit down here an' I'll let you give it a try."

Lonnie took the silk thread, pressed the penny against it, and held steady, the bottle a few inches above the ground. Sure enough the gold finder began to swing, a little bit at first and then in sweeps of four or five inches. And it was swinging toward the pile of copper ore, just the way it had when Old Man Dick had it.

Then Old Man Dick prospected for gold. For gold he held a ten dollar gold piece, something he was really proud of, to the string and the gold finder began swinging toward Old Battleship.

"There's a big pile of gold in that thing, and one of these days I'm gonna dig for it. You can help me and we'll both be rich." His lips were drawn into a fine line, his bald head jutted out on his long skinny neck, and his brow was crinkled, making him look like a greedy vulture.

"Well, I'll help dig."

Lonnie actually had his doubts about the gold finder. One day he had mentioned it to Walt who gave him one of his wide-eyed stares, the tears running down his cheeks a little.

"Well shit, you don't believe in that thing. That old man couldn't find his ass with both hands on a clear day and you think he can find gold with a crazy bottle and a piece of string."

"Well I tried it an' it works."

Walt hawked and spit then mumbled, "Jesus Christ. I knew measles was ketchin' but I didn't think bein' crazy was."

Lonnie was upset and doubtful. He asked Fred Clafin about it. Fred paused, looking thoughtful before he said, "Everybody goes around looking for something. It's Old Man Dick's way of looking for something, and that's important, to be looking for something."

All the same, even though he had just demonstrated that the gold finder could find copper when a penny was used, Lonnie had his doubts. When they got back from the prospecting trip nobody was at home, and Daddy's car was gone. Lonnie decided he would find out if the gold finder really worked.

He took three milk buckets and filled one of them with Mama's sterling silver, and put a lid on each bucket. He took them into the living room and put them in three different places. He put his footstool right in the middle between them and called Old Man Dick who was sitting on the bench in front of the bunkhouse.

"Hey come in and bring the gold finder. I got a game that's gonna be fun."

Old Man Dick glared at him without moving.

"Hey come on, it'll be real fun, you just wait and see, it'll be real fun."

Old Man Dick got up and went in the bunkhouse and came out with the Prince Albert can in his hand. When he came in the door, he gave Lonnie one of his sideways glances, his eyes fierce under his long white eyebrows.

"What you gonna do with them buckets?"

"Well, there's a lot of silver in one of them buckets, and we'll see if you can find it with the gold finder. You sit on that stool with your gold finder and we'll see if you can find the silver."

Old Man Dick suddenly looked eager. "Well that's nothing. As sure as blazes I'll find that silver."

He sat down on the stool and took the gold finder out of the coffee can, put a silver dime on the string and let the gold finder down until it was almost touching the floor. Pretty soon it started swinging in a wider and wider arc, right toward one of the buckets.

"There she is," his voice broke into a cackle.

"Nope, it ain't in that one. Now you hide your eyes an' I'll switch the buckets. Now no peekin'. It won't be fair if you peek."

Old Man Dick had turned a little pale and his eyes were shifty. But he closed them.

"Just to make sure, I'll tie this dishtowel around your head."

They went through the whole procedure three more times, and not once did Old Man Dick pick the bucket with the silver in it. On the last try his hands were shaking so bad the gold finder jiggled up and down even when it was swinging. His face had become drawn and there was a haunted empty look in his eyes. Suddenly Lonnie couldn't stand it. He was feeling real sad for Old Man Dick who was sitting motionless on the stool staring ahead like he was looking but not seeing anything.

"Well shit fire no wonder you couldn't find the silver. I was just playin' a big joke. There ain't no silver in any of them buckets. So how could you find silver when there wasn't no silver."

Old Man Dick suddenly perked up. "I ought to kick your ass for that one, playing a dirty trick on an old man like me."

But Lonnie could see that Old Man Dick felt a lot better. He rubbed the top of his head, carefully put the gold finder back in the Prince Albert can, and headed for the door.

"I'm goin' out and finish that whistle I was whittling for you. But maybe I won't give it to you, playing that dirty trick on me."

After he went out Lonnie grabbed the milk bucket with the silver in it and put the silver back in the brown box that Mama kept hidden away in the bottom of the kitchen cupboard. He worked fast, thinking maybe Old Man Dick might come back in and catch him.

Old Man Dick gave him the whistle anyway, saying it was a goodbye present because the next day he was going to take one of his long walks. After breakfast the next morning, he said goodbye to everyone and headed out with Old Growler leading the way, pulling him along with the invisible rope. Lonnie watched them go, two moving figures, getting smaller and smaller, wavering in the heat warps until they disappeared into a water mirage which hovered over the alkali flats.

CHAPTER 11

Storm

Mama had been jumping up and sitting down more than usual, getting more biscuits, extra ham and eggs, more coffee for Fred Clafin. When she put the coffee pot back on the stove she turned and said it. "I'm going to teach school this year, I've got a job teaching all the grades. Mr. Rutledge, head of the school board, called me last night, and told me."

She stood there holding on to a dish towel, looking shy and afraid. Nobody said anything for what seemed like a long time, then Lonnie broke out. "I didn't know Mamas could be teachers. Does that mean you're going to be my teacher?"

"Yes it does Dummy." Lucy Lemur was looking at Mama, her face shining. "That's really great, Mama."

Everyone at the table immediately agreed except Daddy who kept eating, not looking up.

"If you're as good at teaching as you are at cooking, Blanche, you'll be a great teacher," Fred Clafin was smiling his finest smile.

Everyone agreed again, even Daddy, "Yes she will, she'll be a great teacher." Then Daddy started squeezing his egg and got a little yellow to show. He glanced at Mama. "Blanche could you throw these eggs back in the skillet for awhile? They're a bit bleedy."

Mama jumped up from the table and took Daddy's plate. In a minute or two she handed it back to him, the eggs hard as rocks. Daddy cut into one of them with his knife, and nodded. Mama seemed relieved. She turned to Bartolo. "Do you think Dulcita might be able to come in and help with the cooking and the house cleaning?"

Bartolo stopped eating for a moment, his mustache stopped moving up and down and his muddy brown eyes turned on Mama. "*Sí, señora*, she come, she good cook, not good like you, but good, *muy bueno*, tomorrow, *mañana*, I go home to Tencio, *vamoose mañana*, bring her back, *muy pronto*."

"That's nice, Bartolo," Mama murmured.

And so it was on that dry, hot day as the summer drifted into September. There was no way around it, school was coming. And Lonnie hated it! The whole crummy idea. Well maybe not all of it. He liked recess okay when they would play games like "Red Rover, Red Rover, come over, come over" and "prison base." And the noon hour was great, when they would eat their lunches and then look for arrowheads up on the hill that jutted from the mesa above the school, or ride buggy wheels down the hill, or walk on stilts. But most of it was just a pain in the ass, sitting all day staring out the window thinking about riding and shooting and airplanes.

A week before school started, Lonnie decided to take a ride up to Black Smith Canyon to check on the dead cows. He saddled Baldy and rode over the quarry ridge past Old Battleship, toward the mouth of the canyon.

It was easy to find the way, the closer he got the more the breeze carried the smell of rotting cattle and the birds got thicker; big buzzards circling about, which could sail for minutes on end without batting a wing. Also the closer he got, the more animals he saw. Two fat coyotes broke from a scrub cedar patch and went loping away toward the Zig Zag, three skunks, their tails lifted high, pranced sideways down the trail toward him. The dead smell got so bad he could hardly stand it. He took off his bandanna and tied it around his face but it didn't help much. He sidled around the approaching skunks and into the mouth of the canyon. They lay there where they had fallen, the cows and the calves, most of them were just bones. As he looked, eyes peered out of the cavernous belly of one, and a badger came scooting out, took a look at Lonnie and then went back in, having his dinner and living in it too.

Lonnie stood there for a few minutes, trying not to breathe, then turned and went back toward the ranch house. In the distance he heard a strange low rumble and saw a bunch of black and green clouds edging up over the western mesas. As he was watching lightning flickered and three or four minutes later he heard a low guttural rumbling.

Baldy was pulling his old trick again, trying to get enough slack in the reins to make a run for it. Lonnie gave him a little and he took off, first at a trot, then a slow gallop and finally in a dead run. No holding him now, and Lonnie didn't try to. He hung on and listened to the rhythmic beat of Baldy's hooves on the hard ground. After about a mile, Baldy gradually slowed down on his own until he was just walking along, breathing hard. Lonnie whacked him on the ass with the loose reins, but he kept moseying along, taking it easy. To the west, the rumbling was much louder, the clouds real crazy looking, deep black, moving every which way, with bulbous swellings of green, billowing and swirling. He whacked Baldy again with the reins and this time he jumped to it fast. They passed Old Battleship and could see the Spire sticking up over to the right and far away the ranch buildings looking like little boxes with trees around them.

Baldy slowed down and speeded up three more times before they got there, with the storm coming after them fast. Just as he got to the barn there was a deafening "bang" like a thousand two-inchers going off. Smoke and dust rolled away from where the lightning rod cable on the windmill went into the ground. Then wherever Lonnie looked, across the lower pasture, up toward the near mesa, millions of spurts of dust puffed up and fused together until the entire floor of the valley seemed to smoke and churn. The day turned dark, relieved by jagged ribs of lightning followed in rapid succession by sharp "blams" which mixed in with the roar of hail striking the tin roof of the barn. The rain began, coming in white sheets obscuring the mesas and softening the snap and pop of thunder, the beat of hail and the wind which caused the barn to creak and shudder.

Lonnie climbed the ladder to the second floor of the barn, where he had built himself a hideout by stacking bales of hay until he had a cozy little room where he kept his dirty books. He crawled through the long opening into the total darkness, smelling the hay, feeling his way long until he reached the corner of the room where he found his flashlight.

He turned it on and started looking at his books. The one he liked best was the one which showed Little Orphan Annie getting screwed by her dog Sandy and Daddy Warbucks. He also had one showing Tillie the Toiler getting it from Harold Teen and another one which showed Mutt and Jeff taking turns screwing a goat. It was the funniest one because Mutt who was real tall had a little shriveled up cock while Jeff who was a short little runt had one that would have made a stud horse proud.

Lonnie had another book which actually showed people moving. If you held it just right and let the pages flip fast it showed Little Orphan Annie getting screwed by her dog Sandy.

Lonnie had just finished flipping it, enjoying the action when he heard his brother Sam, his voice barely audible in the roar of hail and rain and booms of thunder. "Lonnie, you little prick, are you up there? You little prick you better answer."

Lonnie put his books and flashlight away and crawled out, taking his own sweet time. When he looked down from the opening there was Sam, wetter than hell, holding a washtub in his hands.

When he saw Lonnie he started screaming. "I knew you were up there you little shit, with that little runt of a horse there in the stall. Get down here right now. I'm goin' to beat the shit out of you for this one. Mama is goin' crazy worryin' about you, and you sittin' up there snug and cozy readin' your dirty books. I ought to show Mama what you've been readin'."

Sam threw down the tub and started up the ladder.

Lonnie grabbed a pitchfork that was hanging on the wall. "You ain't goin' to beat the shit out of me. I'll stick you with this fork." He started making jabbing motions at Sam who was about half way up. "You better not come up here, I'll stick you with this fork!"

Sam stopped climbing. "Well, shit, I'm not gonna beat you up, just come on down and we'll go to the house. Mama is really worried."

Lonnie put the fork back in its place and started down the ladder. When he got down, Sam didn't seem mad at all. He was just standing there looking silly holding the tub over his head.

He grinned at Lonnie. "Now get under here with me and we'll make a run for the house. Get under here or the hail will knock our brains out."

But even as he said it, the noise diminished. No hail now just pulses of rain that came and went as the wind shifted. Then the rain stopped and there was complete silence. The storm was moving away fast. The east end of Black Mesa was still obscured by black streaks of rain in which lightning danced and flickered. Thunder, muted by distance, came through as dull muttering. Then almost as an afterthought a tornado leaned out of the clouds and sent trees and roofs of farm buildings high in the air as it went

threshing and churning along the bed of the Cimarron over toward the Beheimer place.

Just as they reached the door of the house the sun came out,
low in the west but still bright, bringing with it a rainbow with
one foot at the base of the Spire and the other wavering in the
debris of the passing tornado. Except in the northeast where the
storm was still boiling and the tornado still writhing and twisting,
everything was clearing up. The Wedding Cake seemed like it had
just been taken fresh from the oven, its many rings repainted. To
the southwest Old Battleship, new washed, a dark oblong shape
its details draped by shadows, its crown a burst of colors in the
aura of the sun.

Mama was at the door waiting, it looked like she had been crying. Behind her Lucy Lemur was looking pale and relieved. Mama
grabbed him when he got to the door and started hugging him.
Jesus Christ! He wished she wouldn't do that.

"Where in the world have you been? We thought maybe something had happened to you, out there in that hail and lightning. I
was worried to death."

"I wasn't," Lucy Lemur threw her head back and swirled her
black hair. "I knew the little creep was okay. Nothing will ever
happen to the little creep. He's too mean." She gave Lonnie a dig
in the ribs when Mama finally let him go.

"I wasn't doin' nothin'. I just went up to see the dead cows.
Just to see the dead cows."

Lucy Lemur made her disgusted rasping sound deep in her
throat. "Well that's really great. Here we were worried to death
about you and you're up there enjoying yourself, looking at a bunch
of dead cows." She gave Lonnie another poke. But she wasn't looking at him. She was staring out the door, her eyes getting wider
and wider.

CHAPTER 12

Ice Cream

Down below the house, where the arroyo broadened out into a wide grassy and cactus covered pasture, it looked like the earth was moving.

Lonnie ran down the steps past the windmill, sloshing through the mud and small streams of water edged with banks of hail, hearing Sam splashing along behind him and Mama's voice screaming, "Stay away from there! You stay away from there!"

But Lonnie didn't stop running until he was at the edge of it, a brown thick mass moving like molasses but faster, rolling and tumbling, mostly hail at the front with lots of dead cactus and dead branches of mesquite and scrub oak mixed in. As it rolled along fingers of water would dart out a few feet before the rush of trash ran over them.

Sam was looking away toward the west mesas. "We better move back, look at that."

Above them where the pasture narrowed into the gulch of the arroyo, a huge mass of muddy water was pouring out making a moving wall on top of the trash, and coming down from other canyons more walls of water were moving toward them.

The mass at their feet suddenly bulged upward and covered Lonnie's feet. Sam grabbed him and pulled him away. They turned and started running back toward the house where Mama was still screaming and Lucy Lemur was trotting down toward them. She moved quickly through the mud and hail, just floating along, her black hair blowing back in the fresh cold breeze.

Sam and Lonnie stopped when they met her and looked back. Lucy Lemur was staring toward the flooding plain. "Boy look at that, now that's a lot of water, and it's still coming in," she looked up toward the south mesas, "from all the canyons and arroyos, and breaks, from everywhere."

As they stood there, the streams began to converge, wave after wave, until the entire lower pasture was covered by rippling, swirling currents, clear out to the windmill at the north fence. It was rising so fast Lonnie started thinking that it might never stop until the whole valley was filled and everybody was drowned, everywhere.

Just as they got to the pond, Fred Clafin with Dogey and Horse trailing him came riding up, coming in from the line cabin on the topside. They all wore yellow slickers, their wet hats pulled down to their ears. Dogey and Horse got off their horses and tied them to the hitching rail but Fred Clafin sat hunched over in the saddle looking toward the flooded pasture.

Suddenly he spurred his horse into a run down the incline, guiding the horse with one hand and untying his rope with the other. About thirty feet out in the rolling mass of hail and trash a cow was having trouble. She would get to her feet for a few seconds then roll and go out of sight, come up, and roll again. Lonnie could see other cattle, farther out where the current was even swifter, doing the same thing.

Fred Clafin had to beat his horse with his coiled rope to get him to move into it. Lonnie couldn't blame the horse, it was scary as hell. When the horse was in up to its belly Fred Clafin waited until the cow came up, threw his rope and snagged her around the horns. With the horse backing toward the bank he pulled the cow along until she finally found her footing and walked out by herself. Fred Clafin got his rope loose and went back in again. By this time Dogey and Horse were there doing the same thing. Within thirty minutes they pulled out eight cows and missed a few which kept rising and disappearing in the moving trash until they couldn't be seen anymore.

Lonnie heard the phone ringing their ring, three longs and a short so he ran toward the house, but Lucy Lemur, as usual, beat him to it. She was standing at the phone listening, looking excited, saying "Uh huh," "Uh huh," every now and then. Then she hung up the phone and headed for the door, not even glancing at Lonnie.

"Why didn't you let me talk? Who was that? You always beat me to the phone, and you're always listenin' in when somebody else gets a call. That's not nice listenin' in on other people's calls."

Lucy Lemur gave him a whack as she went past him. "Who would want to talk to you, you little thief. What I still can't figure out is why you would want my fingernail polish. You and your dead cows!"

"It was Daddy," Lucy Lemur announced to Mama and Sam, as they came into the kitchen. "He can't get home. He's stuck across the river, over at the Beheimers. They lost both of their barns and a bunch of shingles blew off their house and two of their horses got killed. Daddy's going to stay there tonight, and maybe get back tomorrow if the river goes down."

They all looked up as Old Bartolo came in the front door carrying a tub-ful of hail. He set it down in the middle of the kitchen, then went into the pantry and brought out the ice cream freezer. His eyes were twinkling as he announced, "Hey, we lucky, big storm pretty bad, but some good, *muy bueno*. We gonna have some ice cream."

He went out the door and came back in a few minutes with a sack of salt that he kept next to his bunk in the bunkhouse, not fine white salt but pieces about the size of some of the hail. "Hey Lonnito, you take the ice cream freezer apart, I'm gonna do my big job."

Lonnie loved the ice cream freezer. He would take it out sometimes and examine it, the wooden outer bucket, the inner metal one, the paddle, the crank, but most of all the gears under the bulb at the top of the cover. He would put it all together and turn the crank and watch the paddle go in one direction and the inner bucket go in the other. Then he would imagine he was making ice cream, turning the crank fast at first and then slower and slower as the ice cream got harder, as it always did when they made it.

They didn't have ice cream very often, maybe two or three times a year when Daddy would bring a big hunk of ice home from Clayton. Then Old Bartolo would do his job getting the ice cream freezer ready, chipping up the ice with an ice pick and getting the salt out of the bag.

Although Bartolo called it his job, he didn't do much. Mama mixed everything together that went into it and Lonnie and Lucy Lemur turned the crank which Old Bartolo tried to do sometimes but couldn't because of rheumatism in his elbow which kept getting worse and worse. But Old Bartolo was the one who enjoyed the job most, and was always there first with his salt and ice, and eager expression as he watched the whole thing taking place.

Mama started mixing up a bunch of stuff to go in the freezer bucket; five eggs, a gallon of milk, three tablespoons of vanilla, two cups of sugar and finally half a gallon of rich cream that Lonnie had collected from doing his job at the cream separator.

Lonnie also liked turning the cream separator. It turned real hard at first but pretty soon as it went faster and faster making a high pitched whine, it got easy. When he had it going "lickety, split" as Old Walt was always saying, Mama would pour the milk into the big bowl on the top of the separator and two streams would start coming out, a small stream of yellow cream from the top drain and a white stream of white skim milk, which Mama let sour so she could make cottage cheese, from the lower drain.

Mama poured all the stuff she had mixed up in the mixing bowl into the metal inner bucket of the ice cream freezer and handed the bucket to Bartolo. He held it in his hands for awhile, looking down at it with his lips moving like he was praying over it, then carefully placed it inside the wooden bucket. Just as carefully he placed the paddle in the metal bucket, put the lid with the gears in it in place and connected the turning crank. And it was ready to start making.

Lonnie could hardly wait. He started turning the crank, listening to all that wonderful stuff slosh around inside while Bartolo added the hail and the salt. As he turned it, Lonnie could almost see through the metal of the lid, could see the paddle going in one direction while the metal bucket went in the other.

In the beginning the turning was easy, all that stuff just slopping around inside, but when it started to freeze the turning got harder and harder. Lonnie turned it for about ten minutes while Bartolo kept putting in more hail and salt, packing it in good around the metal bucket. It started getting real hard to turn and Lonnie felt his arm getting tired.

He hollered at Lucy Lemur who was standing there watching. "Hey, it's your turn. I'm gettin' tired. It's your turn."

"I won't help you unless you tell me why you stole my fingernail polish."

"I told you I didn't steal your ol' fingernail polish." Jesus Christ! She had a memory like an elephant.

As the handle kept getting harder and harder to turn his arm started feeling like it had when he held it out for twenty minutes to win Old Bartolo's silver dollar. He felt tears about ready to start when Lucy Lemur pushed him aside and started turning the handle. "Well if you're going to snivel about it, just forget it. I don't care anything about the fingernail polish, I just don't like having a little brother who is a thief." With that she gave him a look which made him feel worse than he already did and turned back to the ice cream freezer, pulling hard now to get the handle around. Finally she got up and announced, "It's done."

After supper they all had some ice cream, a big bowl full for each of them. As Lonnie put each spoonful in his mouth and let it melt some before he swallowed so he wouldn't get a headache, he was sure that never in his whole life would he taste anything as good as that ice cream. And he never did.

CHAPTER 13

Western Hospitality

Early the next morning, Lonnie went to the picture window in the living room and looked across the valley toward the Cimarron River. It was coming over its banks and in some places had spread out until it looked like a lake.

As it turned out, it was the biggest flood anybody could remember. The Cimarron kept rising until it covered all the lowland within half a mile of it. It washed out the bridge next to Kenton and three houses in the lowland near the Wedding Cake.

Lonnie was glad for the flooding. School was supposed to start on Monday but there were so many bridges and roads washed out that just a few people could get there. The phone rang the general call and Mr. Rutledge announced that there wouldn't be any school for a week.

That Sunday, Lonnie was relaxing in his hideout reading his dirty books when he heard a car coming. He crawled out and looked out the upper window of the barn. Jesus Christ! It was the Thompsons.

It always happened when everything was going right, here would come the Thompsons, and he would be saddled with Toad. The car stopped in front of the house and Toad got out. He really looked like a toad with his new green suit and bulging eyes and the way he kind of shuffled along instead of walking like everybody else. There was no way out of it. Lonnie heard Mama calling his name and soon he was leading Toad around. How do you entertain somebody who is as big as a barn and has the brain of a pissant?

Lonnie took Toad out to the barn to show him Baldy. But Toad wasn't much interested. He kept looking at the milk cows, particularly one which was half jersey and had big soft brown eyes. "Hey," Toad wanted to know, "Did you ever fuck one of them cows?"

"Sure, lots of times, want to try it? It's great." Lonnie figured it would be okay since he had to entertain Toad. Fred Clafin was always saying that in the West a guest should always be treated just right. He called it "Western hospitality."

Lonnie tied the cow with the gentle eyes to a post and provided Toad with a rickety bucket to stand on. Toad climbed on the bucket, dropped his pants around his feet and started banging away, with Lonnie smirking and giggling, holding the rope. But he didn't smirk long. He saw the tail of the cow rising, and to his horror saw the huge inundation slowly and inexorably take place, right down into Toad's trousers. Toad didn't miss a stroke, he just kept pumping, his movements becoming more and more frenzied until a kind of misty inward look suffused his eyes.

Lonnie couldn't believe it. What was he going to tell Mama and Daddy? And the Thompsons? Well he solved the problem. He told Toad to fall in the horse tank, and he did, new suit and all. They washed his pants out and it took a lot of washing. Fortunately the suit was green, so even if they didn't do a very good job, nobody ever knew the difference.

That afternoon after the Thompsons had left Lonnie started feeling guilty. He tried to get rid of it by thinking about how he was a Golden Bat and about how he had shot the cow, but it kept coming back. He even tried looking at his dirty books but it didn't do any good. All he could think about was what a shit he was, and he kept hearing Lucy Lemur's voice calling him a thief. Finally he went up on the quarry ridge and got out his treasure box. When he saw his piece of petrified wood, it got even worse, thinking about how he had stolen Lucy Lemur's fingernail polish. That he *was* a thief!

As he sat there on the quarry ridge watching the valley darken with coming night the sound "eeeeooooo," "eeeeeoooo," of the bull-bats as they came out of a dive somehow brought back to him all the bad things he had done; throwing the cat against the wall, spraying high-life on the pigs, shooting the cow with marbles, putting the two-incher up the chicken's ass, tying the string around Mike Collin's prick, helping Toad fuck the cow, stealing the fingernail polish. His guilt became a fierce ache in his chest and, for reasons that he could never understand, he started thinking about that really bad time when Daddy whipped him. Never before had he been able to think about it without trembling but now in his misery it seemed strangely comforting, that bad time.

CHAPTER 14

Bad Time

It happened when Lonnie was just a little kid, when they all lived on the Roberts farm down in the flat land next to the Cimarron river, back before Daddy bought the Ranch. Daddy was the manager of the Roberts farm for the first Citizens Bank of Trinidad which had foreclosed on the whole outfit because Mr. Roberts, who was an old man, couldn't make payments on the money he had borrowed.

The Roberts farm had a lot of different kinds of fields; alfalfa, wheat, corn and something called maize that came in neat bunches and looked like little shotgun pellets when it was harvested.

The reason all this stuff could be raised was the irrigation ditch which ran from a dam on the Cimarron river, three miles up from the farm. When there was a little rise in the river the dam held the water back until it could rise high enough to run down the irrigation ditch. Then all the fields would be irrigated, and practically anything could be grown because the land was so rich.

In the fall, when everything had to be harvested, Daddy needed a lot of help and would hire practically anybody who came along and needed a job. And it was just about that time that the Wilkes family came down the road.

Lucy Lemur saw them coming first and came rushing into the kitchen where Mama was struggling to fix enough supper to feed all the hired hands.

"Something's coming Mama, something real strange."

Lonnie ran to the window and sure enough it was quite a sight. There was a wagon coming down the incline leading to the arroyo where the water ran across the road when it rained. It was being pulled by quite a team, an old swaybacked pinto horse and a skinny steer, hooked up in tandem with the steer leading the way. Four goats and a large fat pig were coming along behind, being led by long pieces of rope.

But the most amazing thing, as Lonnie could see when they crossed the arroyo and started up toward the house, was the people. They were black! There were five of them, a skinny black guy who was partly bald and who had a rough looking black beard, a roly poly black woman with a white rag tied around her head, wearing a ragged brown dress. And three children! Two girls, one about thirteen and another about twelve, both with their hair fixed a funny way so that each of them had about ten braided strands sticking out all over their heads.

And then there was a big husky black kid about fourteen who was walking behind the goats and the pig whacking them along with a long switch he was carrying.

Daddy hired Mr. Wilkes to help with the fall harvest and Mrs. Wilkes to help Mama with the cooking and cleaning, something she really needed. Mrs. Wilkes was always looking at Mama with a big smile, her teeth and eyes flashing white in her black face. "What you all wan' done now, Miz Wilson?" And when Mama told her she would do it fast and would be right back with "What you all wan' done now, Miz Wilson?" It wasn't long, just a few days, until Mrs. Wilkes got everything down, the cooking and cleaning done in no time and without Mama having to tell her a thing. Mrs. Wilkes made great cornbread and she had a way of doing frijole beans cooked with side-meat which were almost as good as Old Bartolo's who hadn't started working for them yet.

As it turned out Mr. Wilkes was a great worker too. He could do practically everything, run the go-devil for getting weeds out of the corn, fix the hay baler when it broke down, grease wagon wheels, fix harnesses, and handle a team of four horses, as even Daddy commented, better than anybody.

Lucy Lemur became great friends with the two black girls, the younger one named Flatima was really cute with her flashing eyes and white teeth and her ability to climb trees and find bird eggs. She could climb high and fast up the great maple trees that towered over the farm building and find bird eggs by the dozens. She would go from nest to nest putting the eggs in her mouth so she could climb with both hands and come down the tree real easy. Sometimes her mouth would be so full of eggs that her cheeks would be pooched way out with a lot of little lumps in them.

Lonnie thought he was a pretty good climber and he was for a five year old kid, but nobody was as good at climbing or finding birds eggs as Flatima. She was real proud and a little bit superior about her ability to climb and bring down eggs better than anybody.

One day, she found a bunch of robins' nests way up the biggest maple tree, the one that towered over the windmill and made the rest of the trees look small. She came down the tree with her cheeks pooched way out and then walked around showing them off to all the other kids as proof that she was the best. When she came up to Lonnie she looked so smug and superior as she bend down over him that he whacked her in both cheeks with both hands at the same time.

Then he wished he hadn't done it. She opened her mouth and spewed the whole mess in his face. But that wasn't the worst of it. All the other kids, including Lucy Lemur and Sam and Ka Dong (which was the nickname they gave the big black kid), started laughing at him and commenting.

Sam was first. "Hey, look at Lonnie, he must be part Chinese his face is so yellow."

"Yeah, I know'd he wasn't black, and I figured he wasn't white. An' now we all know, he's a yaller kid, jus' like them Chinas," Ka Dong observed.

It was as embarrassing enough with all that yellow stuff running down his face without having to listen to all that shit they were handing out. Lonnie ran over to the horse tank, took off all his clothes and dived in, washing himself as he swam along. When he got out, they were all still laughing at him except for Ka Dong who was looking at him funny.

There was something crazy about Ka Dong. He wasn't feeble minded but he sure acted like it. He was always thumping people, particularly Lonnie, on the head saying, "Ka Dong, Ka Dong" as he did it and it hurt like hell. According to him, he spent lots of time screwing women, particularly the real good looking ones." He winked at Lonnie. "Old Ka Dong doan like ugly wimmin," he added, thumping Lonnie on the head for emphasis.

The other girl's name was Althea and she was beautiful. She had skin that was blue black and the face of a girl Lonnie had once seen in National Geographic magazine. And she was a worker. She was always helping Mama and Mrs. Wilkes do all kinds of things but the main thing she did was the washing for everybody. Hour after hour she would stand over the wash tub scrubbing things down on the washboard until they were bright and clean, then she would hang the wash out on the clothesline and gather it in after all the clothes had dried. Not only was she good at washing clothes she was also great at ironing them. And what Mama couldn't believe, and she said so many times, was how Althea could sew. She patched everything that had holes, darned a bunch of socks and sewed on hundreds of buttons.

But Ka Dong was a pain in the ass, as well as the head. He was such a bullshitter, always telling big lies about things he had done, and places he had gone. For instance, Lonnie couldn't really believe that Ka Dong had, as he maintained, been to Chicago and had shook the hand of the President of the United States.

Then one day it happened, the really bad thing that Lonnie didn't like to think about, out under a haystack that looked like a toadstool after the cows had eaten away at it.

"Hey Lonnie," Ka Dong had said, "let ol' Ka Dong show you sumpin'. I's gonna give you a lessin in cock suckin'." And Lonnie had gone along, letting Ka Dong suck his cock. It didn't feel bad but nothing happened.

"It's your turn to do me now," Ka Dong had pulled his cock out, hard and throbbing, and Lonnie had sucked away until his mouth was filled with the rhythmic spasms of Ka Dong's coming.

Why Lonnie bit down he never knew. But he did. Ka Dong started screaming, and ran across the field to the house, holding his cock in his hand. Lonnie had hidden in the hay, burying deeper and deeper until Daddy found him. Yanked him out and stood over him glaring down with a look on his face that Lonnie had never seen before. Then Daddy started whipping him with the reins from an old bridle. Whipping him across his back and arms and face, all the time shouting, "You want to be a cock sucker? You want to be a cock sucker?" With Lonnie screaming "No! No! No!" at the top of his voice each time the reins fell.

Lonnie crouched down on the ground with his hands over his head feeling the bite of the reins on his back, hearing Daddy screaming about him sucking cocks. Then he heard another voice, Lucy Lemur's; she was screaming too. The whipping suddenly stopped and Lonnie looked up in time to see Lucy Lemur, her hair wild about her face, her eyes streaming with tears, throw herself at Daddy and start beating him with her fists.

"You leave him alone! You leave him alone," she screamed. "Do you want to kill him? I hate you! I hate you!"

There wasn't any more whipping. Lonnie got up and edged away, looking for a place, any place, to hide, feeling the searing fire on his back and face. Every now and then little convulsive screams would break from his lips. He started running until he wound up at the house where Mama was waiting. She put a mixture of coal oil and lard on some of the welts, and iodine on the ones that were bleeding, all the time wailing, "Oh, Orlando Ray! Oh, Orlando Ray!"

That evening the Wilkes family disappeared, going down the road in their wagon, carrying some extra things Mama had given them. But that wasn't the end of it. After that Daddy didn't look at him. It was almost as if he wasn't there, or anywhere. And Daddy didn't ask him to sit on his lap anymore.

And that's the way it was for weeks and weeks until one evening Lonnie was hanging around in the corner of the sitting room hoping Daddy would look at him. When Daddy looked up and saw him there a strange expression came over his face. He got up from his chair, came over and picked Lonnie up and hugged him. He took Lonnie back to his chair and rocked back and forth until Mama came into the dark room and lit an oil lamp.

After that Daddy never whipped him again. Ever. And Lonnie decided that no matter what happened he would never suck another cock. And he never did.

Lonnie put his treasure box back in its place but not the piece of petrified wood. He carried it down the hill to the house and stood for a long time at the windmill looking at Lucy Lemur's window where the light had just come on. He knew she didn't like for him to come messing around her room but before he knew it he was knocking at her door.

It opened suddenly and there she was staring down at him, looking mean. "What do you want, you little creep? What are you bothering me for? You really pulled one today letting Anthony fall into the horses' tank. Or did you push him in?"

Lonnie couldn't think of anything to say. He held the piece of petrified wood out toward her. She looked startled then her face softened. She reached out and took the piece of petrified wood. Looked at it carefully and smelled it. Then she handed it back to him. "Well it sure is beautiful, and it smells good. If I had known you were going to do something really important with my finger-nail polish, like paint a rock, I would have given it to you."

"It's not a rock, it's a piece of wood." Lonnie's voice shook a little. "A piece of a tree that lived a million years ago." Lonnie looked at it and ran his fingers over its smooth surface. "A million years ago."

Lucy Lemur opened the door wide and stepped out into the hallway, her eyes gentle with concern. "Yes it is," she said almost in a whisper. She bent down and gave Lonnie a kiss on the head. Jesus Christ! He ran down the hallway into the kitchen where Mama was getting dinner ready. Suddenly he felt great!

CHAPTER 15

Range War

Because of the flood there was an entire extra week of no school and then, early in the morning in the middle of September, they all got ready and waited for the school bus. It actually wasn't a bus, just Mr. Rutledge's rickety truck fixed up with wooden benches in the back. Mama and Lucy Lemur got in front with Mr. Rutledge while Sam and Lonnie climbed in the back and joined the rest of them, the Beheimer kids, the Veeder kids, the Eddleman kids, Toad Thompson and the Morgan kids; Bobby Leo, that son-of-a-bitch Jimmy Joe, and Eula Gay, who always bothered the hell out of Lonnie because she insisted on sitting next to him.

He guessed Eula Gay was pretty with her bright blue eyes and wide mouth always in a little self depreciating grin with her teeth showing. For the life of him, Lonnie couldn't understand why she liked him so much and was always trying to get close to him and to touch him. But that was the way things were, floods, shooting cattle, school and Eula Gay. He sat down in the corner clear across the bus from her hoping it wouldn't happen, but it did. Before the bus got started up, she was there beside him touching him occasionally with her shoulder when the bus made a turn. He leaned against Bobby Leo who shoved over to make more room. Jesus Christ! Having to go to school was bad enough but why did it have to be complicated with Eula Gay?

School, just one boring day after another, sitting there looking out of the window thinking about riding and shooting and airplanes. The only thing that made it worthwhile was recess and the hour they got off at noon when they could play games like "Red Rover, Red Rover, come over, come over," or "prison base" or hunt for arrowheads on the hill which jutted out from the mesa on the southwest.

There were only twelve kids in one large room with a pot bellied stove in the middle. Mama had to teach all eight grades, but there wasn't anybody in some grades and only one or two in others. The kids were strung out all over the place with the ones in the same grade sitting together. Mama would go up and down the line pointing and talking and sometimes scolding when somebody fucked up.

Lucy Lemur was the smartest student. Even though she was only fourteen years old she knew the whole works and spent her time helping Mama with the other kids, particularly the little ones like Bobby Leo and the stupid ones like Toad Thompson and Wayne Veeder. She had a special desk up front in the corner where she could be close to Mama and keep her eye on everybody. She did a good job. She had even gotten Toad Thompson interested in drawing pictures which he now did every day, instead of rocking back and forth making crazy buzzing sounds.

And that's about the way it was, day after boring day until it started getting cold and they had to cover up in blankets when they rode in the back of Mr. Rutledge's old truck. The school room was always warm, though, with the pot bellied stove sometimes glowing red. Wayne Veeder was in charge of keeping the fire going and he was good at it. Putting in just the right amount of coal, shaking down the clinkers and keeping the draft regulated. Wayne wasn't feeble minded like Toad, just uninterested in anything that didn't involve hunting arrowheads and keeping the stove running right.

Then one day they had the range war. Lonnie and Bobby Leo had made a circle of rocks around their ranch and wouldn't let anyone come across the fence onto their land. Everybody, even the girls, had some land fenced in by rocks and things were pretty peaceful with people riding stick horses around, including the girls who couldn't ride them very well since they had to wear dresses.

Then one day Jimmy Joe, the prick, decided that all the land belonged to him because the whole works, including the place where the schoolhouse was located, was on his daddy's ranch. He and Sam started invading other people's land and stealing their rocks. Pretty soon a lot of people, particularly Lonnie and Bobby Leo, were throwing rocks. Lucy Lemur was screaming her head off but the war didn't stop until Mama came running out of the schoolhouse with her whipping stick and not before three kids had been hit by rocks. Jimmy Joe was hit right between the eyes.

Mama herded everybody into the school house and made them sit at their desks for the rest of the noon hour while she doctored the wounded. Nobody was hurt much, just some bruises and some lumps. The good part was that Jimmy Joe's head swelled up like he was about to sprout a horn. Mama decided that all the people who had been involved in the war would be punished by having to memorize a poem. She picked "The Last Leaf on the Tree" by Oliver Wendell Holmes, and made them copy it out of a book and gave them one day to learn it.

Lonnie didn't think it was fair, for him and Bobby Leo to have to learn it since it was about a real old guy and they were just little kids but he didn't say anything because it was him who had hit Jimmy Joe in the head with the rock. But Bobby Leo complained, saying it was too long and that he was only in the first grade so she relented and let him substitute "I Shot An Arrow Into the Air." That night Lonnie and Sam practiced on the poem until they both had it down pretty good. They had Lucy Lemur prompting if they needed help and pretty soon they both got through it without a hitch.

The next day was recital day. Mama decided that the whole school would listen, that it would be good educational experience for everybody. She asked Jimmy Joe, whose lump had turned blue, to go to the front of the room and to explain what the poem was all about.

He stood in front of Mama's desk looking queasy and embarrassed then started talking, his voice shaking. "Well its about this old guy who lived so long everybody else was dead, so that he was the last leaf on the tree." He nodded two or three times and everybody applauded.

Mama was pleased. She told Jimmy Joe to go ahead and recite the poem and he started reciting. He did pretty good, only making two or three bobbles, until he came to the line describing the old guy then he really fucked it up. Instead of saying "He had a melancholy crack in his laugh," Jimmy Joe said, "He had a melancholy laugh in his crack."

Lonnie thought it was the funniest thing he ever heard. Everybody was laughing, particularly Lucy Lemur and even Mama. Jimmy Joe stood there with his face red and his eyes rolling like he was looking for a way out.

"Very good Jimmy Joe, that's nice," Mama finally murmured. "You can sit down." Jimmy Joe moved back to his desk, scuffling his boots along the floor.

Mama looked them over and settled on Lonnie who was still giggling about the "laugh in his crack." He marched to the front of the room, turned and recited the first part of the poem in a steady sing song voice without making any mistakes, but the closer he got to the line the funnier it all got and as hard as he tried he couldn't keep the giggles from breaking through.

When he came to the line, he hesitated, took a deep breath and said "He had a melancholy crack in his lap," then broke into high pitched hysterical laughter.

After awhile he stopped laughing and looked around. Nobody else was laughing! Mama was red faced and Lucy Lemur wouldn't look at him. Even Eula Gay was staring down at her desk. Then everybody was looking at Mama. She went to her desk and got the whipping stick and turned around, her face even redder now and Lonnie knew he was in "deep shit," as Dogey Allen was always saying.

Mama was looking at him, her eyes narrowed down to little slits. "You did that on purpose Lonnie. I know you know that poem so I'm going to give you another one to learn, and you better recite it right."

Lonnie was relieved but he didn't think it was fair. "Which poem?" he muttered.

Mama stopped and thought about it, "Young Lochinvar Came Out of the West."

Lonnie was stunned. "That's a cruddy poem, I already read it, and its a cruddy poem." There was a moment of silence. "And I won't do it," he heard his own voice saying.

"Well you have a choice," Mama was standing over him now. "Either you learn that poem or I'll give you a good whipping, right now." She was glaring down at him, "Which is it?"

There was complete quiet in the room, everybody looking at Lonnie. Finally, his voice trembling, "I'll take the whippin'."

Mama stood there for what seemed like a long time then she said, "Go bend over my desk."

Lonnie got up and shuffled along toward her desk thinking maybe he'd better learn that poem after all. He almost said he would learn it when he heard somebody snicker. Probably that son-of-a-bitch Jimmy Joe. Lonnie was glad he had hit him with that rock. Next time he would use a bigger one. Then he was at the desk. He bent over putting his head and chest on its surface that smelled like linseed oil, the way Old Bartolo's harness smelled.

Mama started whacking him and he thought she'd never stop. Once or twice he almost screamed and probably would have after about the tenth whack if Lucy Lemur hadn't started shouting, "Mama, Mama" over and over.

It finally stopped. He stood up and walked back to his desk, tears streaming down his cheeks and his rear end burning. He couldn't see much of anything, but somebody was touching him and pushing something at him. He looked up and saw Eula Gay holding out a handkerchief. She had that funny little grin on her face with her teeth showing, but she was crying more than he was. He didn't want to take the handkerchief but she just stood there poking it at him. Finally he took it and wiped his eyes.

Mama was sitting at her desk breathing hard, looking defeated and bewildered, staring down at her hands. Lonnie suddenly felt sorry for her. Lucy Lemur was glancing at her with a worried look on her face, and all the other kids were sitting completely quiet, staring at the floor or out the window. Finally Mama gave a little shrug, straightened her shoulders and smiled, a pretty wan smile. Then she reached out and tapped the bell for recess.

That evening Mama was extra nice to Lonnie. She made him pull his pants down so she could put some salve on him. It was as embarrassing as hell, but it made his ass feel better. When she finished she gave him a hug and told him that she loved him. He pulled his pants up, gave her a quick "I love you too Mama" and headed for the door.

Somebody must have told the cowboys in the bunkhouse because they kept looking at him funny and grinning. Dogey Allen asked him if he would like to go for a long ride and Horse let go with his whinny laugh. But Fred Clafin wasn't grinning. He punched Lonnie gently on the shoulder and offered him a chew of Climax chewing tobacco. Lonnie took a bite from Fred's plug and shoved it in his cheek and started sucking on it, every now and then going to the door to take a spit. He felt a lot better now, his ass was still burning but not as much. When the gong sounded for supper, he was laughing and kidding around with Bartolo and Old Walt who were also chewing and spitting. They took turns washing their mouths out at the windmill and joined the rest of them for supper. His ass didn't hurt at all when he sat down on the bench next to Lucy Lemur.

CHAPTER 16

Peppers

Daddy took his place at the head of the table and started eating his steak, looking at each piece carefully to be sure there wasn't any red showing. Everybody began to eat then. It was quite a feast. They had fried potatoes, steak, frijole beans, some lambs-quarter Mama had picked from the garden and some sopapillas that Dulcita had made to go with the green chilies, and lots of boiled cabbage, Lonnie's favorite.

Dulcita brought another platter of sopapillas and more frijole beans. She was Bartolo's niece, maybe twenty years old, really pretty, with black hair and black eyes almost as big as Lucy Lemur's. Her skin was a warm brown and she had the whitest teeth she was always showing when she laughed, which was often. She waited on everybody so Mama could eat without having to jump up and down all the time. Dulcita insisted. Also she wouldn't eat with the rest of them, but later when everybody else had left the table.

Lonnie had another helping of boiled cabbage then something about Old Walt caught his attention. Old Walt was staring out without blinking like he always did, biting into one of Dulcita's fluffy sopapillas, when Lonnie startled him by blurting out, "Hey Walt do you ever have any dreams?"

Old Walt jerked in his chair and gave Lonnie a watery eyed look, "Sure I have dreams, I have dreams all the time, almost every night." He looked around the table, "Just like everybody else."

Lucy Lemur was digging him in the ribs with her elbow but Lonnie was too interested to stop. "I thought maybe you couldn't have dreams cause your eyes are open all the time. Even at night. I thought maybe what you was lookin' at while you're asleep might erase the dreams, or maybe the two would get mixed up together."

"Naw, I just dream dreams." Walt seemed eager to talk about it. "I dream dreams just like other folks, just the same way I did before my eyes got open." He looked around the table as if for approval.

Mama smiled at Walt, "That's nice Walt, that's very nice."

Walt seemed pleased and went back to eating. But now Lonnie was staring at Old Bartolo who was sitting at his accustomed place at the corner of the table, his wrinkled face the color of brown crayolas, his long mustache drooping way down so Lonnie couldn't see his mouth working the frijole beans and jalapeno peppers. Over and over again, some frijoles, a bite of red pepper, and the mysterious munching. Bartolo didn't have many teeth left, maybe three or four. They had simply turned black and dropped out, burnt out like clinkers, Lonnie figured, from all those years of eating hot peppers.

"Hey Bartolo, how can you eat them peppers like that? They're hotter than fire, and you eat them like they was radishes."

Bartolo fixed his bleary brown eyes on Lonnie and smiled until his leather-brown face crinkled. "Aai, Lonnito. When I was a little chico, like you, peppers were hot for me too. *Muy calientes*. But I grow old, *muy viejo*. And the peppers grow cold. Every year, the peppers get colder, every year it takes more peppers to get the job done. *Comprende*?"

To demonstrate his point, he took a fiery red jalapeno pepper from the Mason jar, plopped it under his mustache, and munched away without shedding a tear.

Everyone at the table was watching, even Daddy had stopped eating and was staring in fascination. "That's very nice, Bartolo," Mama murmured.

They all started eating again except for Bartolo who sat looking inward, intent on his own thinking. Finally his glance took in everyone at the table.

"*Gracias, señora*, but it is nothing, *nada*. I grow old, *muy viejo*. The peppers get cold. Everything gets cold when a man gets old. *Un hombre viejo* must eat more and more peppers every year, must work harder and harder, *comprende*, to make life taste good." Lonnie couldn't help it. He took a red jalapeno pepper out of the jar and bit down on it. And then he wished he hadn't. The fire raced through his mouth from his lips to the back of his tongue. He grabbed a glass of water and started drinking, gulp after gulp, stopping for a moment to breathe and then some more water. "My

God," he gasped, "that's just fire." He swallowed some more water and felt the fire go down his throat to become a dull heavy pain inside of him. Finally, when he could quit drinking he looked around the table. "I'm not so sure it's good to be young if everything burns so much and hurts so much. Maybe it's better to be old."

Old Bartolo looked at him with his muddy eyes. "Ah, no Lonnito, young hurt, *mucho dolor*, that's good. Lots of hurt but lots of feel good too. Lots of life! Lots of life! To be young when the peppers are hot. *Muy bueno*." With that he resumed eating, taking another bite of red jalapeno pepper. Everybody else started eating then, except for Lucy Lemur who was staring at Old Bartolo, her huge eyes shining as if lit by an inner light.

CHAPTER 17

Dust

Daddy put his knife and fork on his plate which he always did when he had finished eating and stood up. But this time he didn't leave the table. He stood there clearing his throat and everyone immediately stopped eating and looked at him.

"They'll be comin' in by airplane," he said in a hushed voice.

Lonnie's eyes suddenly bugged out. "Who? Where"" he and Lucy Lemur said in unison.

"The oil men, to look over the land. Tomorrow at four, they'll be comin' in. They'll land in the lower pasture, so you two boys, and Lucy too, be sure all the cattle are out of the way."

He stopped talking and just stood there, then of all things, he did something he seldom did; he smiled. "I'll bet they'll let you look at their airplane, and maybe sit in it." He glanced at Fred Clafin. "When you finish supper let me see you." With that he turned and left the room.

Fred didn't mess around long finishing supper, he never did when Daddy needed to see him. He got up, nodded to Mama and disappeared into the hallway.

"Boy, that's somethin'," Sam shouted. "An airplane landing right out there in the lower pasture."

"Yeah, that's really somethin'," echoed Lonnie. He was so excited he couldn't finish his supper. He sat there gaping, thinking about airplanes. He was always drawing them, Fairchilds, Luscombs, Ryan STs, and his latest accomplishment, a Staggerwing Beech, which was really good, he knew because Lucy Lemur told him so.

Every now and then an airplane would fly over the Cimarron valley. Whenever he heard the sound of one Lonnie would stop in his tracks, his head cocked, listening. Only last week one had come over, flying high sounding like a big mosquito in the far distance when it first appeared just over the Wedding Cake. The dim speck grew larger until he could make out the wings and fuselage, it looked like a Stinson Reliant, cutting across Old Battleship making its high droning sound that became lower and quieter, ebbing away until he lost sight of it.

Fred Clafin came out of the living room just as everybody was getting up from the table. The cowboys with Fred Clafin leading the way went out the door. Lonnie was gazing out the window at the dim light just showing through the half open door of the bunkhouse. He turned to glance at Sam who was still sitting at the table. "You think they'll let us sit in the airplane, maybe even take us for a ride?"

Sam looked offended that his thoughts had been disturbed, a kind of "don't-bother-me" look which really pissed Lonnie off. "How the hell should I know?" Then more gently, "Hey Lonnie, I hope so, wouldn't that be somethin'."

"Yeah, that would be somethin'," Lonnie said again. "Tell Mama I went out to the bunkhouse and, that unless she wants me, I'll sleep in Old Man Dick's bed."

"Jesus, I don't know how you can stand sleeping in that dirty stinkin' bed, it smells like dog piss." Sam grinned at Lonnie. "But I guess that's okay because that's the way you smell all the time!"

"Fuck you," said Lonnie absently, still thinking about the airplane.

Around three o'clock in the afternoon on the Saturday of the coming of the airplane, Lonnie and Sam were out in the lower pasture driving cattle away from a fairly level area where they figured the airplane would land. Lucy Lemur was late, probably helping Dulcita, or maybe messing around with that stuff she kept dabbing on her face and lips, but pretty soon she came galloping toward them with her hair sticking out behind in the wind.

In about thirty minutes they had all the cattle cleared out. The lower pasture was clean of everything except skimpy brown grass, which hid among the prickly pears from the hungry cattle. After the big storm, everything had greened up for awhile but you wouldn't know it now. It hadn't rained for a month and the ground was as baked and dusty as ever.

Lonnie kept stopping Baldy and listening. Once he thought he heard it and then he was sure that he saw it, but it was just one of those little floaters everybody's got in their eyes.

Even as he watched for the airplane, there was a strange changing; the wind which had been blowing from the southwest stopped and it was so still that the grass didn't even rustle. Then the wind sprang up from the north, gentle at first but increasing until there was a strong breeze which had a touch of winter in it.

When Lonnie looked toward Black Mesa he thought something had gone wrong with his eyes. Black Mesa was growing taller! There was no doubt about it, as far as he could see, up and down its entire length Black Mesa was getting taller and bigger!

Lucy Lemur had noticed it and was staring with her eyes even bigger than usual and then Sam joined in the looking. Not only was Black Mesa getting bigger, part of its top seemed to be spilling over like a dark brown liquid, rolling and billowing, filling the canyons, blotting out the caprock. Tongues of darkness tentatively moved ahead of the mass of it, flowing across the plains on the north side of the Cimarron, reaching the Wedding Cake then obscuring it completely.

Sam started shouting, "Jesus Christ! Let's get out of here. Head for the house."

Lonnie let Baldy have his way and he was immediately off at a dead run with Lucy Lemur and Sam close behind, steadily gaining on him until Velvet and then Old Dutch passed him.

Lonnie looked back over his shoulder and the fear came, even worse than when he was alone in the dark of the cave. Black Mesa didn't exist anymore. Nothing could be seen but the dark tide flowing over it, down its sides boiling and rolling across the floor of the valley toward him. Even as he looked some of it reached the Cimarron River, seemed to pause for a moment then rushed forward hiding the cottonwood trees.

Ahead of him Lucy Lemur and Sam had reached the corral. They jumped off their horses and led them into the barn. Fred Clafin was standing by the windmill, a strange mix of emotions on his face. Lonnie brought Baldy to a stop beside the windmill, looking at Fred Clafin in wide eyed terror.

"What is it, Fred, what is it?" he gasped looking at the rolling darkness, feeling the cold of the rising wind.

Fred Clafin started cranking the windmill off, turning the winch that caused the fan to angle inward toward the vanes until the brake came on.

"Well for Christ's sake Lonnie," Fred Clafin managed a big smile. "There's nothing to be worried about, its just dust, you know dirt. You've had dirty hands and a dirty face for most of your life, and it hasn't hurt you. Now get that horse to the barn, and get back to the house before it hits."

Lonnie sat in the saddle without moving, thinking how silly he had been being scared of a little dirt, listening to a funny clicking and buzzing that was coming from the windmill. Suddenly he saw pulses of blue flame arcing across in a number of places, but mostly between the cable winch and the pipe leading down into the well.

Fred Clafin suddenly backed away from it, then turned back to Lonnie. "Goddamn it get that horse to the barn, like I told you. Quit sitting there looking stupid."

Lonnie was hurt and shocked. He didn't say anything, and became frightened again. Fred Clafin had never talked to him like that before. He turned Baldy and gave him a whack with the loose reins. Just before Baldy started moving fast Lonnie looked back at Fred Clafin. He was staring at the blue flames which kept arcing between the cable winch and the pipe, with an odd look of fear on his face. Lonnie knew it then, Fred Clafin was scared, that explained it, otherwise he wouldn't have hollered at him like that.

Sam was waiting for him at the barn door, holding it open, screaming for him to hurry up. Lucy Lemur was screaming at him too, looking pale and big eyed. Lonnie rode inside and unsaddled Baldy and even took time to rub him down a little.

"Come on, you little shit, there's no time for that. It's comin', it's comin'!"

"Let's go now, and stay together," shouted Lucy Lemur above a strange whining sound that seemed to come from the roof of the barn.

Together they ran toward the house where Fred Clafin was holding the door open. They reached it just as billowing dust turned everything to darkness, so dark they couldn't see a thing until Mama lit the Aladdin lamp. Even then there was a smokey haze in the room and it was hard to breathe without gasping.

Fred Clafin got a bunch of towels, dampened them and handed them out. "Tie these around your nose and mouth, it'll make it better."

Lonnie thought it was funnier than hell seeing them looking like that. He wasn't afraid anymore and could breathe okay through his towel. He went over to Dulcita who looked pretty pitiful with nothing but her tear filled eyes showing. She was kneeling by the stove praying in Spanish, crossing herself and counting her beads.

Lonnie patted her shoulder. "It ain't nuthin' but dust Dulcita. It won't hurt you. See I'm not scared." Dulcita got up, gave him a little hug, and started fixing supper.

Mama and Lucy Lemur went from room to room lighting the oil lamps and Fred Clafin started a fire in the main stove in the living room. They needed it. It was so cold in the house Lonnie thought he could see his own breath, but maybe it was just more dust. It was still pitch black outside and the wind made an eerie moaning sound in the eaves of the house, but the stove was putting out plenty of heat. There was still a haze of dust in the room but nobody seemed to mind. Mama started helping Dulcita fix supper and Lonnie, after some prompting from Fred Clafin, played a duet with Lucy Lemur on the piano, "There's an old spinning wheel in the parlor." They had practiced it a lot and it sounded just right for a dark day.

The phone rang their ring and, for a change, Lonnie beat Lucy Lemur to it. It sounded like Daddy, but there was so much popping and cracking on the line he couldn't understand a thing he said, so he had to let Lucy Lemur have it after all. She listened for a long time, shouting "What," "What?" every now and then. Then she called to Fred Clafin and handed him the ear piece. He said "yes" three or four times and hung up the phone.

Lucy Lemur reported, standing straight, looking from face to face like she was giving a recital, "He's worried about the men. He's glad everybody here is okay. He wants us to call him as soon as the men come in. He's glad Fred is here with us. He says nobody should go out tonight, not even to the outhouse." She looked impishly at Fred Clafin. "We'll have to use pots."

CHAPTER 18

Lost

Fred Clafin went to the kitchen and lit a coal oil lantern. He opened the front door, went out for about ten seconds, then came back in shivering and wiping his eyes. He looked at Mama. "It's really cold, and there's so much dust and wind I couldn't see a thing. Emmett's right to be worried about the men. If they didn't make the line cabin . . ." He stopped and shrugged his shoulders.

Nobody said anything for a long time then Mama asked, "Did they take coats with them?"

Fred Clafin shook his head, "I don't know for sure, but I don't think so."

That evening after supper, Lonnie kept staring out the picture window toward Black Mesa thinking about the airplane, wondering if it had gotten lost in the dust storm.

"I guess we'll never see that airplane now," he said aloud.

"Sure we will, maybe not for a few days, but it'll be here, you can bet on it." Fred Clafin looked up from the chess board where Lucy Lemur had just placed him in check. She always beat everybody except Daddy who never lost even though he hardly took the trouble to watch what was going on, and would just sit there with his lips moving thinking about something else.

"Do you think it got lost in the dust storm?" asked Lonnie.

"Not a chance, they'd be way above it, and wouldn't have any trouble getting away from it."

Lonnie felt better. He kept looking out the window thinking it was funny that they couldn't see night coming on because it was already dark.

The next morning it was cold. In just one day it had changed from warm to winter with a cold wind coming in from the north still bringing dust which came in swirls and eddies across the lower pasture. But it wasn't dark anymore. Lonnie could catch glimpses of the bunkhouse as he looked out the kitchen window.

Mama and Dulcita were busy sweeping up the dust and brushing it off everything before starting breakfast. Fred Clafin came in from the bunkhouse looking worried. He had his sheepskin coat on and was wearing an airplane pilot's cap with the flaps snapped together under his chin. His face, where his beard didn't cover it, was red and chapped from the cold.

Mama glanced up from putting wood in the cook stove. "They didn't come in did they?" She was looking worried too, standing there with a stick of wood in her hand.

"No Ma'am, they didn't, and if they don't show up soon, we'll make the general call, and have everybody out looking for them."

Lonnie was still staring out the window looking toward the barn. Vaguely coming out of the dust he saw them, shadow figures, horses and riders becoming clearer as they rode up to the hitching rail.

"They're here," Lonnie shouted. Then he looked again and saw that there were only three of them. They looked real funny, with blankets over their heads and around their shoulders. They tied up their horses and headed for the front door taking their blankets off as they came. Lonnie had the door open and they tramped in, went through the kitchen to the big stove in the living room.

"Where's Walt," Fred Clafin shouted at them. "What's happened to Walt?"

No one said anything for a moment. They all took a wet towel Mama handed each of them and wiped their faces and hands. The towels soon got pretty muddy but they looked a lot better, particularly Bartolo, whose face had turned back to brown leather.

Dogey Allen finally turned to Fred Clafin. "We don't know. We were ridin' the breaks like you told us when we saw the dust storm comin'. We got back to the line cabin just before it hit. We took turns going out the door and firin' our rifles, but he never showed up. This morning we took the blankets from the line cabin and started ridin'." There was a long silence then Dogey added, "We kept lookin' for him on the way in but we didn't see him."

Fred Clafin glanced at Lucy Lemur who was staring at them, her huge eyes misted with tears. "You go ring general, Lucy, tell them Walt's lost and they all better come."

Lucy went to the phone and rang five shorts. Lonnie could almost see them picking up the phones all up and down the valley. Then Lucy started shouting out the news. Shouting was necessary when you called general because every receiver that was taken off the hook weakened the transmission.

Finally, she hung up and came to the table where everybody was setting down for breakfast. They had ham and eggs and biscuits and red hog gravy, which was mostly just grease with some streaks of red running through it, and lots of hot coffee. There wasn't much conversation, everybody eating and thinking about Old Walt out there somewhere in the cold.

"Can I go?" Lonnie was looking at Fred Clafin, "Can I help look? I want to go too; can I help look?"

Fred Clafin glanced at him and then around the table. "Everybody but the ladies of the house," he smiled and bowed a little to Mama. "The rest of you get your heavy coats and caps on, and your mittens, wear chaps if you have them, and long-handled underwear."

"Why can't I ride? I want to ride too," Lucy Lemur was looking intently at Fred Clafin.

"Well, you can't," he said, his voice a little harsh, and then more gently, "Lucy, we need you at the phone, that's important, while your Mama and Dulcita are cooking and we're out there looking."

He smiled at Lucy Lemur who kept staring at him, her face red, breathing hard. She looked like she was about to say something, but she didn't.

Mama, who was just getting up from the table, paused, looked at Lucy Lemur then at Fred Clafin. "Oh! Let her go, Fred, I can take care of the phone, she'll be more help out there riding with you, looking for Walt than she would be here."

Fred Clafin didn't say anything, he nodded his head a couple of times and got up from the table, turned back and said, "Okay, let's move it. Get your winter clothes on and get your horses saddled, Lucy and Lonnie will ride with me. Sam can go with Dogey and Horse. Bartolo, you stay here and cook up a lot of beans and stew for the other riders. A bunch of them should be showing up soon."

They were all saddled up and ready to go when they heard a horse coming in. At first it couldn't be seen in the dust but finally Lonnie could make it out, real dim at first, just a moving shadow which kept getting clearer and clearer the closer it got. When it was just a few yards away, there it was walking towards them, holding its head to the side to keep from stepping on the reins which were dragging on the ground.

"Look at that," shouted Lonnie, "he ain't got no saddle. It's Walt's horse but he ain't got no saddle on. Where's Walt and what happened to the saddle?"

No one said anything, they just kept staring at the horse which had come to a halt by the corral gate, turning its head to look back at them. Fred Clafin shouted at Bartolo who was walking toward the barn to take care of the horse and they started moving out.

Baldy kept trying to turn around and go back to the barn in spite of a lot of whacking. Fred Clafin and Lucy Lemur were becoming vague in the dust mist so he whacked Baldy some more and he finally broke into a trot.

It was easier to see now. When Lonnie looked back the ranch buildings were fairly clear and far ahead he could make out the caprock of the near mesa. Then the sun broke through, not giving much light and no heat, a blood red ball with a lot of fuzz around it.

It seemed to get colder as they rode along. Lonnie was wearing his long-handled underwear, his sheepskin coat and sheepskin hat but he could feel the cold wind hitting his legs and hands even through his chaps and mittens. Lucy Lemur was wearing her white fur hat and her white fur jumper suit. Her skin was touched to a fine blush by the cold and her big eyes were dancing and sparkling under the fur hat. Lonnie couldn't help thinking how pretty she looked and noticed Fred Clafin glancing at her every now and then.

They were moving in a slow trot toward Black Smith Canyon which was now called Bone Canyon because of all the bones left over from the Big Shoot. In the distance Lonnie could see other riders cutting across in front of Old Battleship and still other vague moving shapes coming in around the base of the near mesa.

"Boy, I'll bet Old Walt will sure be surprised when he sees how many people are out lookin' for him."

Lucy Lemur glanced down at Lonnie, her face suddenly convulsed by grief, almost like she was going to cry. "I hope he sees them, he's been out here someplace in this cold, all night long in this cold."

She glanced at Fred Clafin who was slightly ahead of her moving easy in the saddle like he always did, like the saddle and his big black stallion were a part of him.

"Do you think he made it through the night? Do you think he might still be alive?" her voice broke a little, and Lonnie really thought she might start crying.

Fred Clafin slowed his horse until she was beside him. "It's not good Lucy, he didn't have warm clothes and he didn't smoke so he didn't have any matches to light a fire. I don't think he made it. But Old Walt's a pretty tough guy, maybe he made it."

They were in the mouth of Bone Canyon trotting through the bone piles, headed across toward the Zig Zag. As they went up it got a lot clearer and a lot colder even though the sun was bright enough to cause shadows which marched along with them as they rode along. When they reached the flat land on top of the mesa Fred Clafin stopped his horse.

"Let's spread out now, about two hundred yards apart and look down in the breaks. He might be behind a rock or maybe under a tree." Fred Clafin's voice sounded grim, "He might be anywhere. And keep me in sight."

Lonnie was riding between Fred Clafin and Lucy Lemur feeling a funny ache in his feet and higher up above his boot tops it felt like wind was getting in under his Levis. He tried wiggling his toes but it didn't help much. When they rode past the line cabin Fred Clafin shouted Walt's name at the door, then got off his horse to check. He came out shaking his head, got back on his horse, and they rode on, looking down into the breaks shouting Walt's name, their voices echoing back again and again.

Lonnie was looking down into one of the breaks, thinking about his cold feet and legs when he heard the shots. Dull muffled reports coming from somewhere to the north, one about every ten seconds echoed and reverberated from the walls of the breaks and the canyons. Then he heard Fred Clafin shouting at him. He kicked Baldy into a trot toward the beginning of another break where Fred and Lucy Lemur were waiting, their horses steaming in the cold air.

"They've found him," Fred Clafin's voice was ragged with the cold and dust and maybe something else. "Let's get going, you follow me."

They kept listening to the reports coming in, getting louder as they moved back toward the Zig Zag. Then far below they saw a cluster of horses and riders right next to Old Battleship.

On the way down the Zig Zag they saw other riders spiraling in, maybe twenty or thirty, moving through the haze of dust. When Fred Clafin, with Lucy Lemur and Lonnie trailing behind him, finally got there, a large circle of riders was staring down at something.

The circle opened up and let them through. Just as the sun broke through the dust swirls, bright and almost warm, they were looking down at Old Walt, laying behind his upended saddle with his saddle blanket blown down around his legs. Lonnie didn't want to look at him but he did. Old Walt was lying there not moving, all scrunched up, his arms around his legs. He actually didn't look much like Old Walt. His hat had come off and was stuck in a nearby cactus. His hair was nearly white with dust and so were his face and hands. His eyes were little blobs of mud. It was so crazy it was almost funny.

Lonnie started to say something when he glanced at Lucy Lemur. She was staring down at Old Walt, her eyes wide and dark and liquid like she had big black watery holes in her head beneath the whiteness of her fur hat. She kept staring with big tears running down her cheeks dropping off her chin and disappearing into the white fur of her jumper suit. Lonnie suddenly felt his eyes stinging and a big lump in his throat and was afraid he would start crying like some little sniveling kid.

But suddenly he didn't feel bad about it. Damned if Jake Veeder wasn't crying. He sat on Macon without moving, the tears running down his cheeks. Lonnie let out a couple of sobs and felt better.

Fred Clafin said something to Dogey Allen and Horse and they all got off their horses. Working together they rolled Old Walt into a tarpaulin and lifted him onto Dogey's horse. They had a tough time doing it. Old Walt was as stiff as a board and coiled up like a pretzel, but with a lot of pulling and prying they finally got him uncoiled enough to drape him over and to tie the tarpaulin down at each end under the belly of the horse.

They started for home with Fred Clafin leading Dogey's horse and the rest of them, about thirty riders, strung out behind. Dogey was riding double with Horse and both of them kept sneaking side glances at Lucy Lemur who wasn't crying anymore. She was riding beside Old Walt staring straight ahead, her face pale and drawn in spite of the blush of the cold. Jake Veeder was nowhere to be seen, but Lonnie knew he was somewhere close by, probably still crying.

When they rode down the slope, toward the ranch buildings, Daddy was waiting by the windmill looking down at the ground. He didn't move as they came to a halt in front of him but just kept standing there. Finally he walked over to Dogey's horse, untied the rope and lifted Old Walt off. Fred Clafin opened the door of Daddy's car and Daddy put Old Walt carefully inside, rearranging the tarpaulin. But even as they all watched, Old Walt slumped over in the seat and coiled back into the same kind of knot he had been in when they found him. Then Daddy got in the driver's seat and with Fred Clafin beside him drove down the road through the lower pasture, creating a plume of dust in the cold air.

Everybody started talking then, talking about Old Walt and the life he had led. Laughing about the time Old Walt had been the watchman at the county jail, how embarrassed the sheriff had been when Tom Eddleman, the county's resident drunk, had walked out right past Old Walt who was staring right at him.

The Sheriff, Lonnie's Uncle Doc, came driving up just then and joined in the laughter even though he was the butt of the joke. He even stated that, everything considered, Old Walt was the best watchman the jail ever had. And everybody laughed again.

The gong sounded for lunch. Bartolo had set the table up again with the boards on the saw horses. Mama and Dulcita, with Lucy Lemur helping, brought out fried potatoes and biscuits and Bartolo served beans and stew from the large black pots.

The wind had stopped blowing and the sun was shining, not as bright as it should be because of the lingering dust, but still warm. Lonnie thought it was a good day after all as they stood around telling stories about Old Walt, eating beans and stew and drinking coffee from tin cups which Lucy Lemur kept filled from a big black coffee pot she was carrying around.

Lonnie thought she looked even prettier now. The drawn, sad look had left her face and she seemed to enjoy her job as coffee pourer. She had changed from her jumper suit to a small coat with a white fur collar that matched her white fur cap. All of which accentuated her huge black eyes, black hair and pink lips which seemed a lot fuller and a lot pinker every time Lonnie saw them.

He was sure she had put on some lipstick. He had seen her sneaking around with it, even though Mama kept screaming at her about it. She had her fingernails painted a fine pink, the same color Lonnie had used on his piece of petrified wood. When Lucy Lemur approached Dogey and Horse she paused, not looking directly at them, a little crooked smile playing on her lips. They stood there staring at her with dumb looks on their faces, still holding their cups out toward her, even after she had filled them. But of all things when Jake Veeder held his cup towards her, she filled it and then smiled at him, as if they shared something, possibly tears.

CHAPTER 19

Rising

The next day, school was cancelled for the funeral. To get ready, everybody took baths. Bartolo heated up a bunch of water in his two big pots and the cowboys stripped down and lathered up with lots of lava soap with Bartolo rinsing them off with warm water he kept pouring on them from a gallon bucket. They were out of sight behind the bunkhouse but Lonnie noticed Lucy Lemur glancing out that way through the kitchen window. Lonnie went out and took a look. They sure looked funny standing there naked and shivering with the soap lather all over them. When Bartolo rinsed them off they would rub themselves all over making satisfied sounds, "haaaaaaaa," "haaaaaa" as he warmed them up with the steaming water. Horse looked kind of crazy with the red of his face and the red of his neck coming down to a point in the middle of his white chest, about half way down to where brown curly hair clustered around his prick. His prick was all shriveled up and pulled way in like it was trying to hide in the hair.

But Fred Clafin didn't look funny. He stood there with his arms crossed staring across the valley. The most amazing thing about him was the way his flat belly sloped up to his massive chest and shoulders where muscles rippled and swelled when he moved. He didn't seem cold at all and his prick angled out from the curly bronze of his lower hair like it was proud to be there.

Dogey Allen looked the funniest, like a miserable skinny plucked chicken standing all hunched over holding his arms around his chest, turning blue from the cold. When Bartolo rinsed him off with a bucket of water, he stood there steaming and gasping with relief. "Hey, that's really great Bartolo, gimme some more." And Bartolo obliged with another steaming bucket. Dogey's prick was amazing. The end of it bulbed out like a mushroom and was as blue as a concord grape.

Even Daddy took a bath in a wash tub next to the stove in the kitchen. Lonnie wandered in and got a look at him standing there with his huge gut hanging down, holding his hand over his private parts, as Lucy Lemur called them, while Mama scrubbed him down with life-boy soap and a rough looking rag. Lonnie was next in the tub. He hated washing in water somebody else had already washed in but it was hot and he felt a lot cleaner when Mama, after scrubbing him all over, finally let him out.

After the baths everybody dressed up, the cowboys put on their Sunday boots and clean Levis and shirts. Mama put on her new black dress that she had worn only three or four times to church and Daddy put on his grey suit which he had had for years but which still looked good because he didn't wear it much. Lonnie put on his new boots with three rows of stitching that Tony Spenelli had made just for him and new levis and a new blue shirt. He caught a glimpse of himself in the dresser mirror as he walked past and had to admit that he looked pretty snazzy, with his freckled face washed shiny and his red hair brushed back in a pompadour, gleaming coppery from the Vaseline hair tonic he had put on it.

As a matter of fact, everybody looked snazzy, particularly Lucy Lemur who was wearing a new corduroy pant suit with black stitching along the pockets and swirls of silver embroidery on the shoulders and running up and down the back. She passed Lonnie in the hallway and he got a sudden whiff of her, some kind of perfume that smelled like a mixture of polecat and roses. Her black hair was brushed back and held by a red ribbon with a big bow on the top of her head, which exposed her white neck, and little gold earrings with big rhinestones which sparkled as she moved.

"I'm gonna tell Mama you got perfume on," Lonnie whispered as he passed her.

She stopped short and grabbed him before he could dodge down the hallway. She was really fast when she was mad, and she was mad. "You do and I'll kill you, you little creep, I'll kill you deader than a chicken with its neck wrung, and that's the way I'll kill you, by ringing your scrawny little neck."

"Fuck you," whispered Lonnie, his voice shaking a little. He figured she wouldn't do it, but you couldn't tell what Lucy Lemur would do when she was mad.

She let him go and gave him a big smack on the head which made his ears ring. "If you tell on me, I'll tell her about your dirty books."

After a cold, miserable trip all covered with blankets in the back of Mr. Rutledge's truck, they got to Kenton and the little white-stone Methodist church which stood directly across the street from the little brown-stone Baptist church where most of the sheep herder and cowboy families went to listen to preachers preach about salvation and heaven and sin and burning. Lonnie had been there once and he didn't like it. It scared the hell out of him to think about sin and it scared him even more to think about burning.

People came from miles around for the funeral, in buggies, in Ford and Chevy pickups and a few in new cars, big Buicks and Packards. George Morgan, his wife and kids came in a new Ford Model B with a rumble seat where Bobby Leo, Jimmy Joe and Eula Gay were all covered with blankets.

Finally, the church was full with some people standing in the back and another bunch waiting outside in the cold. Lucy Lemur observed that it was quite a turnout, especially for an old guy who had to turn the thirty dollars he earned every month over to Fred Clafin and was so poor he didn't own anything, not even his horse.

Lonnie was sitting by Lucy Lemur smelling her polecat and roses perfume, thinking that it actually smelled pretty good once he got used to it, listening to the preacher droning on and on about how good Old Walt had been and that everybody should be happy for him now that he was up in heaven. When the preacher finished, he said a long prayer with everybody standing up with their heads bowed.

Lonnie thought it would never stop, but it finally did. It was getting hotter than hell in there with all those people, and the hard seat made his ass hurt. Then the preacher asked if anybody would like to say something. Some people got up and said a few words about what a fine man Old Walt had been. Daddy stood up look-ing real embarrassed but managed to say that Old Walt had been a fine cowboy. Even Lonnie's Uncle Doc, the sheriff, with a lot of subdued snickers coming from everywhere, pointed out what a fine watchman Old Walt had been at the county jail.

Then they all sang songs, "When the roll is called up yonder," "When the saints go marching in," and "Bringing in the sheaves,"

which Lonnie thought was funnier than hell, because Lucy Lemur, with her piercing contralto, sang it as "Bringing in the sheep."

Then Mrs. Eddie started playing "Nearer my God to thee," over
and over on the organ and they all walked up in single file to get a
last look at Old Walt. Lonnie was just ahead of Lucy Lemur inching along in the line thinking a lot of people must have a lot to tell
Old Walt the line was moving so slow, but finally he could look
over the edge of the big wood box.

Lonnie was astonished. Old Walt looked great! He was wearing
a new brown suit and a new white shirt topped off by a red and
blue striped tie with a big neat knot snubbing it up to his neck.
But the most amazing thing of all was the way his face looked,
tanned and healthy, wearing a smile. His eyes were amazing too,
wilted a little but bright and shiny with bits of reflected color from
the stained glass windows.

Lonnie kept looking at Old Walt's eyes and before he could
catch himself burst out, "I'll bet he's dreamin' right now, I'll bet
he's havin' a dream."

"Shut up and move on you little creep," it was Lucy Lemur's
voice grating in his ear.

Other people heard what Lonnie said, some were grinning and
all were looking at Old Walt with a new curiosity. Mrs. Morgan, the
roly poly dumpling wife of George Morgan who was just ahead of
Lonnie, stopped and looked back at Old Walt. Eula Gay on the
other side of Mrs. Morgan was looking back too but not at Old
Walt. She had that crazy wide mouth grin on her face with her teeth
showing as her eyes almost seemed to squeeze Lonnie. Jesus Christ!

"Why Lonnie I think you're right," whispered Mrs. Morgan.
"He could be dreaming."

She smiled at Lonnie who was embarrassed by the whole situation, but couldn't help whispering back. "Well one things for sure,
he sure looks good."

"Yes," replied Mrs. Morgan. "I've never seen him look better."
She gave Lonnie another warm smile and moved on down the line,
herding Eula Gay ahead of her.

Lonnie thought the service would be over as soon as everybody
got a last look at Old Walt, but it wasn't. They all had to go back to
their seats and listen to another long prayer which went on and on
with the preacher saying, in a number of different ways, that they

shouldn't be sad for Old Walt and that even though he was going to be buried it really wasn't goodbye since they would all soon greet Old Walt in heaven where he was sitting at the right hand of God.

Lonnie didn't like to think about dying and all that stuff even if he did go to heaven where he could see Old Walt again. It was getting so hot in the church that it was making him dizzy. He was thinking about maybe slipping outside where it was cold and where he could breathe when Mrs. Eddy began playing the organ again and the preacher raised his hand over the congregation and started saying the goodbye prayer.

All of a sudden a bunch of women began screaming, and the men started making all kinds of crazy sounds, low shudders, startled grunts, nervous laughter. The preacher stopped saying his goodbye prayer and looked at Old Walt's coffin. The preacher's eyes got real big, staring sideways with the whites showing, and he just stood there without saying anything with his mouth halfway open and his hand still sticking out.

Lonnie glanced at the preacher then at Old Walt's coffin and couldn't believe it. Old Walt was sitting up! Slowly at first and then faster and faster until he was in a full sitting position with his eyes staring out over the congregation and that little smile on his face.

After awhile the women stopped screaming and the men stopped making their funny sounds and there was complete silence, everybody returning Old Walt's stare. Then the preacher started talking again saying that Old Walt's rising was a true sign from God that some time before the millennium all of those people who had been washed in the blood of the Lamb would rise from the grave and find eternal life.

A lot of people started praying and even Lonnie felt that God was sending a message then figured maybe, as Fred Clafin said later, that because of the heat in the church Old Walt was just curling back into the same knot he had been in when they found him out there in the cold by Old Battleship. And that he had sat up because the lower part of him was held down by the bottom half of the coffin which had already been nailed shut.

But Lonnie wasn't sure. Later he asked Lucy Lemur if she thought God was sending a message with Old Walt's rising. She gave him one of her knowing looks. "Well, God was either sending a message or Old Walt just liked being in a knot."

Lonnie was even more puzzled. "Well which was it?"

She smiled her crooked little smile. "Maybe it was both."

Lonnie thought maybe she was kidding him. "Do you think God went to all the trouble to send a message by havin' Old Walt tie himself into a knot?"

Lucy Lemur laughed. Her voice took on a sing song cadence. "Anything can happen in the great big plan, God's ways are inscrutable to man."

Jesus Christ! Lonnie knew he would never be able to figure out God. Or Lucy Lemur!

After "The Rising" as it became known up and down the Cimarron Valley, they all went to the graveyard where the women clustered in small groups chatting and the men walked back and forth stomping their boots in the cold, waiting for Old Walt to be put in a big hole somebody had dug. They didn't have to wait long. Pretty soon a brand new Model B Ford pickup truck came through the gate and Lonnie could see Old Walt's shiny brown coffin, with two men riding on its top, gleaming in the afternoon sun.

They let Old Walt down into the hole with three sets of ropes and everybody walked past and threw in some dirt. Lonnie got to throw four handfuls before Lucy Lemur prodded him along. As he threw down each handful and saw it splatter on Old Walt's coffin he half expected Old Walt to break out and rise again, but he didn't.

And that was it except for the long, cold ride home in the back of Mr. Rutledge's truck. It was more crowded because the Morgan children were with them, George Morgan and his fat wife with the nice smile having taken off for Clayton right after everybody got to throw in their handful of dirt.

All the kids in the back of the bus were hunkered down under blankets with nothing but their heads sticking out. Eula Gay had pushed in beside Lonnie and kept rubbing up against him and once tried to take his hand. Jesus Christ! It ruined the entire day having to put up with her. He sure hoped nobody noticed what she was doing but he could tell by the shitty look on Sam's face that he knew what was going on. As the trip dragged on Lonnie got tired of pulling away and let himself relax over against her. He was getting a little sleepy and it wasn't so bad. She did smell good and she was real warm.

Chapter 20

Mama

The next day Mama was sick. Lucy Lemur made the general call and told everybody that Mama was having problems and wouldn't be able to make it to school.

It scared Lonnie. Mama almost never got sick, and here she was still laying in bed at seven o'clock in the morning! He went to the door of her bedroom and peeked in, and then he really got scared. She was just lying there, looking pale and shaky holding a hot water bottle to her stomach.

He was suddenly stung with the thought that Mama might wind up in a hole in the ground like Old Walt and that he would never see her again. He ran out of the house, up to the quarry ridge and took out his treasure box. He didn't trouble about the other things but took out his piece of petrified wood, breathed on it and polished it with his shirt tail. He put the box back in its place and went down toward the house hoping Mama would like the piece of petrified wood, thinking maybe it might make her feel better just to look at it.

When he knocked on the half open door she looked up, hurriedly put the hot-water bottle aside and smiled at him. "Why Lonnie, I was hoping you might come by to see me." She glanced down at the petrified wood which he was holding out toward her. "Why, that's really nice Lonnie, that's just beautiful."

He heard his own voice, as from far away. "It's for you Mama, I painted it for you."

"Well it's just beautiful, and I hope you'll let me keep it for a few days so I can look at it. Put it up there on the dresser by the clock so I can see it good." Mama had a bright perky smile on her face. "But first let me feel it, it looks so smooth and bright."

Lonnie felt a lot better. He handed Mama the piece of petrified wood, and watched as she ran her fingers over it.

Just then Lucy Lemur came in carrying a breakfast tray which Dulcita had fixed up. It had a purple and red hollyhock in a glass of water beside the plate. Lucy Lemur was wearing a cheery smile, her eyes bright with reassurance, but fear lurked at their edges.

Lonnie took the piece of petrified wood from Mama and placed it on the dresser, listening to the solid clunk it made as he put it down. Then he gave Mama a last quick look and headed out the door.

But things didn't seem so bad. By afternoon Mama was up and around helping Dulcita in the kitchen getting things ready for supper, and when supper time came she was at her place at the table nodding and smiling at everybody as if nothing was wrong. But they all knew she wasn't feeling right, Bartolo kept glancing at her and Fred Clafin tried to say something funny so she would laugh. Even Daddy was concerned and got up from the table to pour his own coffee, even though Dulcita tried to beat him to it.

Finally, Mama looked around the table and said, "All of you quit trying to baby me. I've just got a little pain in the stomach, and I can hardly feel it now." She smiled to let everyone know she was okay but Lonnie wasn't sure.

The next morning Mama didn't get out of bed at all and she didn't eat anything but kept lying there holding the hot water bottle. Lonnie was glad there wasn't any school again but really got scared when Daddy put Mama in the car and took her to Clayton. That evening just after dark the phone rang their ring. It was Daddy. Lucy Lemur who did the talking said that Mama was in the hospital and that she was going to have an operation. That they were going to take her to Amarillo to the big hospital there, and that she was going to have her womb removed.

They all waited for more news, but the phone didn't ring their ring anymore and Daddy didn't come home. There was no school for the whole week. Then Mr. Rutledge called and said they had found a substitute teacher and that there would be school the next day. Daddy also called from Amarillo and told them that Mama was fine, but that she would have to stay in the hospital for two weeks. Lonnie was so relieved, he was suddenly almost happy. He climbed up the ladder in the hay barn and crawled back into his hay house. He did his flash book showing Little Orphan Annie getting humped by her dog Sandy three or four times and felt like everything was almost back to normal.

They had a good supper that night. Bartolo cooked up some of his special stew, Lucy Lemur boiled some cabbage and Dulcita made biscuits to go with their beans and fried potatoes. Daddy got home just before supper and told them that Mama had come through the operation just fine and that she was making real good progress. That seemed to make everybody happy, and Lonnie was happy watching them eating and talking and laughing a lot.

CHAPTER **21**

Bus Ride

Monday morning the weather turned warm. The sun coming up over the near mesa to the right of the Spire was bright and free of haze. Lonnie climbed into the truck, already half filled with children and tried to find a place where Eula Gay wouldn't bother him. He sat down between Bobby Leo and a new kid named Carl Wamble whose folks were trying to make a living off forty acres, planting broom corn and maize, irrigating with two windmills that ran night and day. But it didn't do any good. Eula Gay made Bobby Leo change seats with her and there she was again a pain in the ass right at his elbow.

She kept looking at him and finally said in a small smothered voice. "Why don't you like me Lonnie, I really like you and you treat me like you hate me."

Lonnie couldn't look at her, he just kept staring ahead while Sam and Jimmy Joe who were sitting together on the other side of the truck grinned at each other while they cast shitty glances at Lonnie and Eula Gay.

Jimmy Joe commented, "It seems to me that somebody who could go to the back of that cave in the dark wouldn't be scared of a little ol' girl."

"Yeah," observed Sam, "Golden Bats ain't supposed to be cowards."

Lonnie just sat there with his face red but Eula Gay started screaming, "You're the ones whose cowards, both of you, just creepy cowards."

Lonnie hunched down, his face getting redder and redder. Jesus Christ! It was getting worse than ever, a lot worse. He must be a coward or he wouldn't need a little ol' girl to protect him.

Jimmy Joe was laughing his crazy laugh, crowing like a chicken and flapping his arms.

That did it! Lonnie threw himself across the truck, and to his own shock and everybody else's, hit Jimmy Joe in the nose. Jimmy Joe yelped and grabbed his nose while kicking out at Lonnie. By this time the truck had stopped and Lucy Lemur with Mr. Rutledge following close behind came running around to the back. Sam and Carl Womble were holding Lonnie while Jimmy Joe dabbed at his bleeding nose with his handkerchief. Lonnie figured he was really going to get it, that maybe he would have to memorize a whole bunch of poems and probably get whipped with the whipping stick.

Lucy Lemur was mad. She was standing there looking mean with her head hunched down, her big eyes crinkled down to fine slits. She started screaming. "Okay Sam and Jimmy Joe, I know you been picking on Lonnie and Eula Gay, I've been listening to you. You just quit it! You just quit it!" She stopped to catch her breath while Mr. Rutledge stood behind her in bemused silence.

"He hit me in the nose," Jimmy Joe sniffled. "An' I'm bleedin'."

"Well you deserved it." Lucy Lemur gave him a scathing look. "We're going on to school, and there better not be any more trouble back here, or I'll tell the new teacher, and Mr. Rutledge will take care of you."

With that she turned and climbed back into the front of the truck. Mr. Rutledge gave them all a big smile, went around and climbed in on his side, and away they went.

Lonnie couldn't believe he got off so easy. Jimmy Joe kept glaring at him, dabbing at his nose but he didn't say anything. Lonnie glanced at Eula Gay. He didn't hate her, he knew that. And she was pretty, real pretty with her wide mouth and snub nose and blue eyes. She felt him looking at her and squeezed over against him a little.

"I don't hate you," he whispered. "I'm just too young to like girls. Maybe someday when I'm older I'll like you."

Eula Gay seemed pleased. "Well I like you a lot Lonnie, and I'll wait for you even if it takes a long time."

Chapter 22

Vulcanizing

Later, sitting at his desk, Lonnie knew Eula Gay was watching him but he couldn't take his eyes off the new teacher. She didn't look much older than Lucy Lemur but she was taller and heavier. She looked a little bit like Eula Gay except she was grown up. She had a real tiny waist which flared up to large boobs that made warm swells under her blue dress and down to the nicest hips he'd ever seen. She had white skin with just a few freckles here and there and the bluest eyes and hair so blond it was nearly white, except for touches of copper, almost the same color as his own hair. But the thing that was most beautiful about her were her legs, round and firm going down to calves that were kind of fat, going on down to feet which were stuck in beautiful low heeled blue suede shoes. She had a cheery voice and smiled a lot as she asked each of them to stand up and tell something about themselves.

Lonnie's time came and it was embarrassing as hell. "I'm Lonnie Wilson, and I'm going to fly airplanes someday," was all he could manage.

Miss Pringle, that was her name, smiled at him the sweetest smile he ever saw, so sweet he forgot to sit down and just stood there staring at her until some of the other kids started to snicker and Eula Gay began to make small whimpering sounds.

He finally sat down but couldn't think about anything except how beautiful Miss Pringle was, and what a nice smile she had. Later in the day when he stumbled over a word while reading a passage from *Huckleberry Finn*, she came and stood over him and he could smell her. My God, it was his most favorite smell in the world!

He had first smelled it when he was watching Hoyt Eddleman fix a flat tire at the Eddleman garage in Kenton. Hoyt had taken out the inner-tube, pumped it up and found a hole by pushing it under water and watching the bubbles come pouring out like little

130

rapid pellets. Hoyt had scraped the rubber around the hole with the top of the patch can until it was real rough, then he took a funny looking patch and peeled the top off leaving one side black and shiny. After spreading some stuff around the hole in the inner-tube he put the patch on and lit a match to the edge of it. It began to sizzle and smoke and to put out the smell Lonnie liked so much. The smell of vulcanizing! He not only liked the smell, he liked the word so much he said it over and over, and sometimes he even smelled it and saw it sizzling in his dreams. And that's the way Miss Pringle smelled, wonderful, like vulcanizing with a hint of Lysol mixed in with it.

The smell of it, with her hovering over him, mixed him up so much that he couldn't read a word and just sat there hunched over thinking maybe he was going to faint. He leaned toward her and felt his shoulder touch her hip. She changed positions and released more of the vulcanizing and Lysol smell. Jesus Christ!

He steadied himself and tried to read. It was that part in *Huckleberry Finn* where Huck and Jim are watching the bank of the river become dimmer and dimmer as night came on until it became "indistinct," that was the word he was having trouble with. Miss Pringle pronounced it for him and went on down the line letting other kids read, but Lonnie wasn't listening. He kept smelling her lingering presence and watching the swell of her breasts as she paused over each kid.

The worst of it was that his cock was so hard that he couldn't stand up when recess came. He sat there helpless and embarrassed looking blindly down at *Huck Finn* trying not to think about vulcanizing or the way Miss Pringle looked when she bent over. Eula Gay didn't go outside either, but sat at her desk glaring at him. He glanced at her and immediately his cock got soft so he could get up and dash out the door into the school yard where the other kids were running back and forth like crazy, playing prison base.

On the school bus, Eula Gay wouldn't even look at him. She sat on the other side staring out the back of the bus, her face drawn and pale. When the bus stopped at the Morgan house, she started to follow Bobby Leo and Jimmy Joe, hesitated then turned back and let Lonnie have it.

In between sobs she screamed. "I hate you, you dirty little bastard, you little moon eyed bastard, dirty son-of-a-bitch. I'll never speak to you again." With that, still sobbing, she climbed down out of the bus and disappeared.

When the bus started up everybody was looking at Lonnie. Sam was curious. "Boy, you must have done something to old Eula Gay." He started snickering. "What in the hell did you do?"

Lonnie was sniffling a little, "I didn't do nuthin', she's crazy that's all, I didn't do a thing to her."

"Well one things for sure," Sam was grinning now with that smirky look on his face. "She don't like you much, and will probably leave you alone."

Lonnie suddenly felt better, "Jesus, I hope so."

CHAPTER 23

Red Gloves

After they got home, Lonnie went to his secret place in the hay barn and started looking at his dirty books. It was funny, every picture had somehow changed. As he was looking at Harold Teen giving it to Tillie the Toiler his prick got as hard as a rock and he could smell vulcanizing. He thought about Miss Pringle and could actually see her as well as smell her, the mixture of vulcanizing and Lysol, the way her tits thrust against her dress as she bent over, the way her hips and bottom moved when she walked.

Then he heard somebody talking down below in one of the horse stalls. It sounded like Lucy Lemur doing all the talking but somebody else was down there too making grunty throaty sounds. Lonnie looked down through a crack and sure enough it was Lucy Lemur. Her voice sounded weird, husky and so soft Lonnie could barely hear her say, "Now you touch me here and I'll touch you there."

Lonnie saw a hand reach out and start rubbing Lucy Lemur's tits and saw her reaching out doing something that Lonnie couldn't see because the crack wasn't wide enough. Lucy Lemur's voice, even huskier now. "My, you've got a big one, and it feels real good, I'll just rub it a little bit. And you rub me."

Lonnie could see her arm moving back and forth and could see the hand move from Lucy Lemur's breast down to her crotch. There wasn't a sound for a minute or two, then there was a guttural murmuring and Lucy Lemur started making little delighted yelps. There was silence again and Lonnie couldn't see anything. He crawled out of his secret place and eased over to the window of the barn. Lucy Lemur was walking toward the house. She stopped at the wash basin by the windmill and washed her hands two or three times, working up a fine lather, using lots of lava soap.

Lonnie waited a long time, staring out the barn window, waiting for somebody else to come out of the barn but nothing happened. Finally, Sam opened the door of the house and started shouting for him to come in for supper. He crawled down the ladder and looked around carefully. Nobody was in the horse stalls or in the tack room but just as he went out the front door of the barn he saw somebody disappear around the corner of the bunkhouse.

They were all seated around the table when Daddy came up the road raising a billowing plume of dust. He washed up at the basin by the windmill, then took his place at the head of the table. He sat there for a moment with everybody looking at him. At last he smiled, "Mama's going to be okay She's getting over her operation just fine. She'll be home in a couple of weeks."

Lonnie was so relieved he almost cried and didn't notice anything unusual at the table until he looked around and saw all the room they had. He missed Mama a lot and Old Walt and then he saw that Horse wasn't at his usual place beside Dogey Allen. "Where's Horse?" he wanted to know.

Lonnie glanced at Fred Clafin who was sitting there without eating, looking at Lucy Lemur. Lonnie glanced at her. She was picking at her fried potatoes, taking a bite every now and then from a biscuit, her eyes were deeper and darker than they had ever been and her face seemed lit with some kind of inner glow. Lonnie thought she had never looked more beautiful. She sat there staring down at her plate, then suddenly she looked directly at Fred Clafin, a funny little smile on her face that was down-right eerie.

"I better go find him," Fred Clafin's voice was low, almost a whisper.

He got up from the table and went out the front door. After about thirty minutes, when all the rest of them were finishing up supper, he came back in by himself. He didn't say anything for a minute then looked at Dulcita who was waiting by the stove, "Could you fix him a plate, he doesn't feel very well, but I think he can eat something."

When Fred Clafin took the plate from Dulcita, Lonnie noticed something that was real strange. Fred Clafin was wearing gloves which were damp and a little bit red in some places. Everybody was looking at Fred Clafin's hands. Even Daddy glanced up from cleaning up the last of his gravy with a biscuit, nodded briefly to

Fred Clafin, glanced at Lucy Lemur, got up and left the table.

Lucy Lemur stared at her plate looking frightened and guilty. Fred Clafin didn't say anything more, he took the plate from Dulcita, poured some coffee from the big pot on the kitchen stove into a tin cup and headed for the door. Sam jumped up and let him out.

The next day, Horse didn't show up at all. Lonnie helped Fred Clafin carry his meals to him and when Horse sat up in bed to eat Lonnie could see that he had been beaten up pretty good. Both of his eyes were black, he had a couple of teeth missing and dark purple bruises on his cheek and chin. Fred Clafin kept wearing gloves but Lonnie saw that his hands were all covered with bandages when he took his gloves off just before he went to bed.

Not much happened the next couple of days. Lonnie did his best to keep things under control at school. He tried not to look at Miss Pringle or to smell her, and he tried to avoid the evil eyed looks Eula Gay kept darting his way.

One evening, right after they got home on the bus when Lonnie was on his way out to the barn to check up on Baldy, he heard somebody talking in the tack room. It was Fred Clafin's voice.

"I told you to keep away from the hired men," his voice was low, but there was no doubt about it, he was as mad as hell. "And now goddamn it you have messed everything up. What chance do you think a poor stupid slob like Horse, or Dogey for that matter, has with you coming at them. They haven't got a chance! I ought to take these bridle reins and whip the hell out of you like I had to beat the hell out of that dumb Horse."

"Who in the hell do you think you are," Lucy Lemur's voice was loud and shrill. "You're not my Daddy! You're just a hired man yourself. What business do you have telling me what to do? You're not my Daddy! And if you think Horse is so helpless, why did you hurt him? You must be real mean to hurt him like that, since he's so helpless."

There was a long silence then she started again. "I don't like your threatening me, I think you're a goddamn coward, threatening to whip me. I don't think you've got the guts. Here I'll give you a reason." There was a sharp popping sound and Lonnie ducked his head. Jesus Christ! This was all getting pretty crazy.

There was another silence, an even longer one this time. Finally Fred Clafin's voice came through, harsh and ragged. "I guess I deserved that, and you're right I am just a hired man, but your daddy trusts me to look after the cowboys, and to look after you and the other children."

He paused and Lonnie could hear Lucy Lemur sniffling now, "Well you're not my daddy," she said through her sobs, "and you can't order me around. You don't even see that I'm growing up, that I'm not a little bitty helpless girl."

"I know you're not a helpless little girl," Fred Clafin's voice seemed calm now, controlled. "That's just the point, you are a young woman who is deadly attractive, who should know better than going around taking advantage of dumb slobs. It's not fair Lucy," and then with a note of pleading in his voice, "It's not fair to any of us."

Lucy Lemur let out a couple of sobs and Lonnie heard her coming toward the door. He got around the corner of the barn just in time, but he peeked around to see her walking toward the house, her head high, her hips moving rhythmically. She stopped at the wash basin by the windmill and washed her face, then disappeared into the house. Lonnie went into one of the horse stalls and was checking on Baldy when Fred Clafin left the tack room.

CHAPTER 24

Desk

The next morning, Horse showed up for breakfast. He still looked really lousy with all his bruises and black eyes. He must have felt pretty bad too because he didn't look up at all, but just kept staring at his plate as he shoveled his food down. Lonnie sneaked a couple of looks at Lucy Lemur. She was sitting there like she didn't have a care in the world, wearing a red ribbon in her black hair and a new white lacy blouse that showed that her breasts were getting bigger. She glanced at Horse a time or two and Lonnie thought he noticed a little sign of strain or sorrow in her eyes. She didn't look at Fred Clafin at all. Her eyes kind of veered around him as if he had become nothing but a hole in the world.

Daddy finished up his eggs, cooked by Dulcita as hard as rocks just the way he liked them, stood up and cleared his throat a couple of times. There was a sudden silence with all eyes on him. Even Horse, looking like a beat up coon with his black eyes, glanced up from his plate.

Daddy looked around the table. "The airplane is comin' in to-day. It'll probably be here before the school bus gets here so you and your men," he glanced at Fred Clafin, "clear the cattle out of the lower pasture. And they'll need horses. Have three ready. Have 'em out there." Then he glanced at Lonnie who was sitting there pop eyed. "Yes I know Lonnie, you won't be able to see it land but it'll be here three days." He glanced at Fred Clafin. "Two of them will sleep in the bunkhouse, the pilot will sleep in here." With that Daddy left the table and went into the living room.

Lonnie sat there stunned, thinking about the airplane. It was on his mind all the way to school, so he didn't even notice Eula Gay and her mean looking eyes or Miss Pringle with her vulcanizing smell until he had been sitting at his desk for awhile.

Then he couldn't help looking up and there she was, sitting at Mama's big desk more beautiful than ever. Reflections of the morning sun tinted her hair with gold and etched her features with a warm glow. She was wearing the same blue dress she had worn on that first day, a dress that clung to her body emphasizing her small waist, wide hips and the upward swell of her breasts. She was staring at Toad Thompson who was sitting at his desk rocking back and forth making weird humming sounds "eeeyoooong," "eeeyooooong," in cadence with his rocking. The longer the rocking and humming went on the more irritated she became and the more beautiful she got.

She stood up and walked over to Toad. "Stop that Anthony, stop that rocking and humming, immediately."

Toad just kept rocking and humming as if he hadn't heard a thing. He had a far away look in his eyes, like maybe he was looking inwards at his own thoughts, if he ever had any. There was complete silence in the room except for the humming with everybody looking back and forth between Miss Pringle and Toad who was not only humming and rocking but wagging his head back and forth.

Miss Pringle went back to Mama's big desk, picked up a ruler, walked back to Toad and whacked him on the head with it. That stopped his rocking and wagging and humming. Then she grabbed Toad and with one big pull got him to his feel. "All right Anthony, just for that, you are going to be punished. You get under my desk and stay there 'til I let you out."

She started dragging at Toad but much to Lonnie's surprise Toad walked to the front of the room, turned around, looked at Miss Pringle for a moment then got down on his hands and knees and crawled under the desk.

Lonnie felt sorry for Old Toad, then he started thinking about it and when Miss Pringle sat down at Mama's desk again with Toad underneath, Lonnie wasn't sorry for him at all. My God, Old Toad was under there so close to Miss Pringle he could reach out and touch her. He was under there right now staring at her legs and smelling vulcanizing. The more Lonnie thought about it the more he decided he had to figure out a way to get punished. Old Toad stayed under the desk until recess when Miss Pringle let him come out. He didn't look like he had suffered much. He stood there by the desk blinking his eyes with a little smile on his lips, looking just like a toad.

After recess Miss Pringle had everybody even including the little ones play a word game. There were two teams of five kids each with Lucy Lemur leading one team and Jimmy Joe leading the other. Somebody on one team would spell a word and pronounce it. It was the job of somebody on the other team to use the last letter of that word to begin another word.

It had been going on for awhile when Sam, who was on Jimmy Joe's team, said "C A N D Y, candy." Eula Gay who was on Lucy Lemur's team responded with "Y O U, you" and Lonnie, who was on Jimmy Joe's team, saw his chance, "U P, up" he shouted. "U P, up" he started to giggle and repeated it, "U P, up."

A lot of kids started laughing and making comments like "yeah, all over you," "down on your head," but Eula Gay wasn't laughing and Miss Pringle wasn't laughing. She was looking pained and embarrassed. Then all the laughing stopped. Lonnie's giggles dwindled away and there was complete silence with all eyes shifting from Miss Pringle to Lonnie and back again. Lonnie was embarrassed but also hopeful.

Miss Pringle turned to him, "Lonnie, that's not funny, it was vulgar and too much. You get under my desk and you stay there until I let you out."

Lonnie didn't wait around. As he walked to the front of the room he glanced at Eula Gay who was staring at him with her teeth showing and her face twitching. When he crawled under the desk, the smell of vulcanizing hit him. He kept breathing it in, listening to the rest of them playing the word game.

In a little while the game was over and Miss Pringle sat down at the desk with her legs so close to Lonnie that he could touch them with his shoulder if he leaned over just a little. He sat there in the half dark looking at her legs which were round and white with a little freckle here and there and fine blond hairs sticking out that he could barely see. He bent his head way over to the side and was able to see up her skirt, past her knees, past the bulges in her thighs that the chair made and into the darkness beyond. She moved a little and released such a strong whiff of vulcanizing and Lysol he was caught there paralyzed with his head twisted over to the side. But all of him wasn't paralyzed, his prick was getting so big he had to move a little to make room for it in his levis. When he moved he brushed against Miss Pringle's legs and felt his heart actually jump in his chest. For just a moment he felt her legs move toward him. Or maybe he was going crazy! He certainly felt like he was going nuts sitting there enjoying the scenery, as Mama often said when she was looking at sunsets through the picture window in the living room.

Then Lonnie started worrying about what he would do when he had to come out from under the desk. He couldn't stand up with his prick sticking out like that for everybody to see. Just then to his horror the bell rang for lunch.

Miss Pringle got up, leaned over and looked under the desk. "You can come out now Lonnie, I hope you've learned your lesson."

"What lesson is that?" Lonnie asked. He loved the way she looked leaning down like that, her boobs straining against the softness of her blue dress, her blue eyes gleaming in the warm light, a little smile on her lips.

"The lesson not to be a smart alec. You can come out now."

"No Ma'am," Lonnie replied in a small voice. "If its okay with you, I'll just stay under here a little while longer," he paused, "so I can learn my lesson better."

"Well that's up to you," Miss Pringle's voice sounded like she was singing when she was just talking.

Lonnie stayed under the desk worrying about his hard-on, thinking maybe he would have to stay under there all day when he heard Eula Gay's voice above him.

"What are you doing under there? Are you sick or something?" There was real concern in her voice. "Are you crying or something?" There was a long pause and then she said, her voice choking a little, "I don't really hate you." There was another pause, and then her voice, so low he could hardly hear it. "I love you."

That did it, his prick began to shrivel until in about two minutes it was back to normal. He crawled out from under the desk and ran past her out into the schoolyard where everybody was playing "Red Rover, Red Rover, come over, come over."

After the game, Lucy Lemur handed out the sandwiches and boiled eggs Dulcita had fixed for their lunch. She nudged Lonnie a little when she gave him his egg and grinned her impish grin. "U P, up, that's pretty good."

Eula Gay came out of the schoolhouse carrying her lunch in a brown paper bag. She sat on a rock not far from Lonnie and started munching on a sandwich with her big blue eyes fixed on him! Jesus Christ! She's at it again!

Going home on the bus there she was, sitting next to him touching him with her shoulder when the bus went around a corner. He sighed and started thinking about the airplane, hoping there wouldn't be another dust storm or anything else that would keep it from coming. As soon as the bus turned in on their road he began staring out the side window toward the lower pasture, but he couldn't see anything.

CHAPTER 25

Airplane

When the bus got to their house, Lonnie jumped out fast and hit the ground running. He heard it and saw it at the same time, a fast moving speck coming in over the Wedding Cake, making a high pitched noise like a mosquito. As he watched, the speck grew into an airplane, which flew directly over him sounding high at first and then low as it passed over, "eeeeeuuuuuum." It circled three or four times then straightened out, getting lower and lower and lower until its wheels kicked up spurts of dust as they skipped along the lower pasture.

Then there it was! Just sitting there with nothing moving, like it was waiting for something. From over to the right near the lower pasture windmill, Fred Clafin and Dogey rode toward it at a slow trot leading three horses, all saddled up and ready to go. Lonnie headed for the barn and got Baldy saddled in record time trying to beat Lucy Lemur and Sam who were working even faster than he was, as it turned out. They were half way to the airplane by the time he got Baldy out of the barn, and then he started pulling his balky trick, the son-of-a-bitch, just when Lonnie was in the biggest rush of his life. With a lot of screaming and a lot of rein-whipping, Lonnie finally got him going at a slow trot, just moseying along taking his own sweet time.

When Lonnie finally got to the airplane, he couldn't believe it. It was his favorite airplane, one that he had drawn lots of times. A staggerwing Beach! A 250-horsepower rotary engine, an enclosed cabin four seater, with the lower wing sticking out about a foot further than the top one. He got off Baldy and walked up to it thinking it was the most beautiful thing he had ever seen except for Miss Pringle. It smelled strange and wonderful, not as good as vulcanizing but something mysterious like wing dope, exhaust fumes and gasoline mixed in together. He walked around it looking and smelling. Sam and Lucy Lemur were sitting on their horses with amazed expressions on their faces.

As if having waited for an audience to gather, the doors opened and men started climbing out. They didn't have aviator clothes on like Lonnie expected, but were wearing levis and denim jackets and cowboy boots and large cowboy hats just like Fred and Dogey.

Fred Clafin got off his horse and shook hands with them. They all talked awhile and then one of them got back into the airplane and got some stuff, a couple of big bags and two black boxes which he carefully handed down to the others. Then one of them took a sledge hammer and started driving steel spikes into the ground, one under each wing and one next to the tail. He stopped when another guy, a real good looking one who had red hair, sunburned skin and snapping blue eyes called to him. This handsome guy who looked a little like Fred Clafin except younger and slimmer was looking at Lonnie and Sam and Lucy Lemur, particularly Lucy Lemur. Suddenly the guy grinned showing the whitest and straightest teeth Lonnie had ever seen. "Hey, you kids want a ride?"

Sam and Lucy Lemur were off their horses in nothing flat, heading for the steps of the airplane. Lonnie was right behind them. He hardly remembered waiting his turn to scramble up the ladder but he did remember being strapped in and he remembered smelling the leather of the seats mixed in with the smells of exhaust and gasoline. He was in one of the back seats sitting beside Sam watching the guy take a lot of time strapping in Lucy Lemur who was in the seat beside him, smiling at him as he worked the buckles. When everything was set, the guy pressed the starter and the propeller turned slowly over and over until the engine threw off big puffs of grey smoke and burst into a steady roar.

Lonnie, who was sitting directly behind Lucy Lemur was overwhelmed by the sights and sounds and smells. It was almost as good as sitting under Miss Pringle's desk. He looked out the side window as the plane started moving, making a sharp turn before it eased along toward the fence at the north side of the lower pasture. It turned again, straightened itself out and waited for a few moments, with the guy switching some switches back and forth and setting the hands on some dials. He slowly pushed the throttle in and the engine went up the scale from low thunder to a high screaming frenzy that threw long billowing plumes of dust behind them and caused the airplane to shiver and shake. He took his feet off the brakes and the airplane lunged forward putting heavy pressure on Lonnie's back. The landing gear made rapid clunking noises as the tires ran over tufts of grass and little bunches of soap-weed. These noises ceased and one after the other Lonnie heard the landing gear bang back into place.

Suddenly they were in a different world where everything was changed, where, even as Lonnie watched, the cows and horses began to look like little bugs and the house and barns and windmill like little toys. To the north he saw the Wedding Cake shrivel and become small with its many layers looking just like a wedding cake waiting to be sliced. To the south, coming up fast, Old Battleship appeared for a moment with the sharp edge of its prow cutting through the upper pasture before it fled behind. Far to the southwest, almost all the way to Clayton, the pinnacles of the Rabbit Ears came into view, rapidly growing until they were over there just a little way looking more like a girl's breasts pointing toward the sky than something on a rabbit.

The guy flying the airplane seemed to be having a good time. He really was handsome with his reddish curly hair, bright blue eyes, and freckled face as he smiled down at Lucy Lemur, showing his perfect teeth. She smiled back at him and Lonnie saw something different in her face, a beauty he had never seen before, and a knowing, as if transformed by an ancient wisdom.

Lonnie caught a look at the altimeter, he knew about altimeters, they were at 5000 feet and climbing, moving into a quiet and peaceful world, not a ripple anywhere—easy, like moving through oil. The guy pushed the stick forward and pulled the throttle back a little and the engine became much quieter with the plane putting the Rabbit Ears behind at more than 160 miles per hour. Then suddenly they were over Clayton, a little bitty town with little bitty cars running up and down little bitty streets, everything small instead of the big scary place it had been when Lonnie had last been there, the time Daddy took them all to see Treasure Island at the picture show.

The plane made a slow, sweeping turn and everything tilted for awhile until it became level again and straightened out the world. Fast away from Clayton then past the Rabbit Ears again. Almost immediately Lonnie could see the great gash in the earth that was the Cimarron valley with the long ribbon of green meandering down the middle of it where the river ran. They crossed the breaks and canyons, dark shadowy crooked lines leading down to the brightness of the valley with Old Battleship showing up on their left and the Wedding Cake set ablaze by the setting sun. Then ahead the ranch buildings started getting bigger and bigger as the airplane sloped down for a landing. Then he heard the "clunk," "clunk" of the landing gear coming down and the shock and rumble of the wheels running over the rough spots. The plane rolled to a stop and then inched forward until it was directly over the steel stakes that had been driven into the ground.

Dogey and Fred Clafin were standing by their horses looking envious as the handsome pilot walked out. His name was Guymond Moore as it turned out, "Guymond" he said, smiling his bright smile which seemed to make everything around him cheerful, because he had been born in Guymond, Oklahoma and his folks couldn't think of anything else to call him. He released everybody from their seat belts, taking a long time, Lonnie thought, to unclick Lucy Lemur who was watching him with a little smile on her face and her huge eyes wide, as he hovered over her.

Then he opened the door and climbed down waiting on the ground for them to come down the steps. Sam was first. He scrambled over Lonnie, pushed the front seat forward and went down in a hurry, looking like the last place on earth, or above it, he would ever want to be again was in an airplane. Lucy Lemur was next. As she climbed down, Guymond was there by the steps holding his hands up toward her. When her foot reached the second step it slipped and she fell backwards into his waiting arms. They remained like that for awhile, him holding her with her looking at him over her right shoulder.

Everybody seemed to forget about Lonnie. Sam was running toward a clump of mesquite, a funny expression on his face which was sweaty and yellowish green. He started vomiting just as he reached the clump then began staggering around like he was about to fall down. Lonnie looked down at Guymond and Lucy Lemur. He finally put her down and the two of them started walking toward Fred Clafin who was not looking at them but staring toward the ground with a sour look on his face. He wasn't the only one with a funny look on his face. Jake Veeder and about twenty other guys had showed up to see the airplane. As Guymond and Lucy Lemur strolled along together, Jake looked like explosions were taking place inside of him. His face was beet red and it seemed like he was having a tough time breathing. He sat there on Macon huffing and puffing, looking real crazy then, without saying a word, he rode off toward the Veeder ranch.

What the shit? They're all crazy! Lonnie sat back in his seat and enjoyed the smell of the airplane, a fine combination of leather, rubber and gasoline with just a whiff of exhaust. That smell, even years later, struck him every time he got into an airplane and it always brought clearly into mind that first ride in the Staggerwing Beach roaring along past the Rabbit Ears with the town of Clayton coming in sight in the middle of the plain.

CHAPTER 26

Dynamite

That night they had a Mexican supper. Bartolo made enchiladas and tortillas and Dulcita cooked sopapillas as light as air and so tasty everybody kept eating them. Even Daddy bragged about them saying they were the best he had ever tasted, particularly with frijole beans. Guymond Moore and his two friends were there telling stories about prospecting for oil, about how they used dynamite to make little earthquakes that went way down into the ground where the oil was so they could pick up echoes on a machine they had.

Lonnie was all ears at the word dynamite. "You mean you're gonna set off dynamite tomorrow, out in the pasture?"

"That's right, five or six times, in different spots, all over the place." Guymond was looking at Lucy Lemur who couldn't take her eyes off him. She kept staring at him, her eyes soft and glowing, a little smile on her face. Lonnie was looking at him too and thought maybe he was the most handsome guy in the world, with his reddish hair falling around his tanned and freckled face, his excited eyes touching everybody at the table, particularly Lucy Lemur.

"And if your daddy doesn't mind you can come out with us to watch and hear the big 'bangs'."

Daddy seemed excited too. He didn't leave the table even though he had finished eating. He smiled a lot and sipped some of the tequila that Guymond had brought him as a present. He kept nodding his head and sipping and every now and then licking some salt he had sprinkled on the back of his hand.

Fred Clafin wasn't smiling. He kept looking back and forth between Lucy Lemur and Guymond Moore, glancing occasionally at Daddy who was busy sipping and licking. Dogey and Horse just sat there like stumps, not saying anything. Lonnie couldn't help thinking how dumb they looked hunched over their plates, stuffing beans and sopapillas in their mouths, sneaking glances at Lucy Lemur. Bartolo was having a grand time cooking more enchiladas and Dulcita kept laughing a lot walking around keeping all the platters filled.

The two guys who came with Guymond Moore seemed to be having a good time too. One of them was a real fat guy not much taller than Lucy Lemur and the other one was tall and skinny with a long hooked nose and a big Adams apple that kept bobbing up and down as he ate.

Suddenly, to the surprise of all of them at the table, Lonnie began laughing like crazy. But he quit laughing when things got quiet and everybody started staring at him.

"Why are you laughing like that, like a hyena?" Lucy Lemur gave him a mean look.

Lonnie quieted down completely, "Nuthin', I was just laughing at nuthin'." How could he tell people that he was thinking that the short fat guy probably had a big prick like Jeff while the tall skinny one had a little shriveled up one like Mutt?

Just as they finished eating, the phone rang their ring. Lucy Lemur beat Lonnie to it again. She listened for awhile, then to Lonnie's surprise handed him the ear piece and helped him up on a stool so he could talk. He stood there on the stool with the earpiece up to his ear feeling dumb until he heard Mama's voice.

"Are you being a good boy Lonnie?"

He burst out. "I had a ride in an airplane, Mama. We went really high, over the Rabbit Ears, clear over to Clayton."

"That's really nice Lonnie, that's nice, now let me talk to Sam."

Everybody talked to Mama that night, even Dulcita. Mama said she was feeling a lot better and that she would be coming home in a week. Everyone seemed real happy to hear the good news, even the oil men, with Guymond Moore saying he sure hoped he could meet Mama and that she must be a beautiful lady to have such beautiful children. He glanced at Lonnie and Sam, but his eyes lingered on Lucy Lemur who really did look beautiful. She was wearing a tan, tight-fitting pant suit with a lacy collar which opened a good bit to show her white throat. A lavender ribbon in her hair reflected in her eyes to give them a violet glow.

Lonnie was thinking how wonderful it would be to have Mama home and then he had a strange lurch in his chest like he had when the airplane banked and he saw the world tilt. What about Miss Pringle? When Mama started teaching again, what would happen to Miss Pringle?

The next morning Lonnie got up earlier than anybody and had Baldy saddled and ready to go by the time breakfast was ready. Ham and eggs and biscuits, molasses and newly churned butter, fried potatoes, everybody around the table with Dulcita keeping the platters full.

Guymond Moore was telling stories about his college days in Norman, Oklahoma, where he stayed and stayed until he got a Doctor's degree in geology and learned to fly. As he listened, Lonnie became sure that he wanted to be a geologist and fly around looking for oil. He had never seen anyone who was as handsome as Guymond Moore or had such a way with words. The way his eyes took in everyone at the table made it seem as if each one of them was special, as if he was talking just to them. And they all responded. Dogey and Horse even opened up a little and asked some questions and Fred Clafin when he wasn't watching Lucy Lemur cast admiring glances at Guymond got caught up in the conversation. Daddy was interested too and asked a lot of questions about the lease arrangements that the oil company made if it became interested in a piece of land.

"A dollar a year per acre, and you don't have to do anything," the fat short guy announced. He had a round shiny face and a bald head and fat chubby cheeks which bulged up so far his eyes were just slits. He was named Dick and the tall skinny guy was also named Dick. Lonnie was about to start laughing when a dig in the side by Lucy Lemur's elbow calmed him down. But it was funnier than hell, two Dicks, Fat Dick and Skinny Dick.

"But we won't know anything until all the dope we gather has been looked at by the people back in Tulsa," Fat Dick continued, "But your place sure looks good to me."

"Yeah, it looks good," said Skinny Dick, "I like the looks of that dome, that big swell out in the middle of the pasture where we landed." He swallowed a couple of times and his Adams apple moved up and down.

Guymond Moore glanced around the table. "We'll check for echoes out there first and maybe that will give us a hint."

After breakfast they all saddled up and headed toward the airplane. Lonnie got started first since he had already saddled Baldy but soon everybody passed him. That son-of-a-bitch Baldy was doing it again, shunting back and forth trying to get back to the barn. He heard Guymond Moore, who was riding beside Lucy Lemur, say as they passed him what a good night's sleep he had gotten out in the bunkhouse. They had fixed a bed for him in the house but he had decided to spend the night with the cowboys, to pick up, as he said, some western atmosphere. Dulcita had put clean sheets on Old Walt's bed and fresh blankets and sheets on Old Man Dick's bed and on a spare bunk so they all had a place to sleep. They had stayed up until the wee hours of the morning trading lies, with Lonnie and Sam hanging around the edges. Lucy Lemur came out for awhile but Fred Clafin wouldn't let her stay, saying in his gruff but gentle way as he hustled her toward the door that it wasn't any place for a young lady. She gave him a dirty look as she went out the door, but she didn't say anything.

When they got to the airplane, the two Dicks got off their horses and picked up a lot of equipment and loaded it into the back of a buggy Dogey Allen had brought out. Then everybody started out for the top of the dome, maybe half a mile from the airplane, with Guymond Moore and Lucy Lemur leading the way. He was talking, every now and then emphasizing his point with a wave of the hand, and she was watching him like everything he said was made of pure gold. It pissed Lonnie off that they were up there having a good time, chatting and taking it easy, while he was back in the rear kicking the hell out of Baldy just to get him to inch along. Jesus Christ! He could move faster walking than kicking the son-of-a-bitch, and he wouldn't have to work near as hard.

Just as they were approaching the top of the dome, a funny looking truck came up their road, turned at the house and moved across the pasture toward them. It had some kind of tank on the back and something Guymond Moore called a derrick folded over the top of it, sticking way out front. It rumbled past them and stopped at the top of the dome. Two guys wearing coveralls and baseball caps got out and started fiddling around, taking pieces of equipment out and putting jacks under the truck. Then one of them began turning a crank while the other made adjustments on the jacks. By the time Lonnie got there, everybody was gathered around the truck and the derrick was already half way up. It was damned interesting, the more the guy turned the crank the higher the derrick got until it was straight up, maybe forty feet tall.

The guy who cranked up the derrick started the engine of the truck and in no time at all a heavy hunk of round iron was going up and down making the dust rise as it bit into the dry ground. Everybody got off their horses and stood around watching as the "whump" "whump" of the bit cut deeper and deeper until it disappeared completely. The guy in the truck pushed a lever and the bit came out of the hole and leaned over against the side of the derrick. The other guy put a hose in the hole and filled it with water from the tank on the truck. Then they put a long round bucket on the cable and bailed out the mud.

This "whumping" and "pulling" and "pouring" and "bailing" went on for a long time, for maybe an hour while the rest of them, except Fred Clafin, Dogey and Horse who had gone back to the barn, watched and waited. And time passed. It was getting boring as hell when they finally pulled the bit out, stored it away and cranked the derrick back into place. The truck drove off about a hundred yards and Fat Dick with the cheery round face opened one of the boxes and took out a long orange stick, Lonnie figured was dynamite, and started drilling a hole into the end of it with something that looked like a screwdriver. Then he uncoiled about fifty feet of black shiny rope.

When he looked up and saw everybody watching him he smiled, "Slow burning fuse," he said as he stuck a brass metal piece that looked like a rifle shell over the end of it, "Everybody move back now," and they did, clear over to the truck but Lonnie could still see what was going on.

Fat Dick took out more sticks of dynamite and taped them around the first stick until he had a bunch of them in one big blob. He carried this blob to the hole in the ground and let it down, hand over hand, until the fuse got limp in his hand. The truck came back to the hole and one of the guys, the one who had cranked down the derrick, ran water into the hole until it filled up and began running out across the ground. Fat Dick lit the fuse and even from way over where he was Lonnie could see it putting off sparks and hear it making a sizzling sound.

"It'll be about ten minutes," Fat Dick who had driven the truck back announced as he got down and joined the rest of them. Lonnie went over to a tent which had its sides rolled up where Guymond, with Lucy Lemur watching his every move, was working with two black boxes which were on the ground next to some folding chairs they were sitting on. He looked up as Lonnie came into the tent. "Maybe you better move your horse a little farther over that way."

Lonnie led Baldy away from the tent and tied him to a dead cactus, near the other horses. Then he went back to the tent and asked Guymond Moore what he was doing. He glanced up from the black box which Lucy Lemur was watching like she expected to see a snake come crawling out. "I'm going to make a record of the echoes from the bang, with this black box. There's film in there on a roller which keeps turning real slow." He flipped a switch. "There, I've started the roller. When the bang comes the echoes will cause this box to jiggle just a little bit, this jiggle will cause a beam of light to trace the echoes on the film so we can have a permanent record."

He was looking out the side of the tent toward the hole, glancing every now and then at this watch. "It should come pretty soon now."

As if to emphasize his point there was a heavy "thump," not a loud bang at all, and Lonnie actually felt the earth jiggle a little and saw a brown plume of mud and water spew out of the hole. There was a short silence then muddy water started spattering down on the tent, and making little brown spots on the dry ground.

All day long they kept beating holes into the ground and setting off "thumps." They took time out for lunch, beans and fried potatoes and biscuits, that Bartolo brought out in the buggy, then they went back to digging and "thumping."

They were working on the fifth hole when Fred Clafin rode out. He stopped where Lucy Lemur was watching Guymond Moore working with his black boxes. Lonnie was checking on Baldy and couldn't hear what they were talking about but Lucy Lemur was looking really pissed. After shouting at Fred Clafin for awhile, something about his not being able to order her around, she got on Velvet and took out for the house at a dead run.

It was about time, Lonnie was dying to take a piss and so was everybody else apparently because there was a steady stream of guys going out about twenty yards, turning their backs, then standing there with their shoulders humped and their arms out front.

Toward evening after the last "thump" the guys working the truck cranked the derrick into place, coiled up all the hose and drove off heading toward the house and then on down the road. Lonnie was sad to see them leaving. He had had a great time with all the activity, the whump of the drill bit, the bailing of muddy slush and the big "thumps."

Dogey Allen came out with the buggy and the two black boxes and a bunch of tools were loaded into it. And that was it. Everybody who was left got on their horses and headed in, with Lonnie riding beside Guymond Moore and Sam, who was asking questions about the other black box.

Guymond Moore was in a good mood. He kept looking back and forth between Sam and Lonnie as he talked about the box. "Measures gravity. It gives us extra information that might help us make a judgement about the possibility of oil. As we move from "bang" place to "bang" place, I record measurements and then later, in Tulsa, they take the dope from the Gravitometer, that's what it's called, and check it with the dope we get from the echoes."

CHAPTER 27

Goodbye

They got to the barn about then so nothing more was said until supper-time when they all sat around eating a big feast Bartolo and Dulcita had cooked up to celebrate the end of the "banging" and to show appreciation for the three guys who had come in the airplane. The grownups had a choice of tequila or whiskey while there was grape juice in wine glasses for the rest of them.

Guymond Moore rapped on the table until everybody was looking at him. Then he lifted his glass of whiskey which Dulcita had just refilled. "Let us all drink to the prettiest girl on the Cimarron." He was looking right at Lucy Lemur. "To the Rose of the Cimarron." Everybody lifted their glasses, even Daddy and Fred Clafin, and nodded toward Lucy Lemur who blushed until she looked like a rose with her large eyes deep and soft. They all drank, Lonnie taking a big slug of his grape juice thought it was the grandest thing he ever saw and he felt himself bursting with love and pride for Lucy Lemur.

After that, everybody began talking about prospecting for oil and Lonnie started looking bug-eyed at Guymond Moore. "You said you could measure gravity, but gravity is just gravity. When you get on a scale all you're doin' is just measurin' your gravity. How can you find oil with gravity?"

Everybody else apparently thought it was a pretty good question because they all fixed their eyes on Guymond Moore. He glanced around the table, his eyes lingered on Lucy Lemur and then stopped on Lonnie. "Well the strange thing is that things don't weigh the same in different places. In some places things are lighter and in other places they are heavier. So we look for places where gravity is less because oil and the kinds of formations that oil comes in are less dense so that things above them tend to weigh less."

There was silence as everybody thought about this, then Lonnie said, "Well, I know what I would do if I was a fat man," he was looking at Fat Dick. "I'd find a place to live where I didn't weigh so much."

Lucy Lemur gave him the elbow but everybody else started laughing and looking at Fat Dick who was sitting there like a horny toad, with its eyes blinking in its fat face. He seemed embarrassed for a moment then he started laughing louder than anybody.

Lonnie felt good. He kept thinking and chuckling. Then his eyes fixed on Skinny Dick. He started giggling, "And Skinny Dick could find another place," the giggle broke into screaming laughter, "where he could put on a little weight."

Lonnie stopped suddenly, Lucy Lemur had given him the elbow again and this one hurt. No one else was laughing! They were all looking at Skinny Dick who sat hunched over, picking at his food, his face a bright red.

But that was it, the talk started up again and Skinny Dick began to smile a little. Lonnie sat there staring at his plate, feeling like a dumb piece of shit.

After supper Lonnie and Sam went to the bunkhouse where Bartolo had made a fire in the big pot bellied stove. It was nice and warm with everybody sitting around under the light from the oil lantern which was hung from a beam above them. Skinny Dick and Fat Dick were telling stories about places they had been, from Clovis to Muleshoe, prospecting for oil.

Lonnie was so interested, listening and looking at the faces in the lantern light that he didn't notice at first that Guymond Moore wasn't there. Then Lonnie figured that Guymond must be out there somewhere in the night seeing Lucy Lemur. Fred Clafin must have thought the same thing because he got up suddenly and went out the door. Lonnie followed him. It was a chilly night. The moon was so bright that everything was bathed in a silvery glow; the farm buildings, the near mesa with its cap rock gleaming, the windmill casting moving shadows on the pond.

Fred Clafin was headed for the barn so Lonnie skulked along behind, far enough he figured that he wouldn't be noticed. But suddenly there was Fred right in front of him standing next to the barn door his head cocked to the side. He reached out and touched Lonnie on the shoulder and both of them waited there listening.

Guymond Moore was talking, sounding like he was on the edge of breaking up. "There's nothing I would like more Lucy, and some- day when you're grown up, I'll come back here."

Lucy Lemur was sobbing but Lonnie could understand her. "So you think I'm just a little girl too, like that old man Fred Clafin. I'm a woman, if you'll just let me show you, I'm a woman." There was a long silence then Guymond Moore's voice came through again.

"You are the most beautiful young woman I've ever met, Lucy, you are my Rose of the Cimarron, and I'll never forget you. But you are just fourteen years old. We are flying out early in the morn- ing and I want you to come out and say goodbye, out at the air- plane."

There was another long silence, punctuated by an occasional sob. "Will you do that Lucy?" There was a note of desperation in Guymond Moore's voice.

"Yes," she finally said. "You know I'll come." Then her voice strengthened a little. "If you'll kiss me goodbye."

"It's a promise Lucy." Guymond Moore's voice suddenly sounded almost joyful. "I'll give you two kisses. Now we better go in before somebody misses us and starts wondering where we are."

Lonnie suddenly felt Fred Clafin's hand on his shoulder push- ing him along. Together they walked fast toward the bunkhouse and were inside listening to the bullshit stories when Guymond Moore came in. He sat down on one of the bunks, his eyes shift- ing like they couldn't focus on anything. The lantern light striking from above brought out gleams of copper and bronze in his hair and touched his face with sadness and regret. And Lonnie felt sad too, sad for Lucy Lemur.

The next morning Lucy Lemur didn't show up for breakfast. Dulcita went to her room and came back shaking her head, saying that Lucy didn't feel very good but that she might eat something later. As they were eating, Fred Clafin and Guymond Moore sat stiffly, not saying anything, glancing occasionally at the hallway. Lonnie was worried too, it wasn't like Lucy Lemur to be sick. Maybe she was coming down with something, maybe the scarlet fever. But down deep he figured she was just sad about Guymond Moore, about his going away, flying off to somewhere else.

Daddy looked up from squeezing his eggs. "How long before we'll know somethin'?"

Guymond Moore jerked and glanced up at him in surprise. "Know something? Oh, you mean about the survey. About two months I guess. But I can tell you one thing. The readings from the dome look promising. And a couple of other places too. I don't make the decision but it looks good to me."

Guymond Moore seemed relieved to be talking. "I think there's a salt bloom under the dome out there, and we sometimes find oil in such places," he paused, "not often of course, every well that's drilled is a chancy operation. Only about five percent actually produce enough oil to cover expenses."

Just then, Lucy Lemur came in from the hallway. She was wearing a white pantsuit which let everybody see that her figure was developing good, small waist, hips getting broad like a woman's hips, boobs swelling out almost as big as Miss Pringle's. She had done something to her eyelashes making them stick out further and there were dark circles under her eyes that made them look bigger and blacker than ever. She was wearing lipstick, Lonnie was sure of it, and when she sat down he caught a whiff of her. Some kind of perfume, like flowers with just a touch of the way a skunk smells mixed in. Her black hair had been brushed until it gleamed, flashes of dark light as she turned her head. It was tied up in a red ribbon that cast reflections of color to her pale face.

Everybody at the table was looking at her, even Daddy stopped eating for a moment and stared. "My you're growing up Lucy," he murmured, then almost as an after thought, "I wish you wouldn't grow up so fast."

Lucy Lemur didn't say anything. She started eating the pancakes Dulcita brought her, thanking Dulcita and smiling down at her plate as if she was thinking happy secret thoughts.

After breakfast, everybody saddled up and headed for the airplane except for Dulcita and Bartolo who came out in the buggy. Daddy came out, riding Old Squirrel who pranced around like he was doing something important even though he looked swaybacked because Daddy weighed so much. Baldy was out ahead of everybody, trotting along without Lonnie having to beat on him, not trying once to go back to the barn. There was no figuring the son-of-a-bitch!

They all gathered around the airplane watching the two Dicks loading stuff into the storage compartment. Guymond Moore came around shaking hands. He thanked Daddy for all the hospitality and the other guys, particularly Fred Clafin, for all the help. He told Bartolo that he was the best cook in New Mexico and Dulcita that she was the best cook in the southwest.

When he came to Lonnie, he did a funny thing. He put his arms around him and gave him a big kiss on the forehead. Jesus Christ! Lucy Lemur was last. He put his arms around her and gave her a kiss on the forehead. But that wasn't good enough. She pulled his head down and gave him a kiss on the mouth that lasted so long Lonnie thought it never would stop. Finally she let him go and he just stood there without moving, with a far away look in his eyes. She was looking funny too. There was a little smile on her lips and her eyes seemed filled with an ancient knowledge, as old as woman.

Guymond Moore shook himself like a dog does, turned and climbed up the steps of the airplane. The two Dicks were already in their places, buckled down. Dogey and Horse untied the ropes and the propeller started going around real slow until the engine started putting out grey smoke and raising a lot of dust. Everybody waved and shouted goodbyes as the airplane trundled away to the north side of the pasture, then turned and headed right for them. Lonnie was just about to duck when it took off and went roaring overhead, pulling up at a sharp angle. It turned and flew past them just a few feet above the ground. For a moment Lonnie could see the three of them waving and looking. Guymond Moore's handsome face was fixed there staring down, trying to catch a final glimpse, Lonnie figured, of Lucy Lemur.

Then everybody got on their horses and rode toward the bunkhouse, that is everybody but Lonnie and Lucy Lemur. Lonnie was on Baldy waiting but she just stood there, holding Velvet by the reins. Lonnie glanced at her and then wished he hadn't. She was staring toward the spot where the airplane had lingered for a moment, growing smaller and smaller until it disappeared from sight and sound, staring through sightless eyes, her face deathly pale with tears running down her cheeks.

Lonnie couldn't stand it. He got off Baldy, went over and pushed her a little. "Hey, he'll come back, you wait and see, Old Guymond will be comin' back." He laughed a little as he poked her on the shoulder. "I know you think I'm a little piece of shit, but I know some things. He'll be comin' back."

Lucy Lemur was looking at him now, smiling through her tears. "Well at least you're right about one thing, you are a little piece of shit." She whacked him a good one and he suddenly felt a lot better and he knew one thing for sure which he would never admit to anybody. He sure did love Lucy Lemur.

CHAPTER 28

Punishment

The next morning on the way to school, Lonnie started thinking about Miss Pringle, about how she wouldn't be around very long with Mama coming home. But at least she would be around for a few days so he would get to see her and maybe if everything went right he could sit under her desk again. Eula Gay was sitting beside him leaning over against him every time the bus made a turn or hit a rough spot. She was wearing some kind of perfume, sickly sweet stuff that made him want to sneeze.

The bus swerved and she pushed over against him, and a wave of perfume hit him. "Why do you wear that stuff?" he leaned away from her. "You're only eight years old and you shouldn't be wearing that stuff. That's for older women." She drew away from him, looking hurt.

He sat there feeling guilty, then said, "A pretty girl like you don't need that kind of stuff." Then he wished he hadn't said anything, she looked so pleased sitting there, giving him moon-eyed looks.

The bus stopped at the schoolhouse just then so he was saved. He clambered out, ran up the steps just in time to see a gorgeous view of Miss Pringle's bottom moving rhythmically back and forth as she erased the blackboard. Miss Pringle tapped the bell and everybody took their seats. Lonnie was thinking about what he might do to get put under Miss Pringle's desk when he glanced at Lucy Lemur. She was looking sad and forlorn, staring out the window as if she was searching for something, and Lonnie figured he knew what it was. An airplane!

Lonnie was on the edge of firing a spit ball with a rubber band, thinking maybe that might be enough to get him punished when somebody, Toad Thompson as it turned out, hit the floor behind him. He had been excused for number two and was coming back to his desk when Jimmy Joe who had been sitting there with a sneaky look on his face put his foot out and tripped him.

Old Toad really made the floor tremble when he hit. He lay there with a bewildered look on his face making little snuffling sounds. Miss Pringle ran over and helped him up. He sure took a long time getting to his feet, leaning on her a lot and acting like he couldn't get his legs to work right. Finally he was back at his desk and Jimmy Joe, with a satisfied look on his stupid face, was climbing under Miss Pringle's desk. The son-of-a-bitch! Lonnie kept thinking about him under there looking at Miss Pringle's legs and enjoying the vulcanizing. He thought about hitting the son-of-a-bitch in the head with another rock. A bigger one!

Lonnie didn't get to sit under Miss Pringle's desk at all that day, nor the next one either. Somebody was always getting punished before he could think of anything bad enough. Sam got put under the desk twice, once for throwing an eraser at Gwen Veeder and another for smacking Bobby Leo in the side of the head with a spit ball. Even Toad Thompson managed to make it again, for letting a loud fart, a dull heavy report which resonated through the room and smelled terrible. Lonnie couldn't help wondering how somebody who smelled as wonderful as Miss Pringle could endure the possibility of such a bad smell close to her. But Jimmy Joe got punished most, at least four times, Lonnie counted and hated him more every time he made it.

After three days of no success Lonnie noticed something funny. One evening before supper he asked Lucy Lemur about it. "Why is it that none of the girls ever have to be punished by sitting under Miss Pringle's desk?"

She gave him one of her wise looks, her eyes twinkling a little which partly erased the sad look she wore around all the time now. "Well what do you think?" she asked.

He thought about it for awhile and then said, "Yeah, I guess I know, it's because boys are a lot meaner than girls."

She actually smiled at him, and he was glad that he had said something that made her feel a little bit better, even if she was giving him that superior look she sometimes wore when she thought he was being stupid. "Sure, that's it, boys are a lot meaner than girls. And a lot dumber!"

Her face took on a crafty foxy look as she glanced at him out of the corner of her eyes, which made him wonder if he had fucked up, and how. But she gave him a little punch as she passed him on the way into the kitchen, so he felt better. But not much, he was too confused about Miss Pringle, about her going away, about ways which might work for getting under her desk.

CHAPTER 29

Baldy

The next morning Lonnie decided to take a ride to the Kierkendahl. Some old guy had homesteaded there and had died just in time for Daddy to buy it and make it a part of the ranch. There was an old ranch-house, mostly fallen down, that Lonnie liked to explore, finding all kinds of crazy things like old horseshoes, some Indian head pennies, funny colored bottles, a glass cutter, and some steel balls. The way to get there was to go a little way past Bone Canyon, then past the Zig Zag, then up a small canyon until the trail suddenly tilted down and wound up in a little narrow valley with the old ranch-house at the far end.

Lonnie took a look at the bones again as he went past the mouth of Bone Canyon; not skeletons anymore, just bunches of bones scattered everywhere, lots of skulls with eye holes empty and teeth glistening white, sticking out of jaw bones. There were still some animals around, two coyotes went loping away up the canyon, horny toads were lying on some of the rocks soaking up the sun. On the west side of the canyon near some huge brown boulders two skunks were moving across, picking their way among the bone piles.

Going up the Kierkendahl canyon he saw a cotton tail rabbit for a moment before it whisked away and disappeared in a large clump of scrub oak. He took his twenty-two out of its scabbard, ready in case, but he didn't see it again.

At the top of the trail where it began slanting down into the Kierkendahl valley, he turned and looked back. Everything was like a clear bright picture; the green ribbon of the Cimarron River, the Wedding Cake, Old Battleship, all framed by the mouth of the canyon. There were some funny looking clouds showing above Black Mesa, whitish grey, hugging the top of the rimrock, but he didn't get worried. It was a little bit chilly even with his sheepskin coat and sheepskin hat on but he had a blanket and a tarp tied behind his saddle, and he had some matches in a little tin container that went "plop" when he pulled the top off. Fred Clafin had made everybody take this stuff when they went out riding. He maintained that Old Walt would still be alive if he had had these things with him.

Lonnie stopped in front of the ranch-house, half of its roof now crumbled in, and tied Baldy to the hitching rail. The windmill was still working so he took a drink from a tin cup, almost ice cold with a slight taste of rust. He was about to go in the front door of the ranch-house when he heard the rattler, a big diamondback, coiled up against the side of the house, its tail buzzing so fast it looked like a blur. Lonnie got his twenty-two out of the scabbard again and took careful aim. There was a sharp "splat" and the rattler's head lurched sideways. It writhed around for awhile then turned over exposing the white of its belly. But it wasn't dead yet, its rattle kept going off every few seconds.

Fred Clafin said you should never touch a rattler until after it makes its last twitch, so Lonnie waited around listening to the buzzes which kept getting weaker and further apart until there was nothing. He poked it with the barrel of his rifle, still nothing so he picked it up by the tail and took it over to a stump and draped it over. He got out his Barlow, adjusted the tail on the stump just right and started sawing off the rattles. As he heard his knife grating through the bone he counted them, fifteen rattles, some big snake and old, fifteen years, one for each rattle. Just as he put the rattles in his shirt pocket he noticed the snow, huge flakes that went sailing down, swirled by a rising wind that was getting colder.

He got on Baldy and headed out watching the snow thicken and swirl in the rising wind. By the time he got half way to the trail out of the Kierkendahl he couldn't see the mesas on each side of him, and in no time flat he couldn't see much of anything. The snow was so thick and the wind blowing so hard that he had to keep brushing the snow out of his eyes just to see the ground. And then after a few minutes he couldn't see anything at all except the blowing snow which came in slantwise right in front of his face.

He thought about going back to the broken down ranch-house but figured he probably couldn't find it, and anyway Baldy wouldn't want to go back that way. Finally since he couldn't see anything anyway, he tied the reins together and hooked them over the saddle horn. Old Baldy didn't seem to mind the snow, he just kept moving along at a fast walk as if he knew where he was going.

What the shit! Lonnie turned in his saddle untied the blanket and tarp and draped them around him. He went along that way for awhile with the icy snow blowing in his face, then put the blanket and tarp over his head and face and stuck them under his legs to hold them in place. It wasn't bad, completely dark but it was a lot warmer and the smell of Baldy coming in under the blanket and tarp was comforting, almost like company.

He sat there in his saddle feeling the movements of Baldy under him, a slow walk now, moving steady but taking short steps and making lots of short stops like he was going up hill. Then suddenly, the wind came in so hard it almost blew Lonnie from the saddle. He hunched down and felt Baldy leaning into it, moving slower now, hesitating a little before each step like it was really rough going. Then, just as suddenly, the wind stopped blowing so hard and Baldy started moving even slower lurching from side to side as he took each forward step as if he was going down hill. Lonnie figured they must be going down the Kierkendahl trail and the wind wasn't blowing as hard because of the cliffs on each side. He tried peeking out from under his cover but couldn't see anything, the snow hit him in the face and everything was pitch black. Jesus Christ!

He covered up again, leaned back and let Baldy just keep walking. Once or twice Lonnie thought he heard gun shots, so low and muffled that he wasn't sure about it. But mostly nothing at all happened but the increasing cold which kept rising up his legs and running up his arms in spite of the blanket and tarp. He tried rubbing his hands together and moving his legs back and forth but nothing seemed to help much. But he wasn't really cold, or maybe he was getting numb, or maybe just tired. The slow swaying motion in the saddle, the mild shocks of Baldy's feet striking the ground as he plodded along seemed to go on for hours.

Lonnie pulled the covers more closely around him listening to the dull roaring of the wind, the creak of his saddle. After a long time Baldy began to move faster, changing from a slow walk to something that was halfway between a walk and a trot. And then he just stopped! Lonnie waited for him to start moving again and then he heard something different. There was a low whistling sound and a distant "chug" "chug" and suddenly he knew where he was and what he was listening to; the wind in the eaves of the barn and the sound of the sucker-rod in the windmill going up and down.

He peaked out from under his cover and could see a dim square of light through the swirling snow, the light from the kitchen window. Then there was another light flickering around in front of him, shining directly into his face.

Suddenly Old Bartolo pulled him from the saddle and started hugging him and shouting, "Lonnito, we all think maybe you die in the cold. You one tough *muchacho*," Bartolo started laughing, at least Lonnie thought he was, kind of a cackling giggle. "You one tough *hombre*."

Bartolo let him go and started firing his rifle, an old 38-55 Winchester that made loud booms in the night. After he had fired eight times he turned back to Lonnie and started hustling him toward the house. "We go in now, get some warm, *mucho calor*, and some supper. Bartolo take care of Baldy, he some horse, *bien caballo*! He come home in the snow and the dark."

Dulcita was waiting for him at the door with some more hugs and some hot chocolate. She took off his blanket and tarp looking at him like he was some kind of alien from outer space, like in Buck Rogers. Jesus Christ! She kept pawing over him so much it was embarrassing. He pulled away and took off his sheepskin coat and sheepskin hat. The hot chocolate tasted good, really good, and the big mug felt great in his cold hands. They heard eight more shots from Bartolo's rifle, and then some answering shots from way out in the night. Lonnie had only finished half of his hot chocolate when they started crowding in the front door.

Lucy Lemur was first. She came over and gave him a hug then started screaming at him. "You little piece of shit, you had us all worried to death, out there in the night and this blizzard."

Sam was screaming at him too, something about being a selfish asshole that didn't have any consideration for others, and that it was a good thing that Mama and Daddy weren't there because if they were they would have been so worried, he stated at the top of his voice, that they would beat the shit out of him.

Dogey Allen and Horse didn't say anything, they were too busy sneaking glances at Lucy Lemur who looked like a snow princess with her shining black hair, flashing black eyes and lipstick red mouth standing out against the white fur of her jumper suit.

Even Fred Clafin got in on the act. He came up to Lonnie, looking stern, almost mean, and stared at him for a long time before he finally said, "I want you to remember one thing. You know how you're always picking on that little horse. I know he picks on you too but you remember, you never forget that if it wasn't for him, you would probably be out there dead right now, froze to death like Old Walt."

He relented a little, gave Lonnie a grim smile and started for the door. He stopped and glanced back at Lucy Lemur. "Call general Lucy and tell everybody that his horse brought him home." With that he gave Lonnie another grim smile and went out the front door toward the bunkhouse swinging an oil lantern.

All Lonnie could do was just look back and forth between them and sip his hot chocolate. What a fucking mess, all he did was take a nice ride, and it wound up like he was some kind of fucking criminal, like Old Al Capone. For Christ sake!

CHAPTER 30

Looking Up

The next morning nobody said anything about his big ride through the blizzard. They were all smiles and even the weather had turned warm overnight so that the little bit of snow that had caused all the trouble didn't last very long. He felt sure he would think of something to get himself put under Miss Pringle's desk but he didn't come up with anything. Jimmy Joe beat him out again, and then of all things Bobby Leo couldn't stop giggling when Lonnie fucked up the poem he was reading hoping maybe it would be enough to merit punishment. He had to watch in total frustration as the little runt strutted up to the front of the room and disappeared into paradise.

That night he couldn't sleep worrying about it, trying to figure out a way to spend a little time under Miss Pringle's desk. He was out in the bunkhouse lying in Old Man Dick's bed smelling the clean sheets Dulcita had put on for the oil man, listening to the cowboys snore and fart. One in particular kept farting as regular as clockwork, once every few minutes, probably Old Bartolo, his bunk was over that way. Lonnie was wondering if all those hot peppers Bartolo mixed in with his beans were at least partly responsible for the continuing farts that sounded a little like the reports from his 38-55 Winchester, when the solution to getting under Miss Pringle's desk came to him. A solution so simple he wondered why he hadn't thought of it before.

The next morning he tried it. When the bell rang for everybody to come in and take their seats, he stayed out in the shit-house, just sitting there on one of the holes with the bad smells circling around him. Pretty soon he heard Lucy Lemur calling his name but he didn't move thinking the longer he waited the more punishment he would receive. Before long everybody was outside yelling his name, some sounded like they were going up the hill in the back while others were just running around the schoolhouse screaming. Finally when the noise was at its loudest, he ambled out of the shit-house and down to the front of the schoolhouse where everybody got really quiet when they saw him. Jesus Christ! They were all looking at him like he had just come back from the dead.

Eula Gay came running toward him, grabbing at his hand and looking into his face as she made little whimpering sounds, repeating, "I thought you had died, I thought maybe you had died."

They were all gathered around him now. Miss Pringle was feeling his forehead saying that he had a fever and that he better come in and lie down. Everybody trooped inside, with Eula Gay on one side of him holding his hand and Miss Pringle on the other, helping him along. She took a blanket and a pillow from a closet and made a place for him in the corner of the room where the blackboard ended. And there he was lying on his back with a bunch of eyes looking down at him.

"Do you hurt someplace?" Miss Pringle's voice sounded really concerned as she bent over him. He got a whiff of her and tried to look sick. "Just a little bit here," he pointed at his stomach and then felt her hand touching him, around on each side, pressing down in different places.

Then she started taking his pulse, and looking even more worried. "My, you must be sick, you've got a very fast pulse." She tucked the blanket in around him, releasing all kinds of wonderful smells. "Well you just lie here for awhile." She glanced up. "The rest of you go back to your desks."

They all shuffled off except for Lucy Lemur who stood gazing down at him with a crooked little smile on her face. The longer she looked at him the more embarrassed he became.

He glanced up at her, "I guess I'm a little bit sick," he thought he sounded sick. "I guess I got the flu, or somethin', I'm feelin' real sick."

"Sure you are," she said in a low voice, "And I know just where." She started to go then turned back and gave him a sharp kick in the ribs.

With that she was gone, and he was alone on the floor looking up at the ceiling, thinking that everything was all fucked up. Jesus Christ! He lay there listening to them do states and capitols feeling like he was some kind of bug being looked at by a bunch of people with magnifying glasses.

When the bell rang for recess Eula Gay came over and knelt down beside him, her blue eyes big with concern. "You do look sick, maybe you've got the chicken pox or something. You got any spots?"

Jesus Christ! "I ain't got no spots, now you just go away and let me be sick here in peace. Anyway," he said more gently as he saw the hurt look on her face, "I'm goin' to get up now." And with that he started trying to get to his feet. Miss Pringle came over and helped Eula Gay steady him and pretty soon he was walking around as good as new.

"Hey, I feel fine now, must have had a little indigestion," he grinned, showing how brave he was. "Probably somethin' I ate."

He was suddenly as uncomfortable as hell with Eula Gay and Miss Pringle looking at him like they thought he might fall over. "Well thanks for lookin' after me. I guess I'll go out and get some fresh air."

Nothing happened the rest of the day. He took his turn at spelling, reciting and doing arithmetic problems at the blackboard, thinking about the way Miss Pringle smelled and the way she looked when she walked, thinking about how dumb he had been, wondering how Lucy Lemur always seemed to know what he was planning even before he did.

CHAPTER 31

Home

When they got home from school, Mama was standing in the open door, smiling and waving. Lonnie saw her and felt like crying, and he didn't even mind it when she put her arms around him and kissed him on the head. He didn't realize how much he had missed her until there she was looking pale and drawn even though she kept giving everybody a big smile. When she walked she took little steps, kind of shuffling along, bent over like maybe something was giving her pain. They all followed her into her bedroom, asking questions and laughing a lot, everybody glad that she was home and that she seemed pretty good if not really great.

Lucy Lemur and Dulcita shooed everyone out and put Mama to bed. She didn't argue about it. She had had a long ride from Amarillo and needed the rest. But in about an hour, she was up helping Dulcita get supper, poking around the kitchen, doing little things like they were really special, lingering over every little job like putting the napkins around and getting the chairs straight.

When supper was ready, she finally let Dulcita sit her at her place at the foot of the table where she watched as everybody sat down, smiling a kind of dreamy distant smile. During supper they all kept looking at Mama who wasn't eating very much but just kept nodding and smiling as people made comments about this or that.

Mama started to say something and then stopped, looking uncertain. Then as everyone was staring at her she said in a rapid low voice. "I'll start teaching again on Monday." They all started talking then, saying Mama needed more rest and Lonnie, thinking about Miss Pringle going away, said that Mama should take more time. Daddy insisted that she should rest for at least a week but she said, "Oh no, I've been resting for too long now, I'm tired of hanging around doing nothing, letting everybody wait on me," she paused, "even though it's been very nice."

CHAPTER 32

Hot Peppers

Lonnie was glad Mama was feeling better, that she was going to start teaching again, but what about Miss Pringle? Tomorrow was Friday. Only one more day to see Miss Pringle and maybe get to sit under her desk. As he thought about it, about her going away, he felt a funny lump in his chest like a hole or something had opened up. That night, out at the bunkhouse in Old Man Dick's bed he racked his brain for some way to get under her desk but couldn't think of anything that wasn't completely dumb.

He dozed off and dreamed about Miss Pringle, felt her close to him, felt her touching him on the forehead, felt her probing his belly with her fingers as she stood over him helping him with some kind of problem. Then he was looking for her, out in a weird flat world full of crazy mirrors which leaned and turned and twisted and cast back strange reflections of him as skinny or fat or with his head on backwards or his arms or legs in the wrong places. She had disappeared among the mirrors with nothing left of her but the lingering smell of vulcanizing and Lysol and the distant sound of her voice saying something that he couldn't understand. He kept calling "Miss Pringle, Miss Pringle," and could hear his own voice echo back like it did from the breaks, lots of echoes overlapping and becoming fused into a louder voice.

Then he saw her clearly for a moment, her face and figure distinct before she went pin-wheeling away into a night sky and became lost among the pinpoints of light where great stars burn. The smell of vulcanizing swelled stronger and a sound grew so loud that he couldn't stand it, the sound that a rubber band makes when stretched taught in a high wind, like the blow hole, pulsating and thrumming.

He woke up suddenly and looked out into the darkness, feeling his heart beat returning to normal, hearing the snores of the cowboys and the yelping of a coyote somewhere out in the night. He lay there thinking about Miss Pringle, about her going away and tears welled in his eyes and ran down his cheeks. He stifled a sob, thinking how silly it would sound if somebody woke up and heard him sniveling there.

The next morning he did a careful job of washing his hands and face in the icy water in the wash basin by the windmill. He took a long time brushing his teeth with Pepsident tooth paste hoping all the yellow would go, and brushing his hair until it gleamed copper in the morning sun. Only one more day of Miss Pringle!

At breakfast, Mama was almost like her old self, smiling and nodding to everybody. Lonnie glanced at her and said, "You sure look fine Mama, but I think you need a few more days rest."

Everyone at the table was suddenly looking at him, particularly Lucy Lemur. Jesus Christ! There she was again with her big weird eyes staring at him, a quirky little smile on her face and a knowing look like she was reading his mind or something. She glanced at Mama and then back at him. "Oh! You think it would be nice for Mama if Miss Pringle stayed for awhile and let Mama take it easy."

Lonnie stared back at her, "Yes I do, Miss Pringle could help Mama a lot, goin' round and checking on all the kids, how their work was comin' at their desks."

Lucy Lemur started to say something but Mama interrupted. "Yes, that would be really nice, but Miss Pringle has to go back to college. They gave her just two weeks leave, to help us out, now she has to go back to Clovis, for her studies. Mr. Rutledge is taking her back on Saturday."

So that was it. That was it! Lonnie didn't say anything more. He sat there staring at his plate, eating a little bit of something every now and then. He glanced up and saw Lucy Lemur looking at him and he knew she knew. But there was a sadness in her face and a glint of moisture in her eyes as she looked away.

Years later. Many years later, he heard a song that said it all, "There is a hunger in every heart." But there at the breakfast table there was just that big lump in his chest, a loneliness and a misery.

The next morning he didn't want to go to school, didn't want to see her for the last time but he didn't want to make it worse by doing something dumb like acting sick. When the bus came he climbed in and covered up with a blanket. When the Morgan children got on, Eula Gay snuggled in beside him. He was so miserable that he didn't push her away. She was warm and soft and smelled of Lifebuoy soap and kept up a continual chatter about something that he didn't listen to.

They all trooped into the school house where the pot-bellied stove was glowing a dull red and Miss Pringle waited, dressed in a new blue dress that snuggled close around her and made her hips and breasts look even lovelier than ever. Her bright blond hair was pulled back tight with a blue ribbon at the back, tied with a large flowing bow. Lonnie sat there stunned because she was so beautiful and because the knot in his chest seemed to be moving, twisting and turning, like the mirrors in his dream.

Just before the noon bell, Miss Pringle tapped on the desk to get their attention. She glanced around the room, her blue eyes touching each of them. "This is my last day of a wonderful experience with you, each one of you, and we are going to do something to celebrate our time together. We are going to have a contest and then after the contest, a party. I baked a cake and Mr. Rutledge made some ice cream. After the contest we'll all have cake and ice cream."

All the kids started clapping and shouting. Even Lonnie felt better. Cake and ice cream! Miss Pringle held up her hand and everyone became quiet. "Now for the contest. We are going to have a two hour lunch period. First eat your lunch and then go up on the hill up there," she motioned with her hand, "and look for arrowheads. The one who finds the largest arrowhead will win a special prize."

She rang the bell. There was a scramble to put on coats and caps and gloves, then everybody headed for the door. Lonnie didn't want to go but he couldn't figure out any way to stay without looking dumb, so he went along. He got his lunch and headed for the hill, moving fast, munching and hunting at the same time. He looked back from the top of the hill and saw Eula Gay trudging along behind him looking like an Eskimo in her fur suit. When she saw him looking at her, she started moving faster trying to catch up with him.

Suddenly he broke into a run, as fast as he could go, through the scrub cedar, scrub pine and cactus. When he was completely out of sight from the others he circled back until he could see the

174

schoolhouse below him, way over to the left. There wasn't a soul in sight. He started running again. He had to see Miss Pringle. He had to tell her what a wonderful teacher she was. That she was really wonderful! He had to smell her one last time!

On the way down the hill he started running so fast, his legs couldn't keep up and he fell down just missing a bed of prickly pear cactus. Jesus Christ! He got up and started running again brushing the dust off as he ran. He ran up the steps of the schoolhouse, opened the door and felt the rush of warm air around him. But no one was in the room. He stood there staring. Nobody! Nothing but little light motes drifting around in the sunlight streaming through the side window and the faint odor of chalk and vulcanizing.

He went out the door and closed it softly. Maybe she went arrowhead hunting too. Slowly he walked around the building scuffing at the dry ground, wishing he had stayed up there on the hill. Then he thought he heard something. A low panting seemed to come from the wood and coal shed which was built onto the back of the schoolhouse. As he got closer he was sure of it, crazy sounds, a low muffled panting and another sound that sounded like a dog whimpering. Slow rhythmic movements.

He tried looking in a side window but it was too high, he could just see the ceiling of the room, rough boards running down at an odd angle. He looked around him and found a large chunk of cedar that had been sawed smooth on each end. He sat it on one end, eased up on it and looked in the window. Everything was vague at first as his eyes kept trying to make sense out of the scene before him. Then in a burst of clarity it came to him. Clearly outlined in the light from the other side window he saw two figures intertwined. There was the face of Jimmy Joe framed by his horny tufts of hair, lips drawn back until his teeth were showing, his contorted face starkly etched in the light coming in from the opposite side window.

And just as clearly etched was the face of Miss Pringle, her eyes staring intently, just below his face. As Lonnie watched the rhythmic movements. As he listened to the moans and whimpers, the terrible knowledge came to him. That Goddamned Jimmy Joe. That Goddamned Jimmy Joe! There on the floor in the wood and coal shed. That Goddamn Jimmy Joe was fucking Miss Pringle!

Stunned, he fell off the chunk of wood, picked himself up out of the dust and staggered around to the front of the schoolhouse. He knew that someday, somehow, he was going to kill that Goddamned Jimmy Joe. Maybe he could catch him out somewhere and shoot him between the eyes with his twenty-two, or maybe he could roll a rock down on him from the caprock when they were out climbing mesas.

He was so blinded by tears that he ran into Lucy Lemur before he even saw her. Suddenly she was holding him, wiping his eyes with her handkerchief, steadying his heaving shoulders. "I know, I know." She hugged him to her. "I know, I understand, and I'll never tell, I'll never tell a soul."

He stood there with his world tilting as it had when the airplane banked over Clayton, feeling a dull pain flaring deep inside of him. He glanced at Lucy Lemur and gritted through his teeth. "I think maybe I just swallowed one of Old Bartolo's hot peppers." Then he actually smiled a little as the lump of pain writhed in his chest.

She smiled back at him. "Yes, I think I swallowed one of them too. Now let's go up the hill and hunt for arrowheads."

"Sure, sure," he finally said.

They walked along together, a young woman and a little boy, looking down at the ground, searching for something beautiful made a long time ago by people who lived nearby.

CHAPTER 33

Spurs

"Hey, Señorita Lucy, you tie this grub to your saddle horn." Old Bartolo was holding a sack up toward Lucy Lemur who was already on Velvet, ready to go.

"*Mucha buena comida*, it's to eat for the cowboys, okay"

"Sure, okay but put it behind me and tie it down. That way I won't have the thing swinging against my leg as I ride."

Lonnie was on Baldy with his twenty-two in his saddle scabbard, thinking maybe he might get a rabbit, or maybe even a deer. He watched as Old Bartolo tied the grub sack on top of the tarpaulin and blanket Fred Clafin made everybody take with them ever since Old Walt froze to death. But it was nice today, an Indian summer day, not a cloud in the sky, a bit cool but the sun felt warm on his legs and shoulders. He glanced at Lucy Lemur. She looked great, dressed in her gabardine pant suit and black riding coat, wearing her black boots, an old floppy hat on her head. She had put her 30-30 in her saddle scabbard, its brown stock gleaming dully in the sunlight.

"Hey, Bartolo, how about cinching me up a little, this crummy little bastard blowed himself up like a balloon when I put my saddle on but I think he has un-blowed now. If you move fast maybe you can cinch 'em before he does it again." Bartolo moved fast for an old man and cinched Lonnie's cinch up two notches before Baldy knew what was happening.

Lonnie felt good even though he still missed Miss Pringle a lot. He wasn't mad at her anymore for fucking that prick Jimmy Joe. For two or three weeks after it happened he didn't know what to think about her, but the more time passed the less he hated her and the more he hoped to see her again sometime.

They started out with Velvet leading the way and Baldy slow poking along behind as usual even though Lonnie was using a quirt on him. The sack held a fresh supply of food for the line camp where Fred Clafin and Dogey and Horse were herding cattle out of the breaks and canyons to the upper corral where they would be collected until the drive down the Zig Zag. They had been at it for a week now and must be about done but they still needed the grub. Velvet was moving ahead at a slow easy pace, a rocking horse motion which is actually what she was, a Tennessee walking horse that could cover ground so fast and easy that Lucy Lemur didn't seem to move in the saddle at all. To keep up, Lonnie had to beat Baldy into a fast trot which was getting easier to do since the farther he got from the barn the less beating it took.

When they got to the top of a high swell in the land about half way to the Zig Zag, Lucy Lemur pulled Velvet in and let Lonnie catch up. They both looked across the valley toward the Wedding Cake. Lucy Lemur was squinting her eyes, whistling a little through pursed lips.

"It sure is pretty, see the cactus has ripe prickly pears and the grass is a little bit green."

It had rained a little two days before but it didn't take much to get the grass growing, even in the middle of November.

"Yea, it is. Maybe we better pick some prickly pears on the way back, so Mama and Dulcita can make some jelly!"

Lonnie started to turn Baldy to follow Velvet who had just started out in her easy walk when he stopped.

"Hey, who's that?" On a ridge over toward the Veeder place a rider sat motionless, silhouetted by the early morning sun.

Lucy Lemur had stopped Velvet and was looking intently.

"It's that crazy Jake Veeder and his big dumb horse Macon."

Lonnie thought it was as eerie as hell. That crazy Jake Veeder who still scared the hell out of him even though he had saved his ass twice, by keeping Sam and Jimmy Joe from beating the shit out of him and by shooting up the line so he could get down from the Spire.

"I'm not afraid of no Jake Veeder," Lucy Lemur murmured, but she reached down and touched the stock of her rifle. "Let's get out of here before the crazy bastard comes up and does his silly little boy act."

She started Velvet off at a fast swaying walk. Lonnie had to beat Baldy into a gallop just to keep up.

Just before they got to the bottom of the Zig Zag, Lonnie turned and looked back. Jake Veeder and Macon were still there in the same place, not moving, a black shape. It was spooky! The dark shadow moved a little and something flashed in the sun. Jesus Christ, he was drinking! Everybody knew there was no telling what Jake Veeder would do when he'd had a few drinks.

They started up the Zig Zag with Velvet no longer able to keep up her rocking horse gait. She was straining with Lucy Lemur easy in the saddle looking back over her shoulder, first at Lonnie and then out beyond. Lonnie figured she was looking for Jake Veeder. She had a funny expression on her face, a combination of disgust and fear. Lonnie felt Baldy heaving beneath him so he pulled up for a short rest. He looked back but couldn't see anything. Jake Veeder had just disappeared as though he'd never been there.

When they got to the line cabin nobody was there. Lucy Lemur wrote a short note and left the grub sack on the table.

"What did you say in the note?" Lonnie wanted to know as they started back toward the Zig Zag.

Lucy Lemur's voice sounded strained. "I told him about that crazy Jake Veeder and that I expected there might be trouble."

"What kind of trouble?"

"If it happens you'll know what kind. If it doesn't happen there's no need for you to know." She had taken her 30-30 out of the saddle scabbard, pumped a shell into the chamber and was riding with it held in her right hand, the barrel resting on the swell of her saddle.

Jesus Christ! Lonnie took out his twenty-two, broke it open and put in a long rifle hollow point shell.

They were almost down the Zig Zag with Lonnie beginning to feel easier when it happened. They had just made the last turn and were headed down toward the pasture when Jake Veeder emerged from behind a huge boulder with two ropes whirling at the same time. Before Lonnie could move, his arms were pinned to his sides and he was jerked out of his saddle. His twenty-two hit the ground and fired, the bullet making a high pitched whining sound as it glanced off a rock. He looked up from where he had fallen in time to see Lucy Lemur pulled from the saddle. But she didn't fall. Jake Veeder caught her before she hit the ground. He took her 30-30 away from her and put it back in her saddle scabbard.

Then he took two short ropes from his saddle bag and hog tied them both, probably in record time, Lonnie thought, even though he was terrified, like when he won the cow roping and hog tying contest at the rodeo last year. While he was hog tying Lonnie he kept talking with his little baby talk voice.

"Well now see here, we jus' gonna put yor hans behin' you an yor legs behin' you an' tie 'em, jus' like you a lil' old dogey caff, which is wat you are, jus' so you doan' caus' no bother."

Lonnie felt his arms and legs being pulled behind him and being cinched up. He was screaming and crying. "You crazy bastard, you crazy bastard, you better not hurt Lucy Lemur. My daddy will kill you and Fred Clafin will kill you."

He didn't say anything more, he couldn't, Jake Veeder stuffed his bandanna in his mouth and turned him so he couldn't see what was happening. But he could sure hear what was happening. Lucy Lemur was screaming and cursing at the top of her voice. "You dim witted son-of-a-bitch, untie me, you better untie me."

Jake continued in his baby talk voice.

"Well if we ain't got a lil' ol' heifer here. A lil' ol' wild heifer, who's been needin' somethin', an' Old Jake gonna give her something'. First I'm gonna untie yor feet." There was a moment of silence between Lucy Lemur's screams and Lonnie could hear threshing sounds and Jake Veeder's voice. "Well ain't this lil' ol' heifer some kicker, but we gotta get them boots off, an' them pretty yeller socks. I bet you wouldn't kick at all if I was that oil man feller." One after the other Lonnie heard two thuds like boots hitting the ground.

"Now we gonna take off them pretty brown britches." Lonnie could hear more threshing sounds and Lucy Lemur's screams echoing from the walls of bone canyon. He couldn't think about anything but what was happening to Lucy Lemur. He glanced up the Zig Zag. Velvet and Baldy had stopped about thirty feet up the trail and stood there with their reins dragging, stomping and whinnying nervously as if they knew something terrible was happening.

"Now we gonna take off them pretty white panties, with that pink lace around em. An' now I'm gonna give you a great big present, jus' like from ol' Sante Claus."

The sounds Lucy Lemur was making became different. Low

moans and high pitched screams, mixed in together. Lonnie could hear rhythmic scuffing sounds and the rhythmic tinkle of spurs jingling. For awhile there was silence, then the heavy crunching, jangling sounds of somebody with spurs on running away from them down the Zig Zag.

Lonnie bent backwards as far as he could and felt his hands touch his feet. He bent more and felt the end of a rope in his hand. He pulled, the rope gave and suddenly he was free. Jake Veeder had used the same breakaway knot he used when he won the hog tieing contest at the rodeo. Lonnie rolled over, got to his feet, pulled the bandanna from his mouth and ran to Lucy Lemur. She was staggering around in the rocky path in her bare feet, her hands still tied behind her back. Her pale face had a greenish cast which emphasized the redness of the blood which ran down her chin from a gash in her lip where she had bitten herself. Blood ran from beneath her black riding coat down both her legs and marred the whiteness of her feet. Lonnie couldn't stand looking at her. He made little whimpering sounds as he untied her hands.

She stood there motionless, her huge black eyes were too bright, staring out, looking everywhere and nowhere. Then to Lonnie's surprise she whistled, high pitched and piercing, and Velvet came trotting towards them down the Zig Zag, her head held sideways to keep from stepping on the reins. When she came to a halt in front of them Lucy Lemur reached up and pulled her 30-30 from the saddle scabbard. Then she turned, rested the rifle on a rock and began firing at Jake Veeder who was headed toward the Veeder ranch with Macon running at a dead run. The shots echoed from the canyon wall and from the breaks beyond. Her third shot brought Macon down. He fell heavily, rolled over twice raising a cloud of dust. Jake Veeder came running out of the dust, zig zagging as he ran. Little spurts of dust rose around him before the bullets went singing away across the dry pasture. Even after there were no bullets left, Lucy Lemur kept moving the loading lever up and down. Jake Veeder shone clearly in the bright sunlight before he gradually faded as the distance grew.

Then they heard a horse coming down the Zig Zag, coming fast, Fred Clafin's big black stallion moving down, lunge after lunge, the rocks flying. He was covered with sweat and foam, blood showed on his side from the bite of the spurs, and bloody foam drained from his mouth. His ears were laid back and his eyes and nostrils were flared when he came to a sliding halt in front of them.

Fred Clafin took one look, then shouted at Lonnie. "Help her get her clothes on. Help her on her horse. Get her home. And give her some of this water."

He threw down a canteen, and went lunging on down the Zig Zag.

Lucy Lemur was pulling on her riding slacks when they heard two pistol shots in rapid succession and looked down just in time to see Macon, who had been trying to get up, go limp. Fred Clafin shot him while passing then went on toward the Veeder ranch.

Bartolo came out of the tack room when Lonnie shouted for help. Lucy Lemur was sitting limply in the saddle, the dried blood streaking her face, her eyes seemingly fixed on something in the far distance. Bartolo helped her from the saddle, then lifted her and carried her to the house. Mama must have seen them come in because the door suddenly opened and she was there holding out her arms with Dulcita standing behind her, looking frightened.

Mama and Dulcita gave Lucy Lemur a hot bath in her room with Lonnie and Bartolo bringing in the water, bucket after bucket, leaving it by the door. Behind the closed door Lonnie could hear them murmuring, mostly Mama's voice but sometimes Dulcita's and once or twice he was sure he heard Lucy Lemur say something.

About then the phone started ringing, first one ring and then another, practically everybody's ring in the whole valley, except for theirs. Lonnie was confused and terrified by it all. Something was happening! Finally he got up on his footstool and took the earpiece off the hook and listened. There seemed to be four or five people talking at the same time but there were so many phones off the hook he could barely hear the voices. But he did make out something about Lucy Lemur and Jake Veeder, and Fred Clafin's name came through. Lonnie hung up the phone and walked out to the windmill where Old Bartolo was standing quietly, looking anxiously down the road. He turned as Lonnie approached.

"Ah, Lonnito, no good, *no bueno. Mucho* bad day. I wait for your daddy to come. I wait for Fred Clafin to come."

"Fred Clafin won't be coming for awhile," Lonnie said, his voice trembling. "I think he went to kill Jake Veeder."

"*Madre de Dios*, Bad day, Bad day."

After about two hours, Lonnie saw a car coming fast up their road. He felt so relieved that he cried a little. But it wasn't Daddy. It was Lonnie's Uncle Doc, the sheriff. He got out of the car, a large square man in a grey gabardine suit, his star flickering occasionally from behind his suit coat. His face was drawn and his grey eyes were bloodshot under his short brimmed Stetson. He glanced first at Lonnie and then at Bartolo.

"Where's Emmett?"

"He's in Clayton. He and Sam went to Clayton to check up at the bank. And he ain't come back yet." Lonnie was still crying a little. "We don't know nothin', except that something' is happening."

"It's already happened." Uncle Doc's voice was strangely hushed. "Jake Veeder is dead. Fred Clafin killed Jake Veeder."

"*Madre de Dios, mucho dolor, muy mal dia.*" Bartolo's voice was almost a wail. "How Jake Veeder die? Fred Clafin shoot Jake Veeder?"

"No, he didn't shoot him." Uncle Doc's voice suddenly carried a note of disbelief and there was a look of amazement on his face. "He didn't shoot him. He beat him to death with his fists!"

Another car was coming up the road, throwing up an expanding plume of dust. This time it was Daddy. He slid to a stop and got out of the car fast. Sam got out too and came around toward them. His face was white and he looked like he had been crying. Daddy's face was grey. He looked sick. A muscle twitched under his right eye.

"How's Lucy? Where is she? Is she hurt bad?"

"Lucy, okay, she be okay," Bartolo murmured.

Daddy headed for the house and everybody followed him. He stopped at Lucy Lemur's door, knocked and waited. It opened and Daddy went inside. He was gone for about five minutes, then he came back out, looking much relieved.

"She'll be okay. But I want Doc Manchester out here as soon as he can make it. You see to that, will you?" He was looking at Uncle Doc. "Where's Fred Clafin?"

"He's in the hospital at Clayton. I got two of my deputies guarding his room. He ain't hurt bad, just some broken ribs and a broken jaw. But he did kill a man. And you just can't go around taking the law into your own hands, no matter what the other person did."

Daddy was glaring at him. "Well I'd have killed the son-of-a-bitch."

Uncle Doc's voice weakened. "Well I guess I would too, but it still wouldn't be right."

Fred Clafin stayed in the hospital for a week and then in the county jail for three days until Daddy could raise bail. When he came home he looked fine, a little thinner and he couldn't eat anything but soup because his teeth were wired shut.

The amazing person was Lucy Lemur. She stayed in her room for three days. Then after Doc Manchester had pronounced her "Fit as a Fiddle" she came out and had breakfast with everyone. She was all fixed up, her black hair pulled back and tied with a red ribbon. A little lipstick on her mouth, just a touch of eye shade, wearing one of her nicest white dresses, the one with the puffed sleeves. She smiled at everyone around the table, then ate her breakfast as if she didn't have a bother in the world.

For months, the Zig Zag episode and the big fight between Jake Veeder and Fred Clafin were the main topics of conversation in the valley. Some people maintained that Fred Clafin had beaten Jake Veeder in a fair fight, and that considering what he had done, Fred Clafin should be given a medal. Others, mainly the Veeder hands who had witnessed the fight, maintained that Jake Veeder didn't put up much of a fight. That he mostly took the beating, as if he was feeling real guilty and needed the punishment.

There was some speculation that the Veeders might do something in revenge. But it didn't happen. Maybe because Daddy and Mama along with Sam and Lonnie went to Jake Veeder's funeral. It was a grave-side service and hardly anyone was there, mostly just the Veeders and their hands, and a few relatives. After it was over Old Man Veeder who was crying came over to Daddy. They stood for a moment looking at each other and then shook hands. And that was it except for Fred Clafin's trial, which took place a month later. The jury found that Fred Clafin wasn't guilty of anything. That he had beaten Jake Veeder in a fair fight and that Jake's death was accidental.

CHAPTER 34

Cactus Burner

Lonnie woke up in the middle of the night with his ass freezing off. Sam had hogged all the feather mattress they had slept under ever since it started getting really cold, leaving Lonnie with no cover except for a couple of blankets. He started pulling and it suddenly gave way and billowed up around him. He lay there in the darkness getting warmer thinking maybe he should give Sam back some of the feather mattress, but what the hell. Let him freeze his ass off for awhile. There was a rumble of voices coming from the living room. Jesus Christ! Somebody must be crazy to be out there talking this time of night.

He got up and tiptoed down the hallway to the door which was open just a crack so he could hear what was going on. Daddy was talking.

"How does it look now Blanche, are we gonna make it through the winter? With you teachin' and the money we got from the government for killin' the cattle, we should make it. But I dunno, what do them figures say?"

Mama didn't speak for a long time. Lonnie guessed she was adding up some stuff. Then her voice came through, so soft he had to strain to understand what she was saying. "It doesn't look very good. With my hospital and doctor bills, and the payment on the mortgage, and the cotton seed cake for the cattle we only have four hundred dollars left. And we're going to need more cake or lots of the cattle won't make it through the winter. And it's only the middle of December."

Daddy didn't respond for awhile, then he said something funny. "Well, some of the ranchers are feedin' cactus."

Lonnie thought that was as crazy as hell. He had seen cows trying to eat cactus and they always got it stuck in their mouths or in their throats so the cowboys had to dig down in there with a pair of tough cowhide gloves to get it out.

It almost seemed as if Mama had heard what he was thinking. "But how can we feed cactus? The spines will lodge in their mouths, and anyway I don't think very many of them would even try."

"We'd burn off the spines," Daddy's voice sounded stronger. "I bought a cactus burner yesterday, and tomorrow I'm goin' to have Fred try it out. Old Man Beiheimer has been feedin' cactus for two weeks now, an' he says once them spines are off, the cattle eat it just fine!"

Lonnie was so cold his teeth were starting to chatter but he remained glued to the door hoping he might learn something that would lessen his anxiety. He knew that things were bad everywhere, for the country, and particularly bad for people in the west where the pastures were drying up and blowing away.

Mama's voice came through again. "Do you think we have any chance for the oil lease? It's been three months now and we haven't heard a thing."

Daddy's voice was a low rumble. "I don't think it's anything we can depend on. Guymond Moore said we would hear in two months, but we ain't heard. Nobody, as far as I know, has heard anything. But if it did come through it would mean over 5000 dollars. A dollar a year per acre, he said. An' we hold the mineral rights on about 5000 acres. The bank holds the mineral rights on the rest of the ranch, but five thousand dollars a year would let us make it for years to come, so maybe you could quit teachin'."

"I like teaching, and it helps a lot." Mama's hurried voice took on a note of pride. "I make ninety-two dollars a month."

"I know, an' I only get fifty dollars a month for bein' county commissioner."

"Well you also get mileage for the car, and that's really important."

"Yea, some car, at the rate its fallin' apart it won't last another six months."

Lonnie couldn't take the cold anymore. He tiptoed back down the hall, got under the feather mattress and snuggled up to Sam's back.

Sam woke up and started screaming at him. "For Christ sake, you're colder than a damned block of ice. How'd you get so fuckin' cold? Move over, you're freezing me to death."

Lonnie moved over feeling himself get warmer as he puffed up the feather mattress around his face. He lay there staring at the ceiling, watching his breath rise like smoke as it became visible in the moonlight coming in through the bedroom window. For a long time he lay there thinking about Mama and Daddy and money, hoping they all wouldn't wind up in the poor house.

The next morning, which was Saturday, it was so cold in the bedroom Lonnie didn't want to crawl out from under the feather mattress. He lay there with it all puffed up around him listening to Sam screaming at him through a crack in the door.

"Get outta there, for Christ sake! Fred Clafin is putting the cactus burner together, and your gonna miss seein' how it works, if you jus' keep laying there playin' with yourself."

That did it. Lonnie snaked out from under the feather mattress, grabbed his clothes and headed for the living room, which was warm and cozy. He moved next to the stove and started putting on his clothes. He had put his boots next to the wall behind the stove and they were as warm as toast to his cold feet. He had his sheep skin coat and sheep skin cap on and was headed for the front door when Mama caught him.

"You don't go out until you've had your breakfast."

He had to sit there and gobble down some scrambled eggs and sausage which Dulcita put in front of him and eat an apple, which he hated, before they let him go.

When he opened the front door the cold hit him. Frost covered everything, the leafless maple trees, the barns and the bunkhouse, even the windmill looked like a Christmas tree full of shimmering lights, ice particles reflecting the cold rays of the sun which had just appeared over the far mesa. The pond was a sheet of ice and the entire pasture sparkled and gleamed, the Wedding Cake wore a bright frosting.

When he went in the bunkhouse, the heat from the potbellied stove hit him, feeling great on his cold hands and face. And there was Fred Clafin with Dogey and Horse and Sam watching him intently, fiddling with a funny looking thing, completely different from anything Lonnie had ever seen before. The biggest part was a metal tank made of shining steel that could hold maybe three gallons. A black handle like the ones used on tire pumps came out its top. There was a hose maybe six feet long that Fred was attaching to a nipple at the bottom of the tank. To the other end of the hose he attached a long straight black pipe with a handle around it.

He looked up. "This is called the wand and that handle all the way around it is what you hold when you're burning cactus."

He glanced back at a drawing for a moment, then reached in the box and took out something that looked like a bed spring, a tight spiral that coiled back into itself. "This is the most important part of the whole thing, it's the part that vaporizes the gasoline, turns the gasoline into a gas. Okay Dogey, you get the five gallon can and we'll fill 'er up. But maybe we better take 'er outside."

Everybody left the bunkhouse with Fred Clafin carrying the cactus burner and Dogey bringing out the red gasoline can.

Lonnie was so interested he didn't even notice the cold. He watched as Fred Clafin turned the pumping handle and screwed the lid off the tank, with Fred giving a blow by blow description of the whole process.

"We'll put in two gallons of gas." Lonnie listened to the "glug, glugs" from the gasoline can, then watched as Fred screwed the lid of the tank back in place.

"Now we pump 'er up. You can do that Horse."

Horse jumped to it, turning the pump handle until it came free, then pumping with the air making little hissing noises as it went in the tank.

Fred looked at Lonnie. "You watch that gauge there on the tank and when it reaches sixty pounds, holler, so Horse can stop pumping."

Lonnie hollered and Horse stopped pumping.

"Well we're ready to give 'er a try. Stand away a little bit, and I'll turn on the gasoline. They all took a few steps backward, watching Fred Clafin as he pressed a valve just above the handle on the wand. A fine stream of gasoline came spraying out of a nozzle at the center of the coil.

"Light 'er up Sam and we'll let 'er get hot."

Sam struck a kitchen match on the steel tank and held it near the coil. There was a sudden swooch and the gasoline spraying inside the coil started to burn.

"Now all we have to do is wait until it starts generatin'. The gasoline goes through the coil, becomes real hot, turns to vapor and pretty soon, we'll be ready to burn cactus."

And that's exactly what happened. Within two or three minutes, a hissing roaring sound came from the coil and a blue flame about three feet long came blasting out.

"She's generatin'," said Fred Clafin. "Yep, she's generatin'," the others said, almost in unison.

Just then, Daddy came out the door and walked over to them. He stood gazing pensively at the flame for a few moments. Then he looked at Fred Clafin.

"Start in the pasture just below the house so we can see what will happen." With that he walked back into the house.

"I'll go on down and start burnin'." Fred Clafin put the cactus burner tank on his back and tightened the carrier strap. "Dogey and Horse, you guys get a couple of bags of cake, and we'll prime 'em. You guys," he was looking at Lonnie and Sam, "come with me and start callin' in the cattle."

Just then Lucy Lemur came out the door. She was all dressed up in her white fur jump suit and brown fur boots. She looked just like a snow princess, Lonnie thought, with her huge black eyes and the black bangs of her hair showing under her white fur hat.

"I'm coming too," her voice had a throaty musical tone just like Miss Pringle's, except lower.

Horse and Dogey came riding out the barn with a sack of cake draped over the saddle horns and swells of their saddles. Sam and Lonnie started whooping and hollering, "Hey yo, Hey yo" and cattle started moseying in from every direction.

When they all got down to the first big bunch of cactus Fred Clafin began playing the blue flame on the different branches causing the spines to flare brightly for a moment before they disappeared. Horse and Dogey opened the cake sacks and let the cake dribble out on the ground as their horses walked along. In about twenty minutes a bunch of cattle had drifted in and were licking the cake up from the ground. Then two or three moved to the first cactus Fred Clafin had burned and started eating, green juice draining from the mouths.

In an hour Fred Clafin burned about 100 cactus and the cattle were eating it as fast as he could burn it. They even seemed to prefer the cactus over the cotton seed cake. Lonnie tried them both. The cactus was bright green, covered with a little bit of white ash where the spines had been. He didn't like it much, it tasked like raw alfalfa. He preferred the cake. It had a grainy texture and crunched when he bit down on it.

Fred Clafin refilled the tank of the cactus burner and kept burning cactus. By lunch time hundreds of cattle were there eating cactus. Finally Daddy came down and told him to stop.

"I'm afraid they might bloat." Daddy was looking at some cows whose bellies were big and round, their mouths and faces a bright green.

But the cattle didn't bloat. As the days went by Fred Clafin started feeding less cake and more cactus, with Dogey and Horse taking turns with the cactus burner. Within a few days the cattle all looked a lot better and Daddy didn't seem as worried.

CHAPTER 35

Check

In the late afternoon just a week before Christmas the phone rang their ring. Lucy Lemur was there first, as usual. Lonnie was watching her. She took the earpiece off the hook and stood listening, then she started to say something but only managed a little gasp, and then a quiet "Yes." Suddenly she blushed clear down to her neck and her eyes became soft and luminous. She finally said, "Yes, it's me, yes I hear you, I can really hear you. Yes, yes."

Then she put the phone down and ran into the living room where Daddy was sitting in his chair staring out the window toward black Mesa.

She was almost too excited to speak.

"It's Guymond Moore, Daddy, and he wants to speak to you."

Lonnie didn't think Daddy could move very fast, but this time he did. He got up from his chair, adjusted his glasses and went to the phone in nothing flat, but not before Lonnie got there and said hello to Guymond Moore. Guymond said "Hello, back," but even as he spoke his voice became harder to hear because of all the phones coming off the hook. Daddy grabbed the phone from Lonnie and said "Hello" two or three times. And then shouted, "Get off the phone everybody, I got an important call here. Get off the phone!"

He waited and then said, "This is Emmett, Guymond, I think I can hear you now." Daddy stood there a long time listening and as he listened his back seemed to straighten and the sag in his shoulders seemed to lift. Finally he said "Yes" two or three times and hung up the phone.

Everybody was in the living room now, Mama, Dulcita, Sam and Lucy Lemur, all crowded around Daddy. And just then Fred Clafin came in the front door and joined them.

Lonnie had never seen Daddy look so happy. He was actually smiling and occasionally let out a small rumble of satisfaction.

"What did he say, what did he say?" Lucy Lemur shouted. "Is it good news? What did he say?"

"It's good news," Daddy said quietly, and then under his breath, "It's about the best news we ever had. They're gonna lease our land. Guymond Moore will be flying in tomorrow with a check and a contract. He should be coming in about two o'clock." He looked at Fred Clafin. "Burn cactus over toward Battle Ship so the lower pasture will be clear of cattle when he comes in, an' check for stragglers that might still be out there."

By noon the next day they started coming in, the word had spread. It looked like everybody in the valley wanted to see the airplane. By one o'clock, twenty-five or thirty cars and pickups and trucks were lined up along the fence in the lower pasture.

It was colder than hell, the sun had knocked most of the frost off of the grass and cactus but everybody had on heavy clothes, the men in their sheep skin coats, the women in their fur coats, the kids bundled up so you could just see their eyes peering out from under their caps and scarves. A lot of fires had been built using dead cactus wood and people were walking from one fire to another visiting or going to their cars and pickups for a shot of booze. There was one fist fight over something that nobody could remember, which Uncle Doc, the sheriff, settled before it got too rough.

Lonnie was having a good time visiting with Bobby Leo but the cold was getting to him even though he had on his sheep skin coat and sheep skin hat. He was sitting close to one of the fires, watching some of the men playing horse shoes, talking to Bobby Leo about how he was maybe going to get to take another airplane ride, when Eula Gay came over with a blanket and sat down beside him. She was grinning her wide mouthed grin with her teeth showing. She was wearing her black fur overalls with a black fur cap and fur boots, all of which made her look more like an Eskimo than ever. She leaned over and brushed against Lonnie, then said in a small voice.

"You look so cold Lonnie and you too Bobby Leo, why don't we all share my blanket."

What the shit! Lonnie was cold and the blanket looked warm so he let her drape it around him. Pretty soon he was feeling a lot warmer not only because of the blanket but because he was snuggled up to her furs. She must have been wearing some kind of perfume, violets and roses with no skunk smell as was always the case with Lucy Lemur.

And just as he thought about her she came riding up, dressed in her white fur pants and coat. A white fur cap was pulled way over her head making her huge black eyes seem even bigger. Her cheeks were red from the cold, and her lips were red, Lonnie figured, not from the cold but from some lipstick she had put on. Velvet was doing her walking horse thing moving toward them in a gait that was so easy, Lucy Lemur didn't even bob in the saddle but stayed steady like she was in an easy chair. Velvet came to stop next to one of the fires, blowing long spurts of steam from each nostril into the icy air. Lucy Lemur dropped her reins, started to get off, then began peering intently toward Black Mesa.

Suddenly Lonnie caught the sound of an airplane and then he saw it coming in over the Wedding Cake growing from a speck until there it was coming right at him, the Staggerwing Beach, going "eeeeeeeeeeeeeummmmmm" as it passed over. It turned and came back over wagging its wings, made another complete turn, lowered its landing gear and sloped in toward the middle of the lower pasture. Spurts of dust rose as the tires skipped along the ground and then suddenly there it was just as before, almost as though it had never gone away.

Everybody started toward the airplane, cars and pickup trucks and horses. It was, as Lucy Lemur remarked later, just like the Oklahoma land rush. Lonnie was pissed, everyone seemed to be getting there before him. Baldy wasn't doing his slow poke thing but his gallop didn't seem to be doing much. Finally he made it, but then Lonnie couldn't get close to the airplane, there were too many people circled completely around it staring up at the cabin.

The door finally opened just as it had before and there was Guymond Moore waving and flashing his great smile. He came down the ladder to be greeted by a lot of hand clapping and shouts, which made him, as he said later, feel just like Lindbergh when he landed in Paris. He stood on the lowest rung of the ladder looking around the crowd, Lonnie figured, for Lucy Lemur, who for some reason couldn't be seen anywhere. Then Lonnie did see her, she had gotten off Velvet and was standing at the outer edge of the crowd looking down at the ground. It was as if she was afraid of something, her face was pale and her shoulders were slumped like her back hurt. But she wasn't that way for long. Guymond Moore walked through the crowd which opened a path for him until he was standing in front of her.

"Well here's my Rose of the Cimarron. She's all grown up and I want a big hug."

Lucy Lemur straightened up then, opened her arms and put them around Guymond's neck. Lonnie who could see them clearly thought she had never looked more beautiful. Her huge eyes were half closed, tears glistening on her lashes. She didn't say anything but just held on to Guymond Moore as if she would never let him go. He didn't try to get away. They remained there for a long time not noticing the sudden silence, the hundreds of eyes; as if they were alone, a completeness that didn't need anybody else.

Finally, Guymond Moore patted her on the back and looked around. He spotted Lonnie, went over and gave him a hug. And it didn't even embarrass Lonnie, he was so glad to see him that it didn't matter.

Now everybody started looking at the airplane. Somebody else was coming out. A little roly-poly man who looked almost as wide as he was tall was climbing down the ladder one careful step at a time. When he reached the ground he turned around blinking at the crowd through thick lensed glasses that made his eyes look too large. He had a neatly trimmed goatee, which Lonnie thought made him look just like a fat goat. He was wearing a long fur coat and a fur hat that had huge ear flaps that stuck out like a pair of fuzzy wings.

Daddy drove up just then, got out of the car and shook hands with Guymond Moore, then both of them went over and Daddy shook hands with the funny looking little fat man, who turned out to be, as they found out later, the President of Cobalt Oil who had, he said as they were all seated around the table having supper, just come along for the ride and to see the scenery and to meet all those good people Guymond Moore had been talking about for so long. He glanced around the table. "Particularly the children and a certain young lady." His eyes twinkled as he looked at Lucy Lemur who couldn't get her eyes off Guymond Moore.

After supper they all went into the living room where Mr. Shorty Belding, that was his name, presented Daddy with a check and both of them signed some papers. Lonnie had never seen Daddy look so pleased. He kept looking at the check and then around the room. Then he made a little speech.

"We all sure do thank the Cobalt Oil company for this here good fortune. And I want Fred and Dogey and Horse to know that this year they will git a bonus for all their fine work."

Dogey and Horse blushed and stared down at the floor but Fred Clafin smiled, showing his white teeth, making him look just like Guymond Moore except older and heavier, having gained all his weight back, with a little extra. Then Daddy handed the check around for everyone to see. Lonnie's eyes popped when he saw it, 5,468 dollars, more money than he ever hoped to see in his life.

When the check inspecting was finished, Guymond Moore brought out a large box Lonnie had helped him carry into the living room. He opened it and started taking out all kinds of presents, a bottle of whiskey for each of the men. As he handed Bartolo his, Guymond grinned, his red beard gleamed in the light from the Aladdin lamp.

"For the best cook of frijole beans in New Mexico."

Bartolo made little clucking noises. "*Gracias, Senior Guymond. Muchos gracias.*"

There was a beautiful scarf for Mama who blushed when Guymond Moore draped it around her neck, blushed and looked hurriedly around the room, suddenly shy. There was another one for Dulcita who smiled her brightest smile as she was also draped. There were books for Sam and Lonnie. Lonnie's book was bright red and smelled great when he opened its pages for a look. It was *The Warlord of Mars*, by some guy called Edgar Rice Buroughs. The same guy who had written all that stuff about Tarzan.

Finally, it was Lucy Lemur's time. A silver and turquoise bracelet, that Lonnie figured must have cost a lot of money. Guymond Moore put it on her wrist while she was standing in front of him, her eyes glowing in the light from the Aladdin Lamp.

Then, Guymond Moore made a speech. "You all must know how important it is for me to be a friend of this fine family. Here in the warmth from your stove and the warmth of our affection for each other. These are just a few small tokens of my affection for each of you, a Christmas present, a week early but it feels like

Christmas now. Tomorrow we have to leave, go back to Tulsa, but I, and I'm sure Mr. Belding, will never forget any of you."

There was a round of applause with even Daddy joining in. Mr. Belding stroked his goatee and said, "Hear, Hear."

Everybody stayed up late that night; the men sipping whiskey, Mama and Dulcita and Lucy Lemur drinking cocoa, and Lonnie and Sam drinking Ovaltine, something Lonnie loved. A lot of stories were told with Shorty, he insisted on being called Shorty, telling some of the funniest about when he first started in the oil business, working as a roughneck—whatever that was. The cowboys thought that was really funny, old Shorty being a roughneck. Later when they were laughing about it, Horse let go with one of his whinnies. "Yea, 'bout as rough as an overused corncob."

Dogey and even Fred Clafin thought that was funny but Lonnie didn't get it.

"What are you all laughing about? What's so fucking funny?"

They didn't say anything but just looked at him with shitty grins on their faces, which really pissed Lonnie off.

When it was really late, about 10:00, everybody, well most everybody, went to bed—with Shorty insisting he wanted to sleep in the bunkhouse, where he could soak up some more western atmosphere.

It was decided that Guymond Moore would sleep on the couch and it was made up for him with Dulcita and Lucy Lemur putting on sheets and blankets and fluffing up pillows.

Long after everyone else had gone to bed, Lonnie could hear Guymond Moore and Lucy Lemur talking in the living room. Lonnie got out of bed and sneaked down the hallway and listened with his ear pressed to the door but their voices were so low he couldn't hear a thing. Anyway it was too cold for listening so he got back under the feather mattress and snuggled up to Sam.

The next morning just as the sun was showing above the near mesa, after a lot of hugs and handshakes and a long kiss, the airplane made its rush down the lower pasture, lifted and zoomed away, getting smaller and smaller until it was lost from sight and sound. After everyone stared at the spot where it had disappeared for awhile they turned their horses and started back toward the ranch-house. Lonnie was almost afraid to look at Lucy Lemur who was riding beside him, fearing that she would be looking lost. Fi-

nally he did glance at her and got a big surprise. She wasn't looking lost. Her head was thrown back, her huge eyes gleaming softly,
her cheeks blushed with the cold, a gentle smile played upon her
face.

"Why you don't look sad at all because Guymond's just gone
away," Lonnie shouted at her. "I thought you'd be cryin'."

Lucy Lemur glanced at him, the smile widening, her eyes sparkling. "Why should I be sad? I'm happy."

"Why in the world should you be happy?"

"Because I know he's coming back." She clucked Velvet into a
fast easy walk leaving Lonnie behind thinking about it all.

Three days later on the third day of Christmas vacation Lonnie
saw something strange coming up their road from Highway 64, a
brand new car which gleamed and sparkled in the late afternoon
sun. The closer it got the more he hoped, and sure enough when
it came to a stop in front of the house, it was Daddy driving. Lonnie
couldn't believe it, a brand new 1934 V-8 Ford, a bright black color
with four doors. Daddy got out and stood beside it as everybody
came rushing out of the house and the bunkhouse. He was smiling, something he had been doing a lot more during the last few
days.

"Can I get in?" Lonnie was turning one of the back seat door
handles.

"Everybody get in." Daddy's voice was a low rumble. "Everybody get in an' we'll take a little ride."

There was an immediate scramble with Lonnie, Lucy Lemur
and Sam in the back and Mama and Dulcita, who was suddenly
timid and held back, being grabbed by Daddy and hustled in the
car beside Mama. And away they went so quiet and easy it didn't
even seem like the engine was running. What Lonnie couldn't get
over was the way it smelled, maybe not as good as Miss Pringle or
the airplane but almost as good.

Two days later, on Christmas Eve, Daddy came down the road
again, and this time he had a huge box riding on the seat in the
back. Fred Clafin and Dogey carried it in the house and lifted something out. A radio! When they got it all set up with the batteries in
place and the aerial strung, they turned it on and it played music
that was so beautiful Lonnie couldn't believe it. Lonnie loved the
radio almost as much as he loved the new car. It had a shiny brown

mahogany cabinet with three dials and the word "superhetrodine" written below the display face which showed which station you were listening to.

Later that evening they were all in the living room with the radio turned to KOA Denver listening to Christmas carols. Daddy was in his big chair, now turned away from the picture window to face the radio. He sat totally relaxed, head cocked to the side, the light gleaming from his glasses, his lips moving in cadence with the music. Mama was sitting on the couch with her eyes closed, her head leaning back, a little smile playing on her lips. Lucy Lemur sat beside her, her head held slightly sideways, the light gleaming from her black hair. Her huge eyes seemed to be seeing something way out somewhere, there was a smile on her lips too, and her face was radiant. She was rocking back and forth a little, thinking happy thoughts, Lonnie figured, about Guymond Moore. Dulcita sat in a straight back chair near the big heating stove, her brown eyes roving the room, stopping for a moment as she glanced at each face. Sam was leaning over the table next to the Aladdin lamp reading the book, *Riders of the Purple Sage* by Zane Grey, that Guymond Moore had given him. Lonnie sat next to the stove near Dulcita thinking about everybody and everything that had happened from the day he became a Golden Bat to the arrival of the new car and the radio. As he glanced around the room at every one he felt a warm tide rise inside of him somewhere. All in all even though some crazy things had happened it had been a pretty good year, and he guessed that maybe this would be about the best Christmas he would ever have. And it was.

Biographical Note

Felix E. Goodson recieved his doctorate in psychology from the University of Missouri (Columbia) in 1954. He taught at DePauw University from 1954 to 1990, where he won several *Best Teacher* awards. He is the author of *The Evolutionay Foundations of Psychology: A Unified Theory* and *Sweet Salt*, a semi-autobigraphical novel recounting several years spent as a World War II Japanese prisoner of war.